Praise for Shocked Earth:

"Written with attentivenes[...] [...]een landscape, community and [...] [...]ful and moving story of love, lo[...] [...] to the future." BEN SMITH, AU[...]

"Exquisitely captures the way our lives and identities are interwoven with the land we live on, and how its destruction will ultimately be our own. A powerful portrait of a family, an exploration of love and grief, it is perhaps most of all an essential call to action – I was both heartbroken and inspired." HELEN SEDGWICK

"This is one of those rare books that gives you the feeling while reading that it has always existed … It reads [as though it is] … already a classic novel." HERMAN KOCH

"A novel with great ambitions, which remains credible." *TROUW*

"I read the book in one breath … you gradually feel the oppression and how people are silenced … The descriptions of nature and land are almost poetic." RIA VAN HALEM

Praise for The Hormone Factory (Saraband, 2016)
LONGLISTED FOR THE LIBRIS LITERATURE PRIZE 2013
NOMINATED FOR THE EUREGIOPRIJS 2016.

"A dark, fascinating exploration of man's nature set during an era of exciting scientific discovery and geopolitical turmoil." *THE LANCET*

"Mordechai de Paauw – womaniser, cheat, and ruthless businessman – is a despicable man, yet the perfect narrator." HISTORICAL NOVEL SOCIETY

"Cleverly and with apparent ease she mixes the fates of the real-life Zwanenberg brothers into different fictional distillations … with the pace of a thriller writer." LESLEY MCDOWELL, *HERALD*

CONT…

"This is historical fiction at its best ... Disturbing on many levels ... The author's theatrical background and meticulous research influenced the credibility and flair of this debut novel ... impeccable tone ... amusing with its dry wit." THE ENTERTAINMENT REALM

"Provides a harrowing insight into the man/woman/machine phenomenon that drove the twentieth century ... this book is populated by truths and secrets that haunt and astound ... fast-paced, won't soon be forgotten." THE SKINNY

"A story written with colour and momentum." DE VOLKSKRANT

"A beautiful novel in which we get the sense of that age of progress in between the two great wars ... Money, power, hormones, science, love, abuse and betrayal are the threads with which the book is woven. A story in which testosterone and oestrogen grab the characters by the throat. A beautiful novel about the proud tyrant De Paauw that is based on imagination, but probably contains a lot more truth than we would like." BRABANTS DAGBLAD

"Goldschmidt's tone is fascinating, picturesque and humorous ... She has written an enthralling story in which she seduces the reader with beautiful sentences." LITERAIR NEDERLAND

Praise for The Vintage Queen:
"Goldschmidt has a fine style of writing and knows how to build a good story. She also knows how to create good and credible characters. A true recommendation." DE LEESFABRIEK

"Goldschmidt is a genuine storyteller. This is a fascinating story from start to finish. Goldschmidt's strength is in her ability to bring her characters to life." NOORDHOLLANDS DAGBLAD

"A gripping portrait of the last decades ... it shows how idealism becomes fierce business. A beautiful book." LIBELLE

"A compelling story with a tragic undertone .... Well-written and worldly." DE TELEGRAAF

Shocked Earth

Saskia Goldschmidt

translated from Dutch by

Antoinette Fawcett

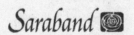

Published by Saraband
Digital World Centre, 1 Lowry Plaza
The Quays, Salford, M50 3UB

www.saraband.net

ISBN: 9781912235681
ebook: 9781912235698

This book was published with the support of
the Dutch Foundation for Literature.

Printed and bound in Great Britain by Clays Ltd, Elcograf S.p.A.

1   3   5   7   9   10   8   6   4   2

For Anita J.

We speak in horror about the consequences,
but we continue to cherish the causes.

Jacques-Bénigne Bossuet

I think human beings are meant to love something.
Not that we're very good at this, but it's what
we should try to do.

Koos van Zomeren

Prologue

Giuseppe Mercalli had spent many years teetering on very edge of volcanoes on the point of eruption, but he died in a fierce blaze in his own bedroom when a paraffin lamp toppled over. He was sitting beside it, working up his notes on earth tremors.

He left us a scale to measure the effects of an earthquake on the ground, and on buildings, animals, and people. The first degree of intensity he described as Not Felt; the last, number twelve on the scale, as Catastrophic.

Mercalli's scale, which is more than a hundred years old now, is still used all over the world, except in a small country in the western hemisphere, won from the sea metre by metre; a land that is little more than a dyked morass with a squelchy clay ground. A land encircled by sky and water, filled with the reflections of shimmering clouds.

Sixty years ago, what was then the biggest gas field in the world was discovered there. Exploitation licences were sold off and the pumping soon began. The country became one of the wealthiest in the world.

A certain Willem Meiborg, an engineer, warned at the time that the ground was being ransacked at too great a rate. He argued for caution or, if that wasn't possible, at the very least to set aside a small proportion of the enormous profits to create a compensation fund, in case the gas extraction caused problems in the future.

His words weren't heeded. In times of euphoria no one appreciates a pessimist. He was a prudent man, but nevertheless, or perhaps precisely because of that, he was destined to be a prophet without honour, a Cassandra of the north.

The tremors could be felt a couple of decades later, but only very lightly at first, and the rare individual who dared to point them out was mocked. But the tremors increased, both in frequency and strength, until eventually a decision was made to carry out some investigations to work out whether the quaking ground might have something to do with the gas extraction, although there were real doubts about that. They used the Richter scale for these tests, a method that measures the magnitude of an earthquake, but does not take into account its effects, which are dependent on the terrain and the depth at which the quakes take place.

It's high time to dig out the Mercalli scale again, so we can work out exactly what has happened to the land, the buildings, the animals, and the people.

We'll go to the farm of Schokland, a characteristic 'Head-Neck-Rump' farmhouse, of the type you can find in the north of the Netherlands, in the province of Groningen. It was named after the former island of Schokland, which was situated in the Zuiderzee. This was the birthplace of a lad who in 1825 lost all his family in the February floods. The boy then left the island, half of which had been washed away, and went north. He must have been a very clever young man, someone with plenty of audacity, although little more is known about him. Yet he left a stately farmhouse to his heirs, with a name that speaks of piercing homesickness. That farm still belongs to his descendants, the Koridon family.

Schokland is a proud farmstead in a sea of clay.

January 1993

To get to Schokland you first have to find the Plus supermarket, the only shop still remaining in the village, and then drive two kilometres down a concrete track. There's just one bend in the road, and here and there the flat land is criss-crossed by ditches edged with stiff reeds. The farm is surrounded by a moat and is built on a *wierde*, a manmade mound, because once upon a time the sea was in charge here.

On the second Saturday of the year 1993, Ootje Rosa Koridon announced that a certain farmer and his wife would be coming to tea on Sunday afternoon and that her daughter was expected to be there. Trijn asked her mother what those people were coming for. Ootje didn't look up from the ironing board, where she was ironing starch into her snow-white tablecloth, but she repeated sternly that they were counting on Trijn to be there and told her to dress nicely.

In the evening, while Ootje was sweeping, mopping and polishing the parlour, Trijn asked her father Zwier what was behind this visit. He tapped out a slow rhythm on the floor with his slippered foot and gazed at the flames flickering behind the blackened mica window of the stove.

'Better not be too rebellious about it,' he said softly, as if his words might pass through the thick walls of the farmhouse. 'She's doing her best.'

'Her best for what?' Trijn continued, whispering. 'What have those old bods got to do with me?'

Then he stopped tapping his foot and said it wasn't only the farmer and his wife who'd be visiting. Their second son would come along too. 'But that's something you don't know. She means well.' He picked up a log, opened the door of the stove, and carefully placed it on the fire.

*

5

Trijn was in the farmyard, watching a faded Volkswagen pickup truck bump slowly up the lonning, then come to a standstill right in front of her. The truck's small cab had hardly enough space for the hefty people who bulged out of it as the door opened: a square-set old farmer; a farmer's wife clothed all in black lace, checking Trijn out from top to toe; and a big-boned young man who thrust his left hand out at her. His right hand was little more than a mutilated claw.

Inside the farm, around the parlour table, the old bods, tea-cups in hand, floundered through a conversation about the first-rate location of this farmstead, surrounded by its own land, about the tornado that had struck one of the islands, and about the plane crash in Faro a month earlier, which had killed some-one from the village.

Trijn paid no attention to the son. He was at least twenty-five – a man who'd lost his youth but not his acne. He kept his lump of a hand on his thigh and listened to the conversation of the old folks, casting an odd glance or two at Trijn. She kept her mouth shut and stared at the patterns in the carpet. Her mother ordered her to come to the kitchen with her to fetch the nibbles and then hissed at her to make more of an effort. The lad was shy, right enough, but plenty of people had told her he was a very decent feller.

When everyone was sitting down again, and Trijn was going round with the bowl of peanuts, and the lad reached out his good hand to grab a fistful, Trijn was struck by the thought that peanuts gave you spots, as she'd once read somewhere.

Because of the sudden silence and the dismayed faces staring at her, she realised that it wasn't a thought, but that she must have said it loud and clear.

The visit was soon over. Trijn realised that in her mother's eyes she'd never be able to do anything right unless she got herself married to a farmer's unprepossessing son. Perhaps it would be better for her to leave. To leave the unspoken reproaches. To leave this boundless landscape and the mist that lingered above the ditches for much too long in the mornings.

And so she left, in the early hours of one Sunday morning, taking only her old school backpack with her, stuffed with a few dresses, her much-too-high stilettos, her make-up bag, her Walkman, the family photo with Jort in it, and Zwier's ancient silver petrol lighter, which she'd nicked from his tobacco pouch on the table, in which she'd left a note for him, saying sorry, twice. Once because she was leaving and once for taking his cigarette lighter with her.

*

In the years before she left Trijn used to like going to Fokko's, at the Wide World. The Wide World was a farmhouse at the other side of the concrete track, a bit south of them, a kilometre into the farmland, at the end of a badly maintained, potholed lonning.

It must have been a very handsome farmstead in the past, but when Trijn used to go there it was a ramshackle mess. The farmhouse shutters were hanging from their hinges, the steps to the peeling front door were worn out, and the windows were dirty. In the living room two rickety benches stood on an old rug, and four electric guitars hung on the wall. These, according to Fokko, had a unique sound. He'd bodged them together from several different cast-offs. The back of the barn section of the farm was chockful of the landlord's rusty tools. The farm was owned by a farmer who lived at the other end of the village and only needed the land to spread his muck on. There was a drumkit and a hodgepodge of sound equipment: an amp, a mixer, gigantic speakers, and a couple of mikes on rickety stands. The tiered seating was made from a stack of empty beer crates. This was Fokko's rehearsal studio, for him and his band, the Wide World.

Fokko was almost thirty and still not married and as far as the village was concerned he was the inevitable village idiot, just as much part of the scenery as their openwork church tower, with its blue spire and graceful arches, visible from a great distance.

Fokko wasn't a farmer, nor your average hard-working citizen. He lived on benefits. He saw the money that came into his bank account every month as a kind of subsidy for his band and as support for the only ambition he cherished: to lead a life that honoured the clichéd image of the old rock star – music-making, drinking, smoking dope, and picking up women. None of these activities led to much. The band occasionally performed in a smoky little room at the back of a village pub, where they played their sets in exchange for free drinks. Their repertoire was made up of cover songs, the famous hits of entertainers already slowly shuffling towards their retirement homes. They played for half an hour as loudly as possible, enjoyed swearing at the audience, and when it was all over they were always disappointed there'd been so little interest from female fans.

Sometimes, for cash in hand or for drink, Fokko would help the local farmers stack their hay bales, spread muck, or pick stones from the arable ground. But the children were forbidden to visit his farm. No one wanted a dope-smoking, hard-drinking, dole-claiming fantasist as a role model for their offspring.

For Trijn the Wide World was proof that there was more to existence than the inevitable farming life: a promise of escape, even closer to home than the village clubhouse, where young people would go and get smashed on Saturday evenings. She and a couple of other kids really liked being around in the barn when the band was rehearsing. The kiddies, as Fokko called them, hung around on the beer-crate stands, drank alcohol, smoked dope, yelled the latest gossip at each other above the racket, read

Fokko's collection of strip cartoons and after the rehearsal sat together round the fire basket in the farmyard. Someone was always strumming a guitar and Fokko would tell them stories about the time when he worked as a general roustabout. Even the job-title impressed them. Fokko had, in his own words, made piles of money in Siberia, doing the kind of work that farmhands do, although he swore that offshore work was much heavier and filthier. He got promoted and became the lead hand, the man at the drill who pumped the oil up, but he was still the lowest-ranked member of the crew. They called him The Worm.

It was a hard life, he claimed, and the guys all did exactly as they pleased. He was the greenhand, and so he was their errand boy and cat. But when they were off-shift and let loose on a city, he'd throw himself at DVC: dollars, vodka, and chicks. Alas, that often turned out to be DVCC: dollars, vodka, chicks, and the clap.

Fokko told this tale so often that it became their custom to roar out these last words with him: 'dollars, vodka, chicks, and the clap.' And then they'd all get the giggles.

Fokko had once narrowly escaped death thanks to an attack of the squitters. This was his most spectacular story. A drunken welder had flouted the rules with the result that burning thermite, a mixture of aluminium powder and iron oxide, had ended up on the ice. Thermite fire on ice.

'Because it burns so quickly,' Fokko would tell his electrified audience, 'the ice turns to gas and is as explosive as hell.' The whole caboodle exploded and all they could do was to wait at a safe distance, because once thermite is ablaze it can't be put out.

'If I hadn't gone to take that shit, just a moment before,' Fokko always closed his Siberia story, 'there'd have been nothing left of me.' Three of his colleagues had burnt to death. Not a bone nor a tooth had remained. They sent sealed coffins back home to their families. He didn't know what was inside them, but there weren't any bodies left to send.

Not long after that Fokko returned to his native town. Then he fell out with his father, jumped onto his scooter and rode into the countryside, on a recce. That was where he discovered a deserted farmstead, the Wide World. After a brief negotiation he got permission to live in the farmhouse for a pretty low rent, as long as he didn't expect any kind of maintenance from the owner.

And that's how hot-headed Fokko became the caretaker of a former farmstead, where he sometimes entertained the local kids with exploding tennis balls he'd concocted with the help of a well-thumbed copy of *The Anarchist Cookbook*. He would place them in the centre of the farmyard and then blow them up, with tremendously loud booms and towering tongues of flame. Fokko's Wide World became a place of refuge for all the local kids longing for a springboard to whoosh them up and away from the cow muck.

And Trijn was going to make that leap. On the beer-crate staging she chatted up a lad with bright blue eyes and curly dark hair. One evening, when Trijn was sitting by the fire, singing along with the rest, he whispered into her ear that she had Freddy Mercury potential. No one had ever told her she had a nice voice before, or that she could sing, or even that she could do anything well at all. Only Zwier sometimes gave her good-humoured compliments when she was reluctantly carrying out the constant and repetitive tasks: all those compulsory jobs she carried out in the knowledge that she'd have to do precisely the same that afternoon, or the next morning, or next week, just as her father had done thirty years back, and her grandfather, and her great-grandfather before him. She knew there'd never be an end to that eternal cycle, that everything she did kept the whole machine working.

So when Harm, with his curly mop of hair, whispered to Trijn that she had Freddy Mercury potential, although she'd rather have been a second Mariah Carey, it seemed that a spotlight was suddenly focused on her, as if someone had truly seen her for the first time.

He took her to what had once been the cow byre. They sat down on a pile of jute sacking and he kissed her more intensely than any farm lad had ever dared. She found it exciting, arousing. He gasped out that he really wanted to have her and tried to get inside, but she managed to stop him with her hand. She whispered: 'Not yet. Not so fast. We've just got to know each other,' but then he started to use more force. She pushed him angrily away, stood up, straightened her skirt and said she was nobody's slut. He grinned, slowly got up, zipped himself up, look straight at her and sang: '*Save the best for last*'.

'If you really fancy me, you can wait, otherwise you're not worth it,' she said mockingly.

'*Don't say you didn't like it, baby*,' he sang and then left, but not before he'd given her his address and whispered in her ear that she was always welcome.

To her surprise he started coming regularly to Fokko's so he could see her. After a few months she brought him home. They sat in the kitchen. Her mother poured the tea, while Trijn served the apple tart she'd made with apples from their own garden and felt embarrassed about the barrage of questions fired at Harm, none of which he could answer satisfactorily. No, he wasn't a farmer's son. His father was a truck driver and his mother was a housewife. He lived in the city, a little to the south. He wasn't interested in farming. He'd never completed any kind of course. He did odd jobs here and there and the only thing he really wanted was to perform with his band. He didn't make any attempt to meet her parents halfway and Trijn saw that her mother's eyes were narrowing more and more and that the line of her mouth was growing thinner and thinner.

Zwier asked if he was interested in anything other than music – football, perhaps, or fishing, or birdwatching. But Harm was only interested in a singing career. 'And in your daughter, of course,' he joked.

That was the point at which Ootje started speaking about their son Jort. Trijn froze. They never spoke about Jort.

If anything at all was mentioned, then they spoke of it as the Accident. Then a painful silence would fall, a silence in which Ootje's reproaches, which she never spoke aloud, echoed through Trijn's head. It was Trijn's fault. It was such a terrible misfortune that the Accident had struck her lad. The one who was going to take things over, a farmer through and through. Her first-born.

Since the Accident, Zwier hadn't argued with Ootje again. All his former bluntness seemed to have been swept away and he became more and more stooped, as if he was carrying a heavy burden.

Trijn felt that she didn't have the right to grieve about Jort's death. That would be babyish, or worse, it would look as if she was trifling with her mother's grief.

At first she didn't understand why Ootje was talking about her brother now, at this awkward moment, with crumbs of apple tart scattered over the plastic tablecloth. What did Harm have to do with Jort? But then Ootje started talking about their farm, which had been in her husband's family for generations. They'd always farmed here, on the land belonging to Schokland. She told him the story of how, thirty years before the farm was built, in 1859, a family ancestor, who was still a child then, living on Schokland in the Zuiderzee, had come to this area after a tidal wave had flooded his island, and how, with a dash of courage and stubborn tenacity, he'd worked himself blue in the face to build up a new life here. They were the stewards of his farm. And, then sounding very hurt, she mentioned Jort's senseless death. As she did this she first looked at Trijn and then at Zwier. Both turned their eyes away.

'And so,' Ootje continued, 'because Trijn has no feeling for dairy farming, she has to find herself a husband who can lighten her burden. Or who can manage the farm alone.' She rounded it all off by concluding that a relationship between Trijn and Harm had absolutely no future and it would be better to put a full stop to it now. Then she stood up, a signal that as far as she was concerned the visit was at an end.

Trijn had no idea what to say. She asked Harm if he'd still like to see the milking parlour. He tagged along behind her but didn't want to go in because he'd get his pointy boots dirty.

She took him to the back of the barn, which was partitioned off from the rest of the building, and had been her brother's taxidermy workshop. He had a small and colourful collection of birds, glued onto twigs or perched on slips of shingle, displayed in cabinets along the walls. There was a honey buzzard, suspended from the ceiling with its wings outstretched. Inside an antique glass display case there were tiny bleached skulls and slender skeletons laid out like miniature construction sets. Jort had always spoken with pride about his Dead Bird Museum.

She'd often watched him skinning, preserving, and then mounting a robin or a skylark. The pièce de résistance was a male peacock. It was perched on top of the cupboard, and its velvety blue tail fanned out over the dark wood. And then one day she'd found a dead great tit and asked him: 'Can you fix it?' He'd handed her a scalpel and taught her how to cut open its abdomen, very carefully. Then he showed her how to scrape the skin clean and how to prepare it. She still kept the little bird by her bed.

Harm stared at the short-eared owl, then went along the cases of bird skeletons, the finches, the peewit, and the robin, the vases filled with brown, white and speckled feathers, the skulls hanging down on cords from the ceiling, their long beaks stabbing into space. He read the article Jort had pinned up on the wall, about a shop in Paris that had an extensive collection of mounted birds, fishes, small mammals and even predators.

'Jort went there once, on a school trip,' Trijn told him. He'd promised her that they'd go there together one day. Harm told her that Jort was a creep, which she indignantly denied.

When he left, she walked along the lonning with him for part of the way. He asked if she agreed with her mother. She shook her head. He hugged her and said: 'I love you'. Then he asked her if she'd go with him, if she'd live with him. She could sing in his band and together they'd be famous. She didn't have to do what her mother wanted, did she? Not anymore.

After that she didn't see Harm at Fokko's farm again. But three weeks later, on a chilly Sunday morning, she left Schokland behind and took the train to the city he lived in.

*

Three years after she'd left, Trijn returned. She trudged up the two-kilometre track, her head bowed and back bent, straight into the cold, cutting wind.

The pushchair was squeaking. There was a kink in one of the wheels. The noise squealed out above the howling of the wind. The net, with the plastic bag full of disposable nappies, kept on ballooning up. The straps of her rucksack, stuffed with adult clothes and baby clothes and little jars and bottles, cut through the winter coat into her shoulders, and Femke was sitting in the pushchair, her little hands stiff with cold, whimpering softly.

When Trijn saw the tall poplars looming up, she slowed down. She could see the dark contours of the farmhouse behind the trees. A light was on. That must be the kitchen light, which had been switched on early on this dark grey day. She longed for the stove and its log fire. She stopped at the edge of the farmyard, as if there was a border post there, or a wall with barbed wire.

The farmhouse looked the same. The big barn doors were shut. She read the name and the year on the keystones in the arches above the doors: *Schokland 1859*. She remembered the moment she'd left, three years ago, when she'd taken the bus and the train and then the bus again, and had found Harm's address, his note clutched in her hand. She thought about that time, a year and a half later, when she'd been in labour for hours and a slippery little creature was put inside her arms, and how she'd burst out crying, a fit of weeping that the midwife had interpreted as being tears of joy, which Harm had too. Even after the baby was born she'd endured everything he did to her, until the day came that he didn't respect the child either.

That was the only reason she was standing here, prepared to go back to her parents' predictable existence. She didn't dare enter the house, but it was starting to rain now, big icy drops. She opened the little door, set in the big barn door, which was always kept unlocked, from early in the morning till the last duties of the night. She breathed in the familiar scent of hay and dung and sour milk. At the back of the old byre, behind the little brick wall, where a place for the calves had been penned off with bales of hay, she took off her rucksack, took out the cigarette lighter, nervously walked into the headquarters and put the lighter down amongst all the clutter on the table. She hurried back to her hiding place, took Femke out of the pushchair, and dug down into the rucksack for a jar of toddler food. She fed her the green mush. A little ginger kitten approached them. The child crowed with delight and the kitten nudged against the child and started purring, and after some time the child fell asleep. Trijn leaned against the hay bales and felt the weariness flow through her.

When it was dark outside when she heard the dividing door open and the clomping of her father's clogs. He talked quietly to the cows, and then the door to the headquarters slammed shut behind him. He swiftly came back, his clogs clattering through the byre, while his deep voice called her name, softly, as if it was a forbidden name. She lifted the sleeping child, stood up, and cautiously stepped forward.

'Over here, Dad.'

'Trijntje?' He repeated her name, then came towards her and embraced her, and the child too. She laid her head on his shoulder and because of her sobs the child woke up and also started crying.

He looked at the little girl and asked: 'And who are you?'

'This is Femke,' she said. 'You're a Grampa now.' She handed the child over to him.

'She says I'm your Grampa,' he said to Femke, who was hiding her face behind her little hands.

'My name is Zwier,' he said, laughing, 'but you can call me Grampa.'

Then he looked at Trijn, all serious again.

'What are you here for?'

She said she'd come to stay, if she could.

It was silent a moment.

'Right,' he said. 'We'll do it like this. I'll take the tot into the house. You wait five or ten minutes, and then come in. Don't expect a warm welcome, but you really are welcome, you know. There's not a day that's gone by when she hasn't thought of you. Aye, that's how it is, right enough.'

She nodded.

And that's the way her new life began, in which everything was exactly the same as her old life.

*

It helped that coming back seemed to turn out well for Femke.

In the year and a half she'd been alive, in the untidy flat in the provincial city, the little scrap of a girl had hardly cried, babbled or laughed at all, as if she was trying to make herself invisible; and Trijn comforted herself with the thought that Femke had been too young still to remember, at a later point, things no child should have to see or go through.

Once Femke was living on the farm she started toddling around and prattling to the calves, the cats, and the dog.

But Ootje couldn't forgive. She no longer bit back her reproaches, but spat them out in spiteful little phrases, like belches. Oh, she'd seen it coming. Trijn had turned a deaf ear to her warnings. Their reputation had been destroyed. But that wasn't their fault. As if she hadn't already had enough blows from life. Losing a child…

Zwier gently resisted this. They should be pleased that Trijn had come back to them, and that she'd given them such a lovely granddaughter. But that couldn't make the lack of understanding between the mother and daughter disappear, and so he got Trijn to come along with him as much as possible, to work in the byres or on the land.

Trijn uncomplainingly did what she was expected to do. The future of the farm had to be secured. Some of the burden of work should be taken from her father's shoulders and that work made amends for the guilt. It wasn't necessary for her to enjoy it. And anyway, the heavy physical farm work helped to push her humiliating experiences with Harm into the background.

In the evenings, so she didn't have to sit on the sofa for hours, watching family shows with her tutting parents, she'd escape to Jort's workroom, the place where he'd prepared his birds.

She'd sit on his stool and look at the article about the dead animal shop in Paris, and she'd remember Jort's tales about that shop in the heart of the metropolis. He'd been astonished that he'd found people there with the same hobby as him. And that they'd even managed to make a profession of it. He'd explored the whole shop in rapture, all the different floors, full of display cases filled with exotic shells or strangely shaped translucent sponges, and birds, and fishes, and even wild animals. She'd

SHOCKED EARTH

really have loved to wander through that unknown world with him, and sometimes she'd picture them strolling through the city together and imagine him showing her the stuffed animals in that fairy-tale shop.

Sometimes she took the birds out of Jort's homemade display cases. She would glide her fingers over the wings and stroke the tails. She'd rummage around in the little cabinets and let liquids run through her hands. And one day, after finding a dead skylark that had crashed into the newly washed parlour window, she did what she'd so often seen Jort do. It was a lot more difficult than she'd imagined, and it turned into a very odd kind of creature, with its eyes skew-whiff, an over-short neck, and legs set too far back, so that the bird tipped forward, but she enjoyed the work and it was only when she was skinning and preparing the dead birds that she was able to think of Jort without feeling guilty.

February 2017

Schokland was once a stately farmhouse, but if you approach it now, via the concrete track, you'll see that half the house is concealed behind safety railings and that the long walls of the barn are supported by props, as if a boat's being built.

A long lane, lined by tall poplars, leads from the concrete track to the farmyard. On one side of the yard there is a wooden barn, and then the feed silo. On the other side there are high doors, the entrances to the tie-stalls and the old byre. Then there's the new shippon, a free-stall barn with space for a hundred dairy cows and two milking robots, which save four or five hours' work per day. A path goes past the byres and shippon and into the garden, which is full of apple trees, plum trees, pear trees and rose bushes. For a few weeks each spring the surrounding farmland, usually dominated by shades of grey and green, is ablaze with them.

If you go inside the farm you'll pass through a small corridor, between the old byre and the new one, and you'll reach the headquarters, a room like a square aquarium. This is Schokland's nerve centre: the canteen, tool store, workshop, office, meeting room and cat nursery combined. And in the middle of the night it's the place where you can warm yourself up again if you have to go and look after a sick cow, or because a cow is calving, or because there's something wrong with the milking robot.

There's a big wooden table in the middle of the room, and on it there are pincers, electric shavers, work gloves, oil cans, pens, string, nails, screwdrivers, spools, post-it blocks, and there's always a jug of raw milk. In the corner there's a computer on a steel desk, and a worktop where the coffee percolates.

On Tuesdays, odd-job day, Brian comes to give a hand. A lad with a backpack, that's how his supervisor from the day centre described him four years ago, when he introduced the young man.

Zwier is sitting at his usual place at the head of the table, reading aloud from the local newspaper. 'This winter,' he says, pointing his finger at what he's reading, 'is the coldest for seven years.'

The milking robot has been checked and rinsed, the teat buckets filled, the youngstock byre has been cleaned, and the feed shared out. Now that the morning's work is over they're drinking coffee and discussing what else needs to be done that day. Trijn grumpily observes that Femke isn't here, again. She must be out on the land, with her binoculars.

'So what are the jobs for today?' Trijn asks Brian.

'Cow shaving,' he says and points to one of the shaving machines.

Trijn nods. 'And what else?'

'Give out the concentrate.' And after a brief silence. 'Feed the calves.' Then he goes silent and grins. Brian has a strong preference for particular jobs. His eyes are twinkling behind the thick lenses of his glasses. Trijn looks at him impassively.

'Mucking out,' he says.

She nods, and when he can't think of anything else, she orders him to go outside and take a good look at the yard. Zwier shakes his head in irritation.

'Don't tease that lad so,' he says. 'It's freezing cold.'

'That'll toughen him up...' she answers.

'I'm tough enough already,' Brian says. He compresses his lips and clenches his fists. He tries to give an angry look from his twinkly eyes, but very quickly a grin appears on his face again.

'As hard and tough as a packet of margarine,' Trijn says.

He grabs his jacket and walks out the door. The old man mutters something. Trijn gives him a dirty look.

'Got anything to say, Dad? Someone taught me that farmers have to be hard on themselves.'

He stays silent. In a more friendly tone she asks him to fix up a plug for the milking robot pump. He goes to the cupboard and gets out a plug and a little screwdriver. Then he searches on the table for a small pair of pincers and sets to work.

Brian comes inside again, shivering. He raises a finger and says that the yard's got to be cleaned. He pushes his glasses back and rubs his finger across his nose. 'Plastic's got to go.'

'Very good,' Trijn says.

'An' the crates.'

'Exactly. Anything else?'

Wrinkles appear on his forehead.

'Clear up the hay.'

'Exactly,' she says. 'And you can begin with mucking out right away. We'll save the best for last.'

'Shaving cows.'

'Yes. But no more punky cows this time. Understood?'

Brian chuckles.

She asks if he's seen Femke outside yet. He shakes his head. 'Femke doesn't like mucking out,' he says. 'She knows when to clear off.'

'I'm afraid you're right, lad.' Trijn sighs. 'And she wants to be a farmer.'

'She's that already,' Zwier says.

'Is the plug finished? Then I'll go and sort out the pump.' Trijn points to the shippon.

She grabs some pliers and a length of twine. 'If Femke turns up, send her to the straw pen to help me out.'

'I can do that, you know,' Zwier offers, but Trijn shakes her head. 'The shaving machine needs a new lead. You could fix that for me.'

She's trying to save her father some work because, since Ootje's unexpected death, he's become much frailer than he wants to admit. Her mother's death shocked Trijn more than she'd thought possible. They'd never had a warm relationship, but with Ootje's death the hope that they could ever be reconciled also died.

23

Brian goes out of the headquarters and Trijn is also giving signs of leaving. As soon as she turns her back, she hears the rustling of her father's tobacco pouch.

'You know what the doctor said,' she says and opens the door.

'Yes,' he answers loud and clearly. 'But a chap has his habits, you know. Baked-in, like clay in a brick. Aye, right enough.'

*

Every step makes the rime crunch. The grasslands have changed to a carpet of glassy frost-spines and little stars of ice, glittering in the sunlight. There's an odd stillness hanging over the countryside. For once no fierce wind shakes the grasses, reeds and poplars round the scattered farmhouses. For once there's no shimmering, surging, rippling, billowing, flapping, rattling and rolling. The clay lies heavy in thick furrows that stretch to far beyond the horizon.

The maar, a winding watercourse, has been changed to a crusty road of ice. From behind the horizon the sky flames out bright blue and brilliant pink. Siepke's Sleepstead, an old sheep barn, seems to float up out of veils of mist. The spindly shapes of bare trees loom up along the country road in the distance.

The air is so cold that it's as if the lungs are closing up, just as a mussel shell closes when danger threatens. In this cold everything is slower and more difficult.

Femke hears a soft whoosh: seven swans flying towards the mouth of the river, tired wingbeats, longing for water. Is the estuary still clear of ice?

The moon, pale and almost full, is still high in the heavens, while the day is already well on its way. She keeps on walking firmly, towards the reedbeds. Two days ago, moorhens and mallards were still swimming around in the little ice hole. The wigeons, tufted ducks and teal had already vanished, flying away from the ice, to the coast or down south. She'd like to understand birds better. How do they warn each other that it's getting cold or that it's time to migrate? How do they know where to meet each other? And who decides when they'll fly up and make that staggering journey? And why does one of them sometimes stay behind? In the winter, every now and then, she sees a solitary bird whose kin have long gone to Africa.

She uses the rubber handgrip to detach the electric wire, steps through the gateway, and attaches it again, even though the electric fence has no purpose in the winter. She walks past the metres-high reeds. Every stem is wrapped in a wafer-thin crystalline layer of ice. The rime has turned the plumy flower spikes into all kinds of amazing, whimsical shapes. There's no sound of ducks quacking, or grunting, or growling, nor the friendly pinging of the bearded tits, not even the honking of geese.

She goes along a reed-fringed branch of the maar, and then the pool comes into sight, glittering in the full sunlight, a dark stretch of icy mirror-glass, with here and there some little tufts of reed-stalks.

In the middle of the frozen pool there's a heap of feathers, an untidy white coating of down. It's an enormous swan. Its long neck is folded back and its head is tucked into its wings.

She throws a lump of clay at it. The clod lands close to the swan, which lifts its head and tries to rise, clapping its wings wildly, but it can't move from where it is.

She steps onto the ice and shuffles towards the centre, and then in the reeds at the edge of the pool she sees another swan, anxiously scurrying back and forth, its neck forming a graceful S, swaying its head from side to side. Its black knob and orangey-red beak are vivid against the bright white. It's hissing and beating its wings.

As she gets closer to the bird desperately flapping on the frozen pool, it tries to fly up, but it still can't free itself.

She hurries home and dives into the barn without anyone seeing her. This isn't the right moment to bump into her mother. She's more interested in dead birds than in living ones. If a bird crashes to death against the spic-and-span farmhouse windows, then Trijn stuffs it into a plastic bag and puts it in the separate dead-bird freezer, before eventually transforming it into a cheerful little corpse in her Dead Bird Museum.

Femke swaps her normal mittens for thick work gloves, grabs the aluminium ladder and a claw hammer, and hurries back to the reedbeds.

The swan is beating its wings and it lashes out at her with its beak as she creeps on her belly across the ladder towards it. The other swan comes closer, snorting and hissing. She makes an abrupt gesture to keep it at a distance, then holds the swan that is trapped in the ice firmly by its neck and presses it down. She is now half lying on top of the paralysed creature. She breaks the ice with the hammer and slowly shuffles back along the ladder. The wingbeats become more and more frantic, and once the swan is freed it slaps its feet helplessly across the icy surface, until it reaches the edge of the pool, wings flapping, and then with loud, indignant grunts it flies up with the other swan, vanishing in the direction of the river delta.

*

When she has put the ladder back into the barn and goes into the yard, Brian calls out to her: 'You've got to help your mother with the pump.' He nods towards the straw pen.

She goes inside, slowly. Her mother is lying fully stretched on her belly. Her dark-blue overalls fall loosely over her long legs and flat buttocks, making Femke think of a scarecrow that has blown over. 'There's no meat on her at all,' Ootje, a rather weighty woman, would sometimes mutter disapprovingly when she looked at Trijn.

Trijn's head is deep inside the drain, from which the sharp stench of cow shit and rot is rising. Femke stays in the doorway, until her mother looks up and asks her what she's been up to.

'Nothing special.'

Trijn stands up and brushes the mud from her hands. Femke is a little taller than her mother. She is lanky-legged, like a newborn calf. She forces herself to keep her head held high.

'And that's all?' Trijn asks.

Femke doesn't answer.

'Nothing special,' Trijn repeats. Femke answers her mother's fierce expression with cold eyes. Don't look away. If you lower your eyes you've lost. Her jaw is trembling with tension.

'It's Tuesday,' Trijn continues.

This is going to turn into one of her mother's rants. Femke freezes, like a rabbit caught in the bright light of car headlamps.

'We were going to shave the cows today and repair the pump. Brian has to be guided and you're not here. You don't say anything. You don't tell us where you're going. You just leave things in a mess.' A short silence falls before Trijn continues. 'We're a partnership, remember.'

'I'm here now, aren't I?'

Biting silence.

Trijn purses her lips and narrows her eyes. Femke hates that expression. She'd like to turn round and go back into the reedbeds, or even better she'd like to put her mother in her place by snapping that she should mind her own business. Being in a partnership doesn't mean that Trijn can still boss her around. But instead of snapping at her mother she nods at the drain.

'Do you need help?'

'Yes. The electric cable has to go through the hole. If you push it through in the milking pen, I'll pull it out here. Then a plug will have to go on it at your end. Earth it.'

The black rubber cable has to go through a small hole under a hatch in the concrete floor. Femke is now lying on the ground, just like her mother on the other side of the wall, and she's trying to fiddle the cable through the hole. The way through is full of clots of earth and straw and manure, and the cable keeps getting stuck in them. Trijn is shouting impatiently at her, asking where it is. She's wriggled countless wires through the wings of dead birds and is much better than Femke at fiddly work. Things only work out after quite some pushing and shoving. Femke cuts off the coloured plastic with a Stanley knife, guides the copper wire onto the contact points, and screws them down.

In the distance the church tower clock strikes twelve. Brian runs in, calls for Trijn, and right after that she pops her head through the doorway of the milking pen.

'Frikandel time. Can you finish sorting out the pump? The cable's already on it. It just has to be set into the drain. And make sure that the float switch is hanging down.'

Femke nods and watches Brian tugging Trijn along with him. Her mother drops everything for that lad. While they're walking towards the farmhouse, Femke thinks to herself that Trijn would probably have preferred a son. Better a simple son than a complicated daughter. Their ease with each other, as they go off to prepare Brian's frikandel sausages, the two of them joking and laughing, is something Femke has never known.

She loves the farm where she grew up and loves the regularity of its life, in which animals play starring roles: mucking out, giving out the feed, milking, sweeping, hosing down, raking, spreading straw in the pens, the eternal cycle of dairy farming, which in its heart of hearts is still the same as it was two hundred years ago, even though automation, mechanisation, and expansion have changed so many things. But she realised when she was still very young that the familiar rhythm she loved was a drag for Trijn, something she'd wanted to escape, and that her birth had forced her mother to return to this way of life. And perhaps that's why Trijn can't stomach it if Femke has any ideas of her own about how to do things.

Femke once saw a TV programme which claimed that a vegetarian driving an SUV is more environmentally friendly than a carnivore on a bike. That made her decide to become vegetarian. But she was betraying her farming roots by doing this, according to her mother. Being a vegetarian, according to Trijn, is something for hypocritical city-dwellers, who weep when a chicken's neck is wrung or if they have to watch a pig being slaughtered, who accuse farmers of being the ones responsible for climate change, while meanwhile acquiring a new set of clothes every season and flying to this or that trendy city every other day, or to the other side of the world for a sun-snack. Every discussion about whether or not to eat meat is eventually cut off by Trijn's remark that if people were meant to be vegetarians, then the good Lord would have made sure that people couldn't digest meat. 'Ever seen a cow tucking into a drumstick? Point proved.'

But if Brian wants to fry frikandel sausages every week, then Trijn makes that happen. Even though after the big quake of five years ago, the living-kitchen and the scullery have become too dangerous to enter, and so they've had to improvise a kitchen area in the parlour.

The sideboard has to make do as a worktop, a Calor gas ring has replaced the cooker, there's a microwave and a jerrycan of water on the broad windowsill, and they have to do their frying outside, on the terrace. The large dark-oak kitchen table from the old living-kitchen, where people have eaten, spoken, and held their tongues for generations, has been lugged into the parlour. The kitchen is now forbidden territory. And more and more cracks are appearing in the byre walls, caused by ever more frequent tremors. Some of the quakes can't be felt, but the farm buildings can't stand up to them. Zwier has got used to sticking a post-it note on every new crack. At first he'd put a different colour on new cracks after every tremor. But very soon the colours ran out and so he now writes down on the little stickers when the crack first appeared. There have already been many official inspections and plenty of reports have been written, but they're still waiting for a solution.

Outside the house Brian puts the frikandels into the fryer basket and drops that into the bubbling oil. Inside the house Trijn is buttering the bread. When Brian calls out, as he will do very soon, 'Everything must go! Everything must go,' which he once heard the hot dog man call out at the cattle market, then Femke and Zwier are expected to go inside immediately and have a frikandel served up to them. And even Femke will take one, because if someone refuses one of Brian's frikandels it really upsets him. And perhaps also because her mother would never forgive her.

*

In the evening Zwier and Femke are sitting together on the little wall in the byre. They're looking at their cows, their milking machines, at the constantly grinding jaws. They're listening to the grumbling of cow stomachs, the snorting and blowing and snuffling, the clanging of the feed rails, the pattering of piss and the clattering of shit, and Femke tells Zwier how she rescued a swan that morning. Zwier sucks at his fag.

'You could've drowned,' he says. 'Birds that get stuck in the ice are usually poorly. They won't survive. That's just how it is.'

'But,' she says, 'is that a reason not to rescue them? Isn't it always worth trying?'

He strokes her head. 'Will you promise me you won't get up to such risky tricks again?'

'What are you two up to?' Trijn calls through the dividing door. 'The coffee's getting cold.'

'Don't tell her,' she says.

They hurry back through the old byre, pull off their boots, and worm their way through the wooden props and into the house.

*

Schokland's herd, one hundred dairy cows, are mainly Holsteins. Zwier once told them that one day, at the end of the nineteenth century, when ships full of poverty-stricken people from Western Europe were crossing the ocean, a cow was put on board too, to provide the first-class passengers with milk during the voyage. When she was hoisted from the hold on the other side of the ocean, the cow made a strong impression on the Yankees. Both her size and her milk yield were unheard of there. From then onwards it wasn't only people that made their way to America, but Dutch cows too, more than enough to breed healthy herds. According to Zwier the Yankees had corrupted the name of Holland into Holstein, but perhaps that isn't true and this breed of cattle are named after the northernmost part of Germany, from where so many people migrated in times of hunger and poverty.

Three years ago, when Femke officially joined the partnership, a new schedule was drawn up for who was responsible for what. Zwier manages the buildings, Trijn is in charge of the land and the feedstuff, and Femke takes care of the livestock.

Sometimes after a farm-study trip Femke will stay behind to nose around in a colleague's cowshed, so she can learn more about the farmer's choice of cows. She now knows exactly which cows give a high milk yield and which calve easily. There are breeds of cow with calm temperaments and breeds that are very skittish, cows that are susceptible to illness and others you can leave outside almost the whole year round. Every farmer sings the praises of his own herd.

Once she was looking around the cowshed of an old woman farmer who was just about getting by. The woman swore by her fifty Meuse-Rhine-Issel cows, good quiet animals, which back in the day she'd chosen for their character, a calm breed. Femke sensed a peaceful, changeless atmosphere there, or perhaps it was more like resignation. The cows moved slowly past each other, without ever hurting each other with their horns. The chickens cackled gently and with restraint. Even the crowing of the cockerel seemed subdued, and in spite of the milking robot, which was the only piece of modernity, it seemed as if time had stood still. Some farmers would scornfully call it a picture-book farm. For them this wasn't a serious business, but a nostalgic fantasy. But Femke liked it there.

She no longer believes in the farming mantra of 'growth', although like Trijn she has been brought up with the post-war credo of 'no more hunger'. But an excess of milk and manure, the overuse of antibiotics, soil exhaustion, species extinction – she's seeing and hearing more and more stories that make it clear they can't continue like this.

Not so long ago the government decided to compensate farmers if they gave up farming. When Femke read about the new scheme she wondered what kind of farmer could let his cows be shot through the head with a bolt, sell up his land, and leave hearth and home to go and live in a terraced house and stare through the curtains at the cow-shaped post-box, waiting for the day he can follow his herd.

To her amazement, after a couple of days the subsidy pot was empty.

She'd never sell up, but expansion doesn't seem necessary to her either – even though the new shippon has plenty of space for more cows – because her mother is convinced that you need to scale up to compete in the world market.

Trijn has in mind a farming business in which all the details of the herd will be read off on a computer screen. The milk yield of each cow, the cell count, when a cow is in heat, all the data could be logged onto the computer via a chip. The antibiotics would be ready on the shelves and the vet would drop in every month. Farming will become a clean business, according to Trijn. A farmer will be a manager. Dirty and time-consuming tasks will be done by robots or contractors. As long as your business is big enough.

'Dairy farming is being destroyed by the whims of politicians,' Trijn asserts, with complete conviction. 'You might well get extra money for organic milk today, but the minute you set your farm up for that, they'll turn everything round again.'

Femke hasn't yet managed to have a serious talk with Trijn about a different way of farming. In the past they would sometimes talk about difficult things by the woodburning stove, the place where, from time immemorial, hands and feet were warmed up, coffee was served, and sandwiches were eaten.

It's strange, Femke often thinks, to miss something that still exists, so close at hand, a few footsteps away from the parlour. But the former heart of the farm, and of their daily lives, has been declared forbidden territory, because it could collapse at any point.

Femke is trying to find a way of carefully introducing a few changes, without creating any arguments, and she's discovered that it's fun to experiment with the breeding programme, which is her responsibility.

She's in the headquarters sitting at the computer. Tomahawk, Goldwin, Baxter, Snowman, Aikman, Jarret: the names of the bulls all seem to have been stolen from hip hop stars, and the descriptions on the semen suppliers' websites could have come from a dating site: *Sunset has a broad head with well-formed jaws, guaranteeing more than enough intake capacity. Fanatic has a high score in terms of weight and looks really good too! Good old Jotan Red is broad in the chest and forelegs. Cricket has an excellent fertility score.*

She likes scrolling through these databases listing bulls whose overgrown bodies make them look like supernatural beings. Walking testosterone cannons. In all the photographs the sires have been trimmed, scrubbed down, and brushed. Their buttocks are all shaven and they've had litres of oil rubbed into them.

She's searching for the right kind of bull. Trijn comes in, looks over Femke's shoulder and asks her which cow she wants inseminated. Femke shakes her head, almost unnoticeably, as if she's shaking off a fly. 'Frieda,' she mutters, while she scrolls through the lists even faster than before, as if she could scroll away her mother.

'Don't go so quick. You can't compare them properly like that.'

Femke reluctantly slows down and then Trijn points to one. 'That one's good. It's got a very good maternal line.'

'It's a Holstein,' Femke answers. At which Trijn gives her a look.

'Exactly.'

'I'm looking for a Montbéliarde.' Femke carries on frantically scrolling. 'They're a sturdy breed. They can be kept out of doors almost the whole year round.'

She forces herself to speak clearly, with confidence. But Trijn isn't impressed. 'We're running a top-rate business now in terms of our milk yield. Grampa has spent years building it up.'

Femke stops scrolling and looks at her mother. 'So all I'm allowed to do is keep things going?'

'Far fewer cows have been on heat this year.' Trijn stares tightly at the computer screen.

'So all I'm allowed to do is keep things going,' Femke concludes and pushes her chair aside. She hurries out of the headquarters, puts on her bodywarmer, and walks out onto the land. The squelchy clay drags at her heels.

*

There's a storm. A fierce wind at sea has reached almost hurricane strength and now it's racing across the vast, wide fields. It's breaking branches from the poplars around the farm, as if they're chicken necks. Roof tiles are skimming through the air like frisbees. The doors and windows rattle in their frames. Dark black clouds empty their rain onto the already drenched land. Water clatters violently onto the roofs. The roaring din and chilly dampness, which in spite of the double-glazed windows and the insulation in the rooms always finds crannies to get through, is making people shiver.

Femke tosses and turns in her bed. In the Koridon family you don't sleep through a storm. A storm, as they know from of old, can cause tidal waves, wash land away, blow roofs off. A storm can orphan a child and leave it all alone. She tries to stop the anxiety by jabbing her nails into her skin, but it doesn't help. When she hears something clanging, she throws off her bedcovers, hurries downstairs, pulls on her boots and waterproof jacket, grabs the torch, and walks through the byre to the door. As soon as she opens it, it's blown out of her hands and smashes against the wall. The straw flies up and the cows bellow. She has to use both her hands to get the door shut and then she starts to check round the various farm buildings, into the wind, her body leaning forward. She could let herself fall over without really falling. She shines the torch into the jet-black night and through the lashing rain she sees the broken pieces of a sheet of roofing, blown off by the wind.

Back in the byre again she dries her face and then does a check inside, taking the dog with her. Some of the cows rub their muzzles against her. She presses on the spot between the horn cores, soft on the outside, hard on the inside, a place they love being stroked.

Then she goes into the headquarters, makes a cup of tea, and sits down on the wooden bench. The storm is roaring less here. Here she is close to the cows and a purring kitten leaps onto her lap and Klaske the dog lies at her feet, her chestnut-red head on her paws, the droopy velvety ears moving back and forth, her dark eyes fixed on her.

She should really go back to bed again. But on a stormy night like this it's cold even under a downie and she'd like to have someone to snuggle against. A strange longing. In Schokland everyone sleeps alone. Zwier lies in his bed in the room where Ootje's bed still stands. The two single beds are separated by an enormous nightstand, which used to form a demarcation line between them, to prevent any kind of unwanted overtures. Trijn sleeps in the bedroom she had as a girl, in her three-quarter bed. Koridons are not destined for closeness. A fear of intimacy has lodged in their genes, perhaps, just like a fear of storms.

She starts when the door of the headquarters opens and Zwier comes in: a crumpled figure, with his grey hair in tangled curls across his forehead, bushy eyebrows, a seaman's guernsey over his pyjama jacket, his blue-and-white checked pyjama trousers bagging around him. He looks older than he does during the day.

'Ah,' he says. 'Are you on night duty too?'

Femke nods. He puts on the kettle and leans against the worktop.

'A roofing sheet blew off.'

'That's right, is it?'

'Only one still, when I checked just now.'

'As long as that's how it stays.'

They drink their tea and listen to the wind, and the mooing of the cows, and the rattling of the wood in the frames, pricking up their ears for sounds that indicate calamity.

'It's one heck of a storm,' Zwier says. Then he puts down his cup. 'I want to show you something.'

He shuffles out of the headquarters into the byre where the youngstock are kept and walks behind the little brick wall, where Femke used to hide herself away. Then he stands still and points. The brick of the wall is cracked from top to bottom, as if it's a piece of paper, or as if someone has wanted to hack out a staircase, right through the brick. An enormous crack, from top to bottom, from left to right. You could stick a hand right through it.

They're used to damage, ever since five years ago, when the earth trembled with greater force than it had ever done before, ever since the evening they were startled by an enormous boom and then a dark, loud rattling and shaking as if a much too heavily loaded truck was racing at top speed through an underground tunnel, that evening when the joists and rafters cracked and the tea whirled in the cups, that evening when the floor tiles cracked, the ceiling lamp lashed wildly back and forth, and the pull bell moaned as if the devil himself was shaking it.

After the first shock an insidious fear crept inside all of them. In the weeks after the great quake cracks appeared everywhere, as if their farm was an old painting that was crumbling into crackleware.

Then there were discussions on the phone and the place was shored up. This was followed by an inspection, which confirmed that the damage had been caused by the tremors, and so they thought the repairs would soon happen. Months passed, which wasn't so strange, since they weren't the only ones affected. Then, unexpectedly, there was a new inspection and this time the conclusion was that it wasn't the quaking ground that had caused the damage, but poor maintenance. After yet another inspection the kitchen, the heart of the home, was suddenly declared to be a threat to life. It was fenced off the same afternoon and its entrance was sealed. They were given just enough time to take the most important things away.

The next report again mentioned poor maintenance and said that this was why they would only be granted a very small amount of compensation, purely as a gesture of goodwill. There was nothing for them to do except refuse to agree to it, and so for more than a year they've been waiting for yet another inspection.

And however much they have to improvise, because they now have to cook in the parlour without a decent stove or worktop, and they're constantly walking back and forth to the old byre, which has become the utility room where they've put the fridge and freezer, and they really miss the wood-burning stove, it all pales into insignificance in comparison to the accusation from so-called experts that the damage to the house has been caused by poor maintenance. Time after time Zwier had said to Ootje that just as it was impossible for a ship to stay still on billowing water, so a house on quaking ground quite simply is slowly torn apart. But it only became clear how that accusation of bad stewardship had festered inside Ootje, as if she had betrayed the trust of the Koridon ancestors, when she fell dead one day, the top half of her body leaning over into the open chest-freezer, a kilo of frozen minced beef still in her hands. Only then did they realise how badly Ootje had suffered, behind that mask of impassivity, under a growing feeling of powerlessness and increasing stress.

The riggers, as the Koridons call anyone that has anything to do with gas extraction, could claim that Mrs Koridon already had a weak heart.

But if they had the words to say it, and the courage, and the hope that it would be of any use, the people living in Schokland could retort that any heart would weaken if that heart has been goaded long enough.

Since Ootje's funeral the three of them, without wasting a single word on the matter, have decided that they're not going to let themselves get too wound up about it. But that hasn't made the disaster disappear. The tremors are more often apparent now, and the ground keeps moving. Just as the tides are caused by the moon, so gas extraction causes earthquakes, and there's nothing that can protect them against this.

But a farmer will never blame the earth for his misfortune. Even though the ground has been skilfully and deliberately sucked dry for the past fifty-four years. Even though there have always been a few lonely voices claiming that this won't go unpunished. But people spoke about such doom-mongers as if they were old-fashioned killjoys who actually longed to return to lives of desperate poverty, as if they were the enemies of progress. And yes, the farmers did want prosperity too, although those who lived close to the gigantic rigging-field, or even on top of it, were the very last to benefit from a gas connection, because it just wasn't profitable to lay pipes to their remote farms. So, while their land was being dug to pieces, and dirt roads and cart tracks were covered with tarmac, which they were meant to feel grateful about, while pipes were laid in their land to bring the flammable stuff to the rest of the country and far beyond, the inhabitants of the clay country were the ones who had to do without that gas the longest, muddling on with their petroleum stoves and propane gas rings. And because the inhabitants of the clay country had long been accustomed to solving their own problems, there was not one of them, neither farmer nor civilian, who spoke against the gas extraction when it began, because they were afraid of being branded as troublemakers or fools. If any of them did feel furious about it, then the most that happened was that their spades were thrust into the earth a bit more forcefully, they tugged at the udders of their cows a little more fiercely, they snapped at their children more frequently, and more people lay awake at night.

*

Femke and Zwier are standing by the back wall, their jaws clenched.

'There isn't even a big crack like this in the kitchen, right?'

Femke looks anxiously from the wall to Zwier and then back again. He shakes his head, leans on her shoulder, and says she should go back to the headquarters with him.

'It'll have to be shored up immediately and be repaired as soon as possible,' he says, lighting his fag. 'I'll do some phoning again tomorrow. I hope they won't have that daft music going on again.'

She sighs.

'Don't worry. Things will work out.'

'You're sure?' she asks.

He nods.

The bellowing of the wind has died down. The storm isn't raging so strongly now.

'Go back to bed,' he nods, 'and I'll put a bit more smoke in my chimney.' He takes a big pull from his fag.

'It's a good job Ootje can't see this anymore,' she says.

'You mean this,' he holds his cigarette up, 'or that?'

He tips his head back.

'Both.'

He nods. 'Aye. Right enough.'

*

Femke drives her Berlingo into the yard. She takes the key from the ignition but stays in the car. The dog whimpers at the still-closed door, her plumy chestnut-brown tail wagging without cease. Femke looks around the farmyard: the gravel-covered ground; the concrete paving in front of the sheds; the truncated pyramid of light green silage bales at the far end; and the feed silo, towering above the roofs of farm buildings. The doors of the barn are open. Inside it's full of tools and equipment. Her gaze glides along the large barn doors and up to the green owl board at the peak of the roof, flanked by graceful white swans with long curved necks, proud ornaments, placed there by their ancestors when the farm was fully paid off. Then the red brick walls of the byres, marred by a few deep cracks that make them seem much more dilapidated than they were before the tremors started.

She looks at the small, always dirty windows, in their cast iron casements, which have filtered the light for one hundred and fifty-eight years already. The blonde wooden props against the walls, meant to stop them shifting further out of true, stand out in their newness against the old splendour. Her eyes rest on the keystones above the doors where the grey-blue letters tell the name and date: SCHOKLAND 1859.

No, she thinks: Schokland 2017.

Thanks to the meeting she has just had, she can see the new course she wants to steer Schokland into, as if a veil of mist has been blown from her life.

She's in a hurry. Even though there's still frost at night and storm clouds rage and howl around the house, even though the hail clatters violently on her attic window and the mornings are icy cold and grey, yet the days are lengthening and as soon as the wind and rain calm down, around halfway through the afternoon, the birds tell you that spring is on the point of breaking out. Then the farmyard air is alive with the sound of chirping, cackling, and quacking, the finches sing out their little tunes, a woodpecker sounds its drum, and in the reedbeds there's the raspy fluting of courting mallards. A brand-new season.

But there's still one problem, or rather two. Zwier has farmed in the current fashion for the whole of his life, and Trijn clings to the idea that the farm has to continuously expand. And their voices have just as much weight in this partnership as hers, even though it's her future that's at stake.

She opens the car door, with Klaske leaping up at her, and walks into the byre to get to the headquarters, which is still more like a workshop than an office and that's how it will stay. She won't become a manager.

Zwier is sitting in his usual spot at the head of the table and is pulling nails out of a plank. He sorts old nails and screws by size into little containers he's made from tins. He uses the nails to create compositions on large plaques of wood. He puts them into different arrangements, on staves sketched out in pencil, as if they're musical notes, scores made of metal. As soon as one of the pieces is ready, he props it against the wall of the tie-stall. There's a whole row of them there by now. He never looks at them again, but immediately starts working on the next one.

Zwier looks up as Femke enters.

She goes to the work surface with a bounce in her step. He narrows his eyes.

'What's up with you, then?'

'Do you want a coffee?' she asks, filling the pot with water. She turns round and grins.

'Something's up,' he observes. 'Have they asked you to be in the Farmer Wants a Wife?'

'Of course not. Don't be daft.'

'Won the lottery?'

She shakes her head.

'I've met someone,' she says. She sits down beside him.

A long-drawn aha! So a kind of Farmer Wants a Wife after all. 'Who's the lucky feller? Do we know him?'

'No, Grampa. It's not a him. It's a woman farmer.'

His face falls and he looks so alarmed that she starts to laugh.

'No, not that. Of course not,' she says embarrassed. 'It's her farm I'm interested in. It's up north. By the sea dyke.'

'Heavy clay up there,' he affirms. 'Does she farm with her father? Her brother?'

42

She shakes her head.

'She's alone and she doesn't even come from a farming family. She started four years back.'

'Oh, an amateur then. Well, they never keep at it for very long. If you haven't grown up with it…'

She fiercely interrupts him and says that the woman knows exactly what she's let herself in for. That she did a degree-level course at the agricultural college.

'What were you doing up there, then? How come you know her?'

Femke says she'd sent the farmer a message after she'd read an interview with her on Facebook.

'But why?' Genuine amazement.

Then Trijn enters.

'Well there you are,' she says, without looking at Femke directly. She goes to the tap to wash her hands. 'Where have you been this time?'

Silence.

'Why do you never say where you're going?'

Femke stays silent.

'You didn't answer your phone. What's the point of that thing if you never answer it?'

And when the silence continues: 'Your sandwiches are still in the room. On the table. I've put some clingfilm on them.'

The words that Femke was so full of stick in her throat. She gulps a couple of times and then says: 'I want to talk to both of you. About the future.'

Trijn abruptly stops drying her hands and stares at Femke, as if she's said something really dirty.

'Talk? What do you mean? I'm busy. I've got to send off the orders for the sowing seed.'

Her mother screws up the hand towel.

'That's exactly why,' Femke says, and she explains that it has to

43

be now, because they shouldn't be sowing silage maize again, but clover, or if that's not yet possible, then alfalfa.

Trijn leans against the worktop. A loaded silence, like air full of electricity before the thunderstorm breaks. Trijn looks at her fiercely.

'What's up with you?'

'Could we perhaps talk a moment?'

'Well, I think we're doing that already,' Trijn says.

'Can you come and sit at the table for a bit?'

'I'm fine where I am.'

'Trijntje,' Zwier says, 'if that lass wants a chat, then let's have a chat.'

Slowly and unwillingly she sinks onto a chair. The coffee machine is perking and Femke stands up to pour the coffee out.

She can feel the eyes of the other two boring into her back.

She serves the coffee, sits down, and addresses Trijn.

'You always think I get too worked up about side issues.'

Her mother looks at her with raised eyebrows.

'The baby roe deer being mowed to bits when we're doing the grass,' Femke explains.

'Oh yes, that,' Trijn agrees, nodding, 'that's exactly…'

'That I want to mow the fields later, because of the birds,' she continues.

'But the quality of the first-cut silage is crucial.'

'That I want to create field margins and use fewer antibiotics and not use artificial fertiliser anymore. Those kinds of things.'

'That's naive, yes.'

'So you don't think I'm a real farmer,' Femke says.

Trijn denies this. Femke has really positive qualities, especially with regard to the animals. In that respect she reminds her of Jort. When Trijn mentions Jort her voice softens, and her words even make Femke smile a little. But the moment in which there was a glimmer of reconciliation is immediately destroyed when

Trijn says that Femke is still wild and impetuous. Trijn asks Zwier if he doesn't think so too. He rolls himself a new fag, with complete concentration, as if he needs all his attention for the task, as if he hasn't already spent fifty years rolling thirty a day.

'Playing deaf,' Trijn grumbles.

'Right enough,' he mutters, licking his cigarette paper.

'Do you remember, Mam, how you put the blame on me because there've been fewer calves born since I've done the inseminations?'

'Blame,' Trijn says, 'that's a bit much.'

'It's not true,' Femke continues. 'I've checked the figures. Not one calf less has been born since I've been in charge.'

'Are you sure of that? I could swear there aren't as many.'

'That's the problem, Mam. You always think you're right.'

It goes quiet in the headquarters. All that can be heard is the soft clicking of Zwier's lighter. And then his breath hungrily sucking the smoke in and blowing it out again.

Trijn says that she may have been wrong about the calving, but the fact that Femke is still interested in things that get in the way of running a healthy farming business shows she still needs guidance.

'You always were a special child, when all's said and done,' she carries on, and it sounds like an accusation. Images loom up in Femke's mind from her primary school years, when Trijn would urge her to invite friends home with her, while she had no idea at all who she could ask. No one ever called her by her name. Lamppost. Bat Ears. Horse Face.

'I'm just worried,' Trijn says softly.

'Yes,' Femke answers and gives her mother a straight look, 'and you should stop it.'

'I'd love to.' Trijn stares at the table as she speaks. 'But it's not so easy.'

'I know how I want to go on,' Femke continues, and then says after a short pause, in an almost solemn tone: 'I want to switch.'

'Switch?'

'You know what I mean. From conventional to organic.'

Now Zwier looks up for the first time and asks her if that lass up by the sea dyke is organic too.

'Who?'

Trijn looks from Zwier to Femke and then back again.

'She's been visiting some lass. She's the one who's put this in her head.'

'That's not true,' Femke says fiercely. 'She hasn't talked me into this. When I take a good look round her place, I can see the kind of farm I'd like to have. I'm not crazy. It can be done differently. Different to what you, or we, have done up to now.'

'Oh, just different, then,' Trijn says scornfully.

Femke thinks about what Danielle told her, that she went to agricultural college because she dreamed of having her own farm. Her parents had tried to talk her out of it, telling her she had no clue what she was getting into, that she'd never make it work, that she wasn't a farmer's daughter, and she had no idea what it meant to have to take on so much responsibility. And then Danielle told her triumphantly that she'd answered an advertisement from a nature organisation needing a manager for one of their farms in the middle of a conservation area. She was the only applicant who didn't have a farming background, and she was the youngest, but she was the one chosen, and now she's working organically. She's busy setting up a farming business that has space for nature. Nothing is wasted. Neither the animals nor the soil are exhausted. Her grasslands are full of flowers and herbs that attract insects and therefore birds too. She's working with a herd that barely needs to be given concentrate anymore. She often works alone, which is what farmers do anyway, but she isn't lonely. She feels herself to be part of an emerging worldwide movement.

Femke had listened to her with bated breath and felt, as she had never felt before, that she was not alone.

'I want it different. Yes. Not because you two have done it badly, but times have changed.'

'We're business people,' Trijn says. 'We have to earn our daily bread.'

'Yes,' Femke answers, 'but that can happen without constant expansion.'

'Standing still means going backwards.'

'That's what they try to tell us,' Femke answers. 'But if we carry on like this, then everything will be destroyed. We're having to get the cows slaughtered sooner and sooner now, because they're forced to produce so much milk. Our grass isn't nutritious enough and so the milk we produce isn't all that nutritious either. The animals need more and more antibiotics, and insects and birds are dying out. I don't like doing it this way.'

And then it's silent. All three of them stir their coffee, looking at the black liquid, like fortune tellers staring into coffee grounds.

Trijn is the first to break the silence.

'It's a kick in the teeth.'

Femke trembles and doesn't answer her mother.

She gives Zwier a sidelong glance: 'For you too?'

He slowly shakes his head, licks his tongue along his lips, and, twisting a rusty nail round and round in his fingers, says: 'I'm thinking it through.' He's quiet a moment and then says: 'If I've got it right, that lass is renting her farm. Right in the middle of a nature reserve. She'll be getting plenty of subsidies for that.'

'Yes,' Femke says, nodding, 'but there are also farm owners who are fed up of things as they are now, and they're switching. Farmers who do things organically, who produce less, who create marsh pools and bio-diverse field margins on their land, who don't overwork their soil. There are even farmers,' she continues, 'who are experimenting with family herds.'

'And then your profit goes down the drain,' Zwier says.

She doesn't even bother to contradict this.

'Perhaps. But we'll be making a farm business that's future-proof.'

He looks up and points the nail in his hand at her: 'You're rattling on too fast. Chucking out the maize and putting in clover right now, well that's just undermining your profits. What I think is if you want to do things differently, then do it with more prudence.'

'But you're not saying no?'

He looks at Trijn as he continues: 'The best farmers know what they want. Our lass has had this in her head for a long time now.'

He nods at Femke and then turns to Trijn again: 'A wild horse runs best if you give it free rein. That's just how it is. It seems best to me that we go along with her in this, then we can keep an eye on her for a bit. Not too quickly, not this year already, but let's not kill the idea right off.'

Trijn stares into space, her lips compressed. A long silence. She sighs.

'I don't know,' she says. 'I'm afraid it won't work. That we'll go bankrupt.'

'We won't. Really,' Femke says with suppressed enthusiasm. 'The time is now. And there's,' she repeats what she heard Danielle say, 'momentum.'

'Act normal, and that's crazy enough.' Trijn shrugs her shoulders. 'Do you really want me to say yes, just like that, to changing the whole way we do things here?'

'No,' Femke answers, 'that's not the case, Mam. But couldn't we just let someone come round, to advise us about it?'

'I won't say no to that.'

Femke stands. 'So I'll ask if someone can come and talk to us.' But the triumphant feeling she had when she came back to their farm a while back has been extinguished, as if a bucket of dirty water has been thrown over her.

*

The next day, with thick rainclouds hanging low over the land, Femke drives back to the farm by the sea dyke, twenty-five miles to the north, on the vast expanse of the newest polderland. Behind the old inner dykes, on the thick clayey soil there, fewer farms and cottages have been hit by the tremors up to now.

She goes into the cowshed. Danielle is sitting on the loader, dealing out the bales of fodder. Femke stands still a moment and watches the small but sturdy figure, the straight back and the dark curls that seem to leap up. Then she walks slowly round the loader, smiles, and hesitantly raises a hand. Danielle looks surprised and then turns off the engine.

'I've done it.'

'What?'

'Talked to them about switching.' And then hesitantly: 'They want to think it over.'

Danielle gives an enthusiastic shriek, as if the switch-over is already a fact, then jumps off the tractor and opens her arms. Femke laughs shyly as she's hugged. Her arms dangle down by her body, like flapping polytape.

Femke doesn't mention that her mother is still full of doubts.

Luckily, Danielle lets go and asks Femke if she can help give out the feed, so they can drink coffee together as soon as possible.

*

In the Dead Bird Museum Trijn is gutting a sparrowhawk. It's not the first time that a bird of prey hunting a songbird has crashed to death against the parlour window, blinded by the chase.

49

The bird is lying on its back on the workbench, wings folded. It has a long, striped tail and outspread yellow talons that look as if they could still grab hold of prey, as if the life hadn't already drained out of it. The head and the beak are still more or less intact.

Trijn is sitting on Jort's stool and with a razor-sharp scalpel has made a vertical incision straight down the brown-grey bars of the breast, and then, with absolute focus, has cut the skin from the body, scraping at it till the last scraps of flesh and fat have gone.

She cuts loose the legs and wings and tendons, and takes out the body, treats the skull with borax to loosen the last scraps of flesh, scrapes the leg bones clean, and then puts the feathered skin into a lye bath, into which she has added a little arsenic, which is very effective against decay.

She remembers taking Femke to school when she was an infant and watching her from behind the fence, seeing the child inch into the schoolyard, full of kids yelling wildly and glowing with apparent self-confidence.

She lays the bird's bloody carcase onto a piece of paper and traces round it with a pencil to get the exact proportions of the bird's body: length, breadth, thickness. She measures it and notes the measurements on the sketch, which is stained with reddish-brown patches. When everything seems correct she pushes the body aside, gets a piece of rigid foam, draws the outline onto it, and then uses a sharp knife to create an artificial body.

In her mind's eye she sees the other girls looking at Femke with hostility, conspiratorially, then turning their backs on her. She sees her child seeking refuge in a corner of the yard, from where she quietly watches this little world that grudges her a place in it. She can never stop seeing that image: the vulnerable little child hiding herself in the darkest part of the playground, as if she was trying to make herself as invisible as possible, like a water snipe flattening itself into the clayey ground, as if it were a little clump of grass.

After that Femke didn't even look at the girls again. As soon as Trijn dropped her at the schoolyard she zig-zagged off, fleeing something, though she never wanted to say why she shot off like that. Or she would look with absolute attention at a twig, a pebble, an ant, or her own finger, as if she was alone.

Trijn cuts the rounded form of the back from the foam and remembers the gossipy little girls, their mocking glances, their little mouths spewing out filth, and the cutting finger-gestures, all directed at her child.

And she stood there every morning behind the fence, her stomach clenched with pain. At home she'd try to get Femke to be a bit tougher: don't slump, don't hunch your shoulders like that, don't give such shy glances, and don't speak so softly. Speak loudly and clearly. That wasn't so difficult, was it?

She makes a notch in the foam rump and puts the model on the sketch. Some more foam needs to be added.

At parents' evenings, during the ten-minute consultations, they always said her daughter was too introverted. That was a constantly returning reproach. But Femke's isolation didn't seem to make her suffer. She hated school, but as soon as she got home she'd skip into the byre, play with the kittens or tie a rope around a calf's neck so she could take it for long walks beside the maar. As she watched her doing this, she'd hear the child talking to the calf as if it was her friend. The calves knew everything about her. And when the cattle buyer took them away, Femke was inconsolable for the rest of the day.

She makes the bird a new neck from wire, wood shavings and thread. Switching to organic. She can't make herself feel enthusiasm for it. She pushes a long piece of wire through the skull.

She can certainly see that the magazines are full of articles about organic farming, and that politicians and city-dwellers are always going on about nature-friendly agriculture, but too often she's seen that such fads are transitory and that everything can be steered in a completely opposite direction when governments and ministers change. Everyone's shouting out about the circular economy now, a posh-sounding term, but for how long will they do so? Till the next election? Till the next milk scandal? Till everything collapses? They wouldn't be the first farming enterprise to throw everything up in the air and then come down to earth with a shock. The way they farm is based on years of experience. They can't just throw that overboard, although she does understand that Femke wants to put her own stamp on the business.

When she was Femke's age she got on the bus and went to the city, convinced that love and happiness were waiting there for her. That's the same as Femke thinking that some farm she happened to pop into one fine afternoon can serve as a good model for their own farm.

She wiggles a long piece of wire through the wings and guides it through the fragile sternum. Then she presses viciously small balls of clay into the eyeholes and goes to the little chest of drawers where she stores dozens of artificial eyes: big black balls with white dots in the centre; balls with a circular white rim; yellow eyes with a black centre; little eyes like coloured pinheads. All those eyes are staring at her.

She has always been worried about what would become of her Femke. A child that seemed to have so little interest in other people. How could she become anything other than an outsider, a loner, someone splintered off from society? Someone like Fokko. Someone everyone tolerates, but a tragic figure.

In the years after her return she never visited Fokko again. His farm, the Wide World, hadn't turned out to be a gateway to an amazing existence, but had been a rat trap, like that friendly-looking little house with its slanting roof, floating on the maar with a piece of apple inside it to lure a muskrat, and then the mesh snaps shut behind it and the floor falls away and it flounders and thrashes and slowly drowns in the underwater cage.

The Wide World had merely been a through station, and not only for her. One by one the members of the band and all the kiddies had dropped out. They reconciled themselves to an ordinary life with a job, wife, and children, and Fokko was left alone on his farm, a kilometre away from the concrete track, alone with his four guitars, the big barn, his beer crates, and his tall stories that no one listened to anymore.

And as the years went by, he changed too. He began to wash his windows and painted the frames and the front door, repaired the half-hip roof and cleared the barn. And one day, to his surprise, he got a small inheritance, left to him by his father, with whom he'd always been at odds but who after his death clearly hadn't begrudged him a little something after all. Then he put his long hair in a ponytail, pulled on a pair of jeans without any holes, and even wore a jacket, and first paid a visit to the owner of the Wide World and then to the bank. And then to everyone's surprise he managed to get himself a mortgage. Fokko himself called it a gift of God, but Zwier said that in the '90s everything was possible and that even the biggest idiot could get a loan, because the banks were dealing out mortgages as if they were slices of aniseed cake. Ootje said people would be sorry one day, but no one understood what she meant by that.

Once Fokko was finally the owner of the Wide World he took pleasure in restoring the farm to its former state. He had found a description in a book of what it had looked like a century ago, and he scratched together some old floor tiles to patch up the floors, and bricks as well, and he even managed to find proper medieval cloister bricks to restore the walls.

He proudly announced that he was living with a pair of buzzards who were nesting high up in one of the poplars by his farmhouse. One of them often sat on a post in the yard, with its wings spread out, as if it was greeting Fokko. He could get quite close to the bird without it flying off, and if he made mewing sounds then the buzzard tilted its head as if it was listening.

Sometimes the birds would perch high up in the old beech tree, eyeing up Schokland's chickens. Zwier had once grabbed his air rifle and tried to shoot one of the buzzards down, but he missed. He shot again and again, each time more angrily, until he'd shot a hole in the silo. The gun-cracks and the bird's fierce mewing as it circled round, high up in the sky, out of reach of the gun, alarmed Fokko who came racing along on his moped. Fokko offered to pay compensation for the stolen chickens, as long as Zwier left his birds alone. For Ootje that was definite proof that their neighbour was still stark staring mad.

Fokko continued to be the village weirdo and Trijn was afraid that her daughter might turn into a female version of him. A lot had gone wrong in her own life and that, perhaps, was exactly why it was so important that her daughter's life should be successful and that Schokland should remain a healthy business. This is the only place in the world where Femke can flourish. And if Trijn has learned one thing in all these years, it's that only farmers who are big enough can't be walked over. No one pays any attention to a hobby farmer. Only a business focused on expansion and efficiency can survive.

She presses the yellow irises with black pupils into the clay eyeholes and the sparrowhawk immediately regains its character. She can start sewing it up.

March 2017

THE SKY IS GREY AND DULL. The vague contours of the old brick factory and its dilapidated chimney loom up indistinctly from the mist. A mute swan is flying eastwards, low across the land, its wings beating powerfully, as if it has a specific aim in mind. The barrier tapes, placed across the meadowland to stop armies of geese gobbling up the grass, hang down like forgotten bunting after a rained-off party. On the grey pool in the distance a few ducks are bobbing. Although all the little birds are warbling nineteen to the dozen, as if they're trying to get spring going, the land seems to be holding its breath and the prevailing mood is one of dejection. A goose is standing stock-still, glued to the reedy border. Its greyish-white breast stands out against the bronze plumes. It seems to be sulking. A second goose wheels in a large circle across the reedbeds, then hastily vanishes. A crow caws loudly and aggressively. The finches provide the background rhythm.

Behind Femke is the farm for which she has such wonderful plans – plans that on a day like today speak only of brash over-confidence. Yesterday the organic farming advisor came to visit and toured the farm with her. She produced all the papers and gave him the data about the extent of their land holdings, the dimensions of the shippon and the byres, and the milk cell count. Trijn and Zwier sat there saying nothing at all, but let her explain everything, as if this wasn't their business too. They only answered if he addressed them directly, a little like reluctant teenagers having to say something in class for the teacher.

The man decided that in its present state the farm could definitely convert to organic farming: the cow-housing is big enough and they have more than enough hectares of land. But he did strongly advise them to sort out their milk marketing and warned them that in the first years their income would drop because of lower grass and milk yields. Moreover, it would be a year and a half before they'd get organic prices. She knew that, of course, but when it was said aloud like that, and she saw her mother and grandfather nodding without making any comments, she felt really downhearted. Should she go ahead with her plans at all, now that Zwier is having to hang around on the phone for hours to report the enormous new crack in the wall? And it'll be days before he manages to get hold of someone, who'll simply promise to send yet another expert, the umpteenth perfectly dressed man who will come and assess the damage, who'll nod, take photos and make notes before getting into his lease-car and pronouncing the infamous sentence: 'You'll hear from us.'

On the other hand, she wants nothing more fervently than to put all her energy into a farming business that will work with nature instead of against it. That's how Danielle puts it, because as nature goes her own sweet way the best thing is to make sure that you're on her side. It would be a farm that doesn't use feed concentrates or antibiotics, a word that actually means anti-life. There by the sea dyke she saw with envy how a young woman, just a couple of years older than herself, was running the kind of farm she dreamed of.

They could wait until an agreement is reached about compensation and reinforcing the farmhouse, until the kitchen has been rebuilt and the woodburning stove, with its little mica panes, has a fire in it again. One day. But will that day ever come?

Trijn drives the van into the farmyard. She's been on a big shopping trip at the supermarket. Femke goes across to help her unload it. Trijn flings the back doors of the van open and hands her a crate. They stow away the shopping without saying a word. As Femke is placing things in the fridge, she comes across a small packet of vegetarian mince.

She goes to the headquarters and starts making coffee. Trijn comes in, and then Zwier, with a pen and memo block in his hands.

'Aha,' Trijn says, 'you're seeing to the admin again.'

He mutters something.

'People in the village are saying that it's all over for Fokko. His farm's going to be demolished.'

'How come?' Zwier sounds surprised.

'Quake damage. But you know that, don't you?'

'But Fokko's farmhouse has a foundation made from those big medieval bricks. They will rebuild it, won't they?'

Trijn shakes her head. 'They've bought him out.'

'How much?'

Trijn shrugs.

'He's not allowed to say. He had to sign a confidentiality clause. But they're saying it isn't enough for him to pay off his mortgage.'

'Disgraceful,' Zwier grumbles.

Femke looks from one to the other, at their tight expressions. She heard once that the miners in the south of the Netherlands would take a canary into the mine with them. If it was lying on its back, claws in the air, they knew they had to move like the clappers to get back above ground. She pictures Fokko and his Wide World as their region's canary. And sees that Schokland could very well be next.

Trijn says he must have brought it on himself. They all know what an awkward so-and-so he is.

'He's no friend of mine,' Zwier says, 'but that farm is even older than ours. From 1849, if I'm not mistaken. It's a real beauty of a farm, and it should be restored. That farm belongs here, like the clay they built it on.'

Trijn shrugs her shoulders.

'Things haven't got that far yet,' she says. 'There'll be a solution.' And then, completely unexpectedly, she says to Femke: 'Shall we just take a look together to see what alfalfa costs? Perhaps for a small piece of land to start with? To see how it goes?'

Femke looks at her in amazement, and then a smile breaks through and she leaps up.

'Hallelujah!' Zwier says. 'So we'll go bust after all. Well, I'll just light myself another fag.' And he rummages around for his tobacco pouch.

*

Trijn is hosing down the farmyard. The sharp stench of cow shit announces the spring. They're now allowed to suck the slurry from the overfull slurry stores again and inject it into the bare land. It's impossible to escape the smell, it penetrates every pore. The washing has to be kept indoors, the doors and windows must be kept shut, and the offcomers who have bought up the farms of bankrupt farmers turn up their noses and spray whole can-loads of air freshener all around. The stench of shit reminds Trijn that she's here, trapped in a life that city folk can so easily manage to avoid. For them, the change of the seasons simply means the difference between drinking in a lounge bar or on a terrace in the sun.

There's a dull droning sound. At the head of the concrete track a column is approaching: metal machines moving slowly forward on caterpillar tracks, like an army of extra-terrestrial monsters. The one in front is a giant grabber, with steel teeth set on an articulated metal neck. Behind that there's a tractor with a drill, like the sting of a giant wasp, and the last colossus is a blue truck with a hydraulic crane and a big orange skip at the back. Slowly and tauntingly the Panzer division of the demolition team comes towards Schokland, with orange lights flashing on the mammoth creatures, fierce flickers warning them that their daily routine will be disrupted.

Zwier comes running from the shippon and asks: 'What the bloody hell is happening now?' He narrows his eyes.

Trijn asks nervously: 'They're not coming for us, surely?'

Zwier spent hours on the phone last week trying to inform someone about the new cracks.

'I asked them to come and take a look, and to shore things up.' And then: 'I'll shoot them off our farm.' His small dark eyes are spitting fire and his cheeks are bright red. He puts his hands on his hips, as if that stance can make him firm enough to resist their superior force. Trijn crosses her arms. A fragile front-line against an enemy of steel.

Then they see the column turn left, onto Fokko's lonning. They give a simultaneous sigh of relief. Zwier lights his stubbed-out fag, takes an angry puff, then looks up at Trijn, who towers a full head above him.

'And you said it wouldn't get as far as this? That there'd be a solution?'

'Oh, as if it's my fault.'

'Come on,' he says, heading for his little pickup. 'Where's the lass?'

For once Trijn knows the answer: Femke is on the land with the contractor.

They drive to the Wide World in Zwier's vehicle. He parks at the edge of the farmyard and steps out. Trijn slowly follows him.

The orange lights are still flashing. The spacious yard is in chaos, filled with demolition machines and a pile of metal fencing, the trappings of forbidden access, retired now and shoved carelessly aside. A man in overalls is guiding the truck into a corner.

The vehicle reverses, its shrill alarm blaring out as if it's trying to warn the last mice and martens to take to their heels.

The man gives a stop-signal and raises his thumb. The vehicle halts. The electronic shrieking stops. The driver starts the hydraulic crane and, guided by the arm-waving of the man in work clothes, the skip is hoisted on rattling chains from the vehicle and set down beside the barn.

The other demolition apparatus is lined up by the side of the house, like ranks of soldiers waiting for the signal to attack. The big steel-toothed maw is wide open.

The centuries-old cloister bricks and the carefully painted barge-boards, the dark green owl board, the dark red floor tiles in the kitchen with their worn-out pathways along which, year after year, generations of women shuffled back and forth, the old tiled chimneypiece, the wooden floorboards that Fokko had repaired and varnished, the green shutters he'd so carefully restored, the wide window seats where he liked to sit on a cushion and gaze out of the window, and the stone front-door steps, where for more than a hundred and fifty years brides were carried in and the dead were carried out, are all on the point of being destroyed.

Fokko's black Mercedes van is parked by the house, remnants of bright-red lettering on its side that once formed the words THE WIDE WORLD. Its doors are open, his household goods are bulging out, and scattered on the gravel around it are all the things that won't fit in: a chair, a half-torn box filled with pans, a crate of LPs, a couple of bin bags stuffed with linen. Fokko is sitting on the tail-end of the van, leaning on his elbows, a bottle in his hands.

Zwier walks towards him, at the same time as the overalls-man, who is gesturing at Fokko and shouting that he and his van and his trash have to leave, that they can't make a start on the job with him here.

Fokko whimpers when he sees them, points at the over-stuffed van and the junk beside it, and then at his house. He bursts into sobs. Zwier claps him on the back: 'Me lad, me lad.'

Fokko looks old and dishevelled. His face is dark and drawn. There's stubble on his cheeks. His ponytail, a limp grey string, hangs down to his back. His eyes are half shut.

The overalls-man approaches and asks if they're family.

'I'm the neighbour,' Zwier answers, 'and who are you?'

The man says that they've got to get on with the job. They need space to do it and this gent was supposed to have been gone already.

'Don't you have one little scrap of feeling in you?' Zwier asks, while the guys from the other machines come closer: the heavy gang, a bunch of muscled thugs.

'It's not nice for the gent,' the man says, and swallows, 'but agreements have been made. Mr What's-his-name-here has signed a contract, he's cashed his compensation, and now it's time for him to stick to his side of the bargain. He wasn't meant to be here today at all.'

'And where's he supposed to go, then?'

'That's not our problem, sir. We're the demolition men. Perhaps he could ask the council for help. Or the Salvation Army?'

The man shrugs his shoulders while his mates wait there in silence, their arms folded.

Zwier asks Trijn to get Femke to bring their van along, so they can load up the last boxes and refuse sacks.

'And where are they supposed to go?' Trijn asks.

'We'll see about that later,' he says, 'but he's got to leave.' And then he yells out at the top of his voice: 'Bloody frigging bloody hell.'

'Sir,' says the man in overalls, 'I can't do anything about this either. Let's try to be a little civilised about it.'

'If we were all a little civilised about it, then you lot wouldn't be here,' Zwier says, and for the first time Fokko raises his head and gives a little grin.

Femke arrives and they load all Fokko's remaining household stuff into the van. He himself does nothing at all, just swigs from his bottle every now and then.

'Where's this stuff supposed to go then, Fokko?' Trijn asks again. He shakes his head, shrugging his shoulders.

'Come on,' Zwier says, 'we'll take it all back home with us. He shouldn't drive, Trijntje. You drive his van. I'll take him back with me.'

Zwier and his pickup are at the front, then Femke, then Trijn. The overalls-man guides them out of the farmyard, as if they're actually waiting for him to direct them. But the pickup stops at the edge of the farm lane, and their whole little column stops with it. Zwier and Fokko get out. 'He just wants a last look.'

As they lean against the back of Fokko's van, they see the roof being drilled right through and the shark's maw gobbling up pieces of roofing. The roof cracks, the beams break like bird bones, the insulation material turns to dust and plunges down, the engine roars and drones and thunders and rages and crackles and crunches: destruction makes a hellish din. Fokko wails. Femke stares. Trijn purses her lips. Zwier's cheeks go red.

And high above this apocalyptic scene, where a hundred and fifty years of history is being guzzled down, bite after bite after bite, a buzzard is circling, mewing, lamenting.

'Come on,' Zwier says, 'this is too awful to watch.' He wipes his tears away with the back of his hand and takes Fokko by the arm, who lets himself be led away like a rag doll. They get into the vehicles and drive back to Schokland in a small funeral procession.

Femke makes up the bed in what used to be the farmhand's room, between the old byre and the farmhouse. Trijn repeats several times that it's not their problem if Fokko doesn't have a house anymore. Till Zwier says: 'Now hold your tongue. We're not going to let a neighbour sleep on the street.'

'He's a boozer,' Trijn says firmly.

'He'll stay with us till there's a solution.'

And that means the discussion is over, for the time being.

*

It's two weeks later and Femke is in the straw pen rubbing a bull calf dry. As she wipes off the meconium the calf's markings appear: a clear red-and-white flecked hide, dark eyes, a soft pink muzzle, eyelashes blonde as angel hair.

Femke leaves the calf at the back of the straw pen and then milks the mother cow. The colostrum spurts into the pail.

She hears Fokko approaching. Everything about him makes a noise: his body, lurching forward with every step, his over-loud sniffing and hawking and talking. Zwier calls him a polter-guest.

As he comes closer the cow starts kicking. Femke makes shushing sounds, milks the last of the beastings out, and stands up.

'Another new-born calf?

Fokko stumps into the milking pen to join her. She pours part of the thick yellowish liquid into a bottle.

'What's it this time?'

The calf is lying in a corner of the straw pen.

She pulls the calf to its feet, clamps it between her legs, makes little hushing noises, and pushes the teat into its mouth. It doesn't want it and pulls its head back. Fokko laughs and the calf jumps.

Femke speaks softly to the little creature, pushes its mouth open, and forces the teat in. The animal bucks and tries to struggle free. Her body tenses and then, using quite some force, she grips him fast. It's a question of persistence.

Fokko laughs loudly.

'A stubborn little thing, that one. It won't be forced.'

'He's got to drink the beastings,' she says, 'but he's already suckled from his mother tonight.'

'He's right. A bottle or the real works. I know which I'd choose,' he says. 'Why don't you just let him drink from his mother?'

Trijn has just entered the shippon.

'Listen Fokko, we can do without folks who tell us what to do. The whole country's doing that already.'

Femke is distracted for a moment and the calf pulls free. She grabs it by the skin of the neck and clamps it between her legs again, opens its mouth, and pushes the teat in once more.

'Just look at that. What a battle.'

'Shut up,' Trijn snarls.

'The more you wait,' Femke says, 'the harder it is to separate them from their mothers.'

'Exactly,' Fokko says, 'so why do you do it, then? Just let them stay together.'

'We're not a play farm,' Trijn snaps, 'but a business. If I were you, I'd go and look for somewhere else to stay, for once, instead of telling us how to run our farm.'

The calf gives in and is now fiercely sucking at the beastings, down to the very last drop. Then Femke lets him go and the little creature takes a few tottering steps.

'Look at that,' she says. 'His front legs are wonky.'

'We won't keep that one,' Trijn answers. 'It's a bull calf, anyway.'

Fokko leans over the animal and sings: 'Little calf, they'll sell you and they'll fatten you up. They'll turn you into veal steak and gobble you up. Your mother's just a dairy cow. You're not important anyhow.'

Trijn laughs. Femke gulps.

'Exactly,' Trijn says, 'and if you have any objections to that, you should become one of those vegan-fundamentalists. Anyway, have you been to see the council yet?'

Fokko nods. 'I'm not urgent.'

'Not urgent? You haven't got anywhere to live.'

'No, but they bought me out.'

'But that money went on paying back your mortgage.'

'You don't have to tell me that, but they say it's not their problem.'

Trijn asks whose problem it is then.

'Yours, I think,' Fokko says with a snigger. 'You don't want me around.'

Trucks loaded up with refuse skips had gone back and forth for days, like an aid convoy in a war zone, in this case not bringing hope but carrying it away. Fokko had spent all that time sitting dejectedly on the bench in the farmyard, staring at the spot where his Wide World was being demolished.

And when the hauling away of the rubble had finished and silence set in, he stood up and walked towards the Wide World, first with slow footsteps, but then quicker and quicker, almost stumbling over his big feet. Femke followed him.

A strong wind was blowing white clouds along the sky, sunlight fell across the land, and the chirruping of sparrows sounded through the air. But on the former farmyard of the Wide World nothing remained, except black, flattened earth, tipped out by the workmen over the dug-up, ransacked yard. A century and a half of history destroyed at dizzying speed.

Fokko collapsed, shook his head, gave a kind of a groan, then long howls. Femke went and sat down beside him. She clumsily placed a hand on his broad back, then took it away again. She stared ahead and pictured their own farm like this, and a metal hand seemed to clench at her stomach.

'Nothing's left,' he observed, and looked at her with glistening eyes. She shrugged her shoulders. At the edge of the farmyard the full-throated song of a thrush rang out.

'What can I do now?'

She stayed silent, and then said carefully: 'But you signed, didn't you? Why did you do that?'

He clenched his hands and beat his fists hard against each other. 'Because the uncertainty was driving me mad.'

His knuckles went red.

'And why don't they give you somewhere else to live, then?'

The shadow of a cloud slipped across the land. She placed a hand over his fist. He gripped it strongly and squeezed it.

'They bought me out. They say.'

She drew her hand back.

'And that's all gone to the bank.'

Femke wondered what would happen to this dead spot now. The most appropriate thing would be to let it turn wild again, to let grass and cleavers and cow parsnip run riot, to let it be filled with shrubs, reeds and water, and be a refuge for insects and reptiles and birds and foxes.

The cloud floated away, the sky cleared, and high above them they could hear the mewing of the buzzards.

They looked up and saw the birds spiralling upwards, wings outstretched, their fanned-out tails pivoting back and forth like joysticks. Circle on circle, spiralling up like corkscrews, lamenting above the emptied-out Wide World. Then the birds went even higher and vanished from sight. A cloud slid across the sun again.

'Come on,' said Femke, 'I've got to get back to work.'

Fokko scrambled up again, picked up a clod of earth, and was going to put it in his pocket, but had second thoughts. 'No,' he said, 'this isn't my earth anymore. This is enemy poison.' And he flung the clod as far away from him as possible.

*

To escape Fokko, Trijn increasingly retreats into her Dead Bird Museum, one of the few places where she won't be disturbed. When she's sitting here, she can imagine that she's ended up in another life. The Dead Bird Museum could be anywhere at all. Birds aren't tied to a particular place. Birds fall from the sky everywhere.

But it's only here that they have to deal with constantly

subsiding ground, with growing cracks. This is the only place in the country where a sense of insecurity is increasing; this region with its dwindling population, this remote corner of the land, far from the seat of government where they've decided to let international companies pump the ground dry.

That massive crack in the byre terrifies her – fractures in the brickwork where their cattle, their capital, are located – and she sees the fate of the Wide World as an evil omen, a prophecy of what is probably in store for them too. And as if that weren't enough there are whispers in the village that one day there'll be an enormous earthquake, bigger than anything they've had before. No one knows when, no one knows how powerful it will be, but it'll definitely come, that's what they're saying.

She shudders.

Fokko crashes into the barn, bawling her name. She can't free herself from the thought that he tempts fate, that his bad luck is catching. She's absolutely convinced that he only has himself to thank for his misfortune, that his obstinacy, insolence and lack of manners have led to the hopeless situation he's in. One thing she's sure of: decent people are treated decently.

Very soon the day will come when Schokland's new quake damage will be inspected and she's scared that Fokko's presence will have negative consequences for them.

'Trijn!' She doesn't react. There's an unwritten law that no one should disturb her when she's in her Dead Bird Museum. But the door is flung open, and Fokko crashes in, and the air thickens. He stands in front of her like an old prophet, holding out both his arms, with a dead buzzard on them, its wings outspread and a necklace of whiteish feathers on its dark-brown breast. The yellow feet with their black talons stab forward like knives.

The big man is wailing. He puts the creature down on the workbench. Trijn looks from the bird to Fokko, and then back at the bird.

'Fix him,' he orders her, blubbering.

A brief smile crosses her face. His command awakens a memory.

'Is that one of yours?'

Fokko nods.

'What happened?'

'He was lying dead by my house.'

'Where?'

'By my house.'

He sounds impatient.

'But your house doesn't exist anymore, right?'

'But he was lying there. On the ground.'

'How come?'

'He crashed against it.'

'Against a tree?'

'No, against my house.'

She tells him not to be so daft. It's really not possible.

'Why isn't it possible?'

'Because your house isn't there now.'

He answers by telling her not to be such a know-all.

Trijn keeps quiet. He really is crazy, she thinks. We have to get rid of him.

The silence continues.

'Well?' he asks impatiently.

She makes a decision.

'That's fine,' she says. 'I'll do it, but on one condition.' She looks straight at him now. 'You've got to promise to stick to it.'

'I've got no money.'

'I don't want money. You don't have to do anything. You just have to go away from here.'

His eyes narrow.

'I don't want you here anymore. You have to leave. And don't bother the others about it. You'll find somewhere else. We've got enough on our plates as it is. Agreed?'

He keeps on staring. She swallows. Straightens her back.

'Agreed?'

'Bitch.'

'Agreed?'

'When will he be ready?''

'In two weeks' time. Come and fetch him then, but I don't want to see you here at all before then.'

He turns his back on her and goes out of the door, jabbing a middle finger up in the air.

She opens the window to let the fresh spring air inside.

*

It's Tuesday. Frikandel day. Odd jobs day. The day the livestock buyer comes round. The day the damage experts will finally come and check things out. Femke is sitting on the loader and is taking the bales of fodder from the yard into the shippon. She dumps them on the ground, then Brian slits open the plastic and gives out the hay. When she's on the loader she enjoys playing a little competition with herself: manoeuvring back and forth as quickly as possible and putting a new load down in the shed in the shortest possible time. Just when she's outside again, as she's picking up a new load of haybales, her phone goes.

'I'm near your place. Have you got time for a quick coffee?'

'Yes, of course,' she says, after staying quiet just a little too long.

'Then I'll be with you in about ten minutes.'

She leaps down from the loader, tells Brian to finish the remaining bales, dashes up the stairs to her attic room, goes to the mirror to take the hairband out of her hair, combs the unruly mop of curls, puts the band back in again, with a few fluffy tendrils escaping it, runs down the stairs, goes into the parlour and sweeps all Zwier's empty shag packets together, puts the roe deer leg with the hoof still on it into Klaske's basket, tidies her study books about organic farming on the windowsill, hears Klaske barking, hastily pulls on her boots, hurries through the byre, and a moment later sees Danielle getting out of her estate car.

'Hi, Femke.'

She holds out her hand, but Danielle gives her a fashionable city-hug.

'Well,' Danielle says, 'at last. Now I can take a look at your farm, hey? You've got a really nice place here.'

Femke hurriedly says that it's not her place, but her Grampa's and her mother's too.

'How long have your family been here?'

She points to the keystones.

'I believe I'm the seventh generation.'

'Schokland,' Danielle reads out. 'Why's it called Schokland? That's a place in the polderlands, isn't it?'

She tells Danielle the story about the island in the Zuiderzee and the tidal wave and the young lad.

'Then he did well for himself,' Danielle concludes.

Femke hesitates a moment, and then asks what she'd like to see.

'Everything,' Danielle answers.

They walk towards the shippon, past the props. Danielle gives the timber a knock.

'Quake damage?'

Femke nods. They walk through the shippon and the tie-stalls, then go into the old byre, where Zwier is examining the wall. He has his memo block and a pen in his hands.

'This is my Grampa.'

'Well, fancy that,' he says, 'a visitor.'

Danielle introduces herself.

'Aha,' he says, 'the lady from the heavy clay.'

Danielle nods. 'Terribly heavy, but very fertile. What are you up to here?'

Zwier explains how he uses the stickers to check if the cracks are getting bigger.

Danielle looks around her.

'All the foundations are under strain,' he explains. 'The house is getting more wrenched out of joint by the day.'

Danielle indignantly cries out that it's these beautiful old cow barns that seem the most vulnerable and it's a disgrace that the government lets this sort of thing happen. Zwier hushes her and tells her that they're going to come and look at it this afternoon. Her agitation seems a little misplaced.

Femke takes Danielle outside. They walk some way along the maar, against the strong wind. Danielle's curls are dancing round her head. Two yellow wagtails skim across the field like speedboats, darting behind and around each other, and then they catapult themselves upwards and vanish out of sight.

'They're the first ones this year,' Femke says joyfully.

'Where would you go if you could fly like that?' Danielle wants to know. Femke shakes her head. 'I don't know. I've never been anywhere. I like it here.'

'But there must be somewhere in the world you'd like to go, right?'

'Along the coast, across the sea, to Senegal or Ghana, where the marsh harriers go. That'd be nice.'

Danielle laughs.

'What about you?' Femke asks. 'Where would you like to go?'

'I've travelled a lot already. South Africa, Nigeria, Peru and Bolivia. I did voluntary work there. I'd still like to visit Antarctica, though, before it all melts away.'

'Why did you start farming then, if you're so fond of travelling?'

'Because I didn't always want to be travelling. I wanted to arrive.'

'Ha!' Femke says. 'So I don't need to go anywhere then. You've been everywhere and you end up in the place where I already am.'

'It's the journey that's important, not the destination,' Danielle cries, giving Femke a little shove. She returns the shove, and they run laughing back to the house.

Brian's call rings out across the farmyard: 'Everything must go! Everything must go!'

Femke hesitates a moment and then decides to invite Danielle to have lunch with them, and while they're walking to the farmhouse she realises that apart from the odd fellow student at the agricultural college, when they had to work together on a project, she's never had a guest at home before. Trijn is standing by the sideboard buttering the bread.

'Welcome,' she says, when she sees Danielle. She shakes hands with her and then turns to Femke.

'The livestock man was here and you'd cleared off somewhere again.'

Femke starts, covers her mouth with her hand.

'I let him take three of the calves,' Trijn continues abruptly, and then turns back to Danielle. 'Are you eating with us?'

Brian flaps around them, urging everyone to sit down. They sort out somewhere for Danielle to sit. My girlfriend, Femke thinks, and the thought pleases her.

Brian goes round the table like a waiter, carrying a dish in his hands, serving out his frikandels. When he gets to Danielle and tries to serve her, she holds her hand over her plate, thanks him, and says: 'I don't eat meat.'

The room goes silent.

Brian stands there frozen with the frikandel speared onto his fork.

'It's not meat,' he says. 'It's a frikandel. I fry them myself.' He nods towards the terrace where the fryer is still standing.

Danielle looks at him and says: 'Sorry, but I really don't eat meat.'

'It isn't meat. It's a frikandel,' Brian insists impatiently, repeating it a few more times.

Danielle looks round the table.

'I haven't eaten any meat since I was eight.' She shrugs her shoulders apologetically.

Trijn orders Brian to stop going on about it, adding with a thin smile that their guest doesn't know what she's missing. Brian says, staring at Danielle: 'Picky pigs don't get fat.'

'Now, now,' Trijn says to Brian and Zwier holds his plate up and asks for an extra frikandel.

They eat in silence, until Danielle asks Femke how far they've got with switching over. Before Femke can answer, Trijn says it's not even certain that they'll ever do so.

Femke would like to say that she's started making a development plan, that she's hoping to start improving the soil next year, that she's already going to sow a small plot of land with alfalfa this year, but she says nothing.

Then Trijn challenges Danielle, asking her what she would do, as an organic farmer, if a cow gets mastitis. Surely she uses antibiotics when that happens, or doesn't she? A typical Trijn question which has only one answer, Femke thinks.

But Danielle answers that the most important thing is prevention. That an organic cow builds up resistance, isn't milked dry, has fewer calves, spends more time outside, and is healthier.

Trijn gives an impatient nod. 'Yes, but if one of them does get ill, what then?'

Danielle smiles.

'Then I usually just wait and see. Did you know that fifty percent of cows get better by themselves? The main benefit of antibiotics is to the pharmaceutical industry. Human beings and animals should keep off them.'

'And that always ends well?'

The conversation is a bit like a boxing match.

'No,' Danielle says, 'not always. But that's the case with conventional methods too. Or don't you ever have to slaughter one of your cows?'

Her tone is friendly, but if anyone's on the ropes it's Trijn, Femke thinks. She eats up her last piece of bread and hopes that the meal will soon be over.

Zwier asks Danielle about the cell count of her cows' milk, but before she can give an answer the bell rings and a moment later three city gents step in. The smallest one is wearing a bright blue waisted suit and a stripy red and blue tie, and perched on his nose is a square pair of glasses mounted in a bright green frame. It gives him a rather absurd look. The other two are tall. One has blond shoulder-length hair, slicked back with oil, and his neck is neatly wrapped with a bow tie. The other one has dark curly hair, and is wearing a broad white tie, stippled with black polka dots, clearly meant to camouflage his sedentary-lifestyle-and-no-time-for-the-gym belly. They're carrying shiny black folders and are completely out of tune in this untidy parlour and with the people sitting at the table, all wearing practical work gear intended for the cold and dirt.

'Good afternoon. Is this the Koridon family?'

*

They introduce themselves as representatives of the various rigging organisations. Businesses have sprung up across the flat landscape like mushrooms as a result of the gas extraction, and they've brought an uncontrolled proliferation of men in suits with them: damage assessment experts, arbitrators, engineers, structural engineers, consultants, lawyers, assessors for the opposing parties, contractors, advisors, all kinds of ground, house, quake and sustainability clever clogs. In this region, where the population is shrinking and there are few opportunities for work, employment in the building, demolition and renovation sector has grown by leaps and bounds since the ground started quaking.

When everyone has shaken hands, Zwier asks if any of them have been here before.

'No, we're here for the first time. We'll take a fresh look at things,' Green-specs says.

'Would the gentlemen like coffee?' Trijn asks, with the friendliest of smiles.

'We'll first do the inspection,' Green-specs says, 'and then we'd certainly like a cuppa.' He gives her a wink.

Zwier goes outside with them. Trijn starts clearing the table and urges Brian to go back to work, sending Femke and Danielle out too.

'Shouldn't you go round with your grandad?' Danielle asks.

Femke answers that he's the one who sees to the buildings.

'Don't be silly,' Danielle says. 'You need to be there. It's about your future.'

The men are walking away from the 'head' section of the house, past the kitchen, falling into more and more disrepair behind its metal fencing, past the shored-up walls, towards the old byre. Danielle walks behind them and Femke hesitantly follows.

They stop within hearing distance and see the men examining one of the cracks, like farmers watching a horse being mistreated. Green-specs photographs it with his smartphone and then says, stabbing his finger: 'See that? The wall is completely out of true.'

The others nod. Bow-tie says something about it being soft soil here, which Polka-dot expresses some doubts about, and then Zwier asks hopefully if Polka-dot agrees with him that the subsidence has been caused by the quakes, and that the quakes are caused by the gas extraction. Polka-dot looks down at him, smiling, and says it's still too soon to come to any conclusions about it.

'Too soon?' Zwier's cheeks turn bright crimson. 'This has been going on for five years now.' His voice breaks.

Bow-tie suggests that they first examine things calmly. 'And then we can chat about it in a moment, over that cup of coffee your wife promised us.'

'My wife?' Zwier casts a perplexed glance from one to the other.

This is when Femke steps forward and puts her hand on his shoulder. They move in a column to the cow-housing. Now and then the men nudge each other, pointing at the blue plastic that's temporarily covering the gap where the roofing sheet blew off, or at the peeling paint, or the molehills. Pens scratch. Smartphones tap.

In the byre Green-specs says: 'Well, that tells no lies.' He's pointing at the post-it notes. 'You've made a very colourful job of it.'

Polka-dot is shaking his head. He's standing there, pointing at a crack. Bow-tie gives a nod. 'Oh dear,' he says. 'That's not good. A loadbearing wall with a great big crack like that…'

Polka-dot tells them they should at least be pleased there are no cracks in the byre adjoining the free-stall barn.

He nods his head towards the big shippon. 'What I mean is, your dairy cattle aren't in immediate danger.'

'But what about the youngstock then?' Danielle asks.

'And who are you,' Green-specs asks. 'Family?'

'I'm a colleague.'

'Oh dear,' the man says. 'Then you'd better leave.'

'Why?' Danielle asks him, while Zwier looks from one to the other.

'Because we're only allowed to do business with those directly affected. That's not something I've just come up with, those are the rules.'

'But why?'

'Because,' the man says, 'that's what the rules are.'

Then he addresses Zwier and continues: 'Confidentiality is a requirement for every agreement we make. And that's why I have to request you to ask those who are not part of this farming business to leave immediately.'

Zwier looks uncertainly at the man. Femke looks nervously from him to Danielle. For a moment it's silent.

'Okay,' Danielle says. 'I'll go.' She pulls Femke along into the yard with her.

'Watch out,' she says. 'All three of them are playing a role. Poison-specs is the bad guy, Mr Dickie-bow is the jobber, and Spotty-tie is the so-called good guy. But there are no good guys in that bunch. Don't sign anything. I'll ring you.'

She gives Femke a hug and walks to her estate car, which has been boxed in by three executive gas-guzzlers. She drives across the grass to get to the lonning, beeps the horn again, waves and is gone.

Femke walks back and sees Bow-tie putting his hand inside the newest crack and then getting a handkerchief out of his trouser pocket and wiping the debris off his fingers. More notes are jotted down and there's much deliberation. Zwier's desperation has increased. He's trembling a little.

'I've got the picture,' Green-specs decides. 'You two as well?'

The other two nod.

'Well,' says Polka-dot, 'I really fancy that cup of coffee your wife promised us. Oh no, she wasn't your wife, I believe.'

Femke would like to tell them that Ootje died because of all the stress and the increasing dilapidation, and especially because of the accusation of poor maintenance, which had secretly upset her so much, but how do you start talking about something like that?

The men walk confidently ahead, still in discussion, and then stand at the door talking.

Trijn has tidied things up inside and the coffee is ready. The biscuit tin is on the table. Zwier sits down. Femke sits beside him. Trijn raises her eyebrows.

'Shouldn't you be working?'

Femke shakes her head. 'I'll stay here.'

The delegation comes in and coffee is served. Zwier is smoking. Bow-tie gives an exaggerated cough. Green-specs clears his throat.

'The situation is very serious. That's clear. There's an acute danger of collapse, and that's not acceptable. But,' he says, stretching the word out and snapping the final *t*, before taking a sip of coffee and giving all three of them, one by one, a serious look, 'I don't want to pretend the weather is nice when it's raining cats and dogs. Your case is very weak. We've already made you an offer, which you haven't agreed to. The problem here is subsidence, that's what many of the cracks prove. Diagonal cracks, hairline cracks. I can't find any link to the gas extraction.'

'But,' says Zwier hesitantly, 'when they came to look at the kitchen they said it was irreversible earthquake damage. How do you explain that?'

'Well, sir, it's a question of progressive insight. However annoying it may be for you, not everything is quake damage. Subsidence, poor maintenance, rotting foundations, fault lines, the water table, faulty construction, I could go on. You should expect most of the renovation work to be at your own cost.'

'But,' Zwier says grimly, looking at Green-specs fiercely now, 'where does that subsidence come from, according to you?'

Bow-tie answers. He says, in a friendly tone of voice: 'Mr Koridon, you're a farmer, you know everything there is to know about clay. I surely don't have to explain to you about ground water extraction, salinity, sea clay, the capacity that clay has for swelling and shrinkage, and softening and settlement, because you know more about these things than we do, and I'm sure that's right. Right?'

'Of course,' he answers proudly. 'We've been farming here for a hundred and fifty years already. The farm has survived storms, floods, and two world wars. We've invested in a new shippon. We stand on solid ground here...'

Green-specs interrupts him: 'That's what you thought, and that's precisely the problem. That clay layer of yours, on which you grow your crops and where your cattle graze, is just a miserably thin little layer. It's soft ground under that, sir. I'm sorry. I realise how terrible it is to hear this, but these are the facts. The ground beneath your livelihood is sludge.'

Zwier seems to be thrown off balance.

Polka-dot suggests shoring things up immediately, at their cost. For a moment it looks as if Green-specs wants to protest, but he yields easily.

'Not because we're admitting any fault on our part,' Polka-dot tells him soothingly, 'let that be clear, but purely as a gesture of goodwill.'

To her amazement, Femke sees the roles Danielle described being played out in reality before her very eyes. Trijn hastens to say that they're happy with Polka-dot's promise and they hope there'll soon be some clarity about the rest, because they have to move on. But she totally understands. They're not the only ones, and the gentlemen must have many more cases to deal with.

'Good,' Green-Specs says. 'So we'll send another contractor this week to shore things up. You'll receive our final offer in around six weeks' time. And once again, and I must stress this, we require complete confidentiality. That's not something I've invented. Those are the rules. Compare it to the kinds of business agreements parents make with their successors: you don't shout those from the rooftops either.'

Trijn nods. Zwier gently shakes his head. The men gather up their papers. Femke feels her heart thudding in her throat. She hesitates. The thudding grows louder, and suddenly, to Trijn's surprise, and perhaps most of all to her own, she asks: 'And what if we don't agree to your proposal, what then?'

Bow-tie and Polka-dot sink back into their chairs. Green-specs stays standing, straightens his back, splays his fingers on the table, and says: 'You're always free to bring someone in for a second opinion. I should add, though, that it's not at all certain we'll pay for that, if we deem it to be inexpedient. And I should warn you that if you do so, the whole business will be put on the back burner. You'll end up in the complex cases dossier.'

Trijn gives Femke a furious look and quickly says that she's sure it won't have to go as far as that, she has every confidence the gentlemen will accommodate them. That it doesn't all have to get so complex. 'Right, Dad?'

Zwier looks from Femke to Trijn to the men. He nods wearily. Then they stand up and shake hands.

The cars zoom off, up the lonning, and Trijn gives Femke a telling-off: how could she think of antagonising the gentlemen like that?

Femke looks straight into Trijn's eyes, shrugs her shoulders, and walks out of the room with head held high.

The wind is rushing, hurling rain onto the land. Femke steps out along the maar, in her waterproof jacket, with the hood up, straight into the wind, and it's singing inside her, so loud that it seems you can hear it above the wind roaring.

April 2017

SPRING IS HERE NOW in all its glory. The temperature early this morning already felt mild, the light was clear and warm, and when Femke opened the shutters and doors to the byres and the shippon, the cows were restlessly walking back and forth, in and out of the robot milking parlour, mooing loudly. Every year there's tension about whether or not to let the cows out to graze on the pasture. Even the points of debate are part of the cycle.

Trijn doesn't think it's necessary at all. They didn't spend an arm and a leg on the new free-stall barn six years ago to no purpose. There's still plenty of space for more cows. Airy, light, roomy cubicles, a feed barrier, underground slurry storage, a grooming machine, milking robots: everything a dairy cow needs has been provided. There's absolutely no reason to send the cows outside still. The fact that people think it's beautiful to see cows in a meadow, and so typically Dutch, is no argument at all, as far as Trijn is concerned. According to her, the cow is used to strengthen the Dutch identity because Dutch people can no longer do that for themselves. Putting the cows onto pasture in the spring is out of date now, superseded, in the same way that electric lighting has replaced oil lamps, computers have ousted typewriters, and hand milking has been swapped for the milking machine. It's labour intensive, unnecessary and risky. Everything should be focused on making the work lighter, and on expansion. That's what gives a farm the right to exist. As far as Trijn is concerned, all the debates about whether to make outdoor grazing compulsory are simply proof that politicians are capitulating to the sentimentality of an unconfident nation.

The battle between mother and daughter has been going on for days now, with snappish comments and loaded silences. But this morning Femke walked straight into the headquarters and said really happily and spontaneously that today was the perfect day to put the cows out to grass, as if there hadn't been any conflict at all. And Trijn was so surprised by Femke's cheerful mood that she didn't want to be a spoilsport.

While Femke and Brian are seeing to the cows, Trijn and Zwier go out onto the land to hammer in the posts. Trijn is wearing her cropped jeans and a denim tool apron, and carrying a couple of metal prods and a large roll of electric fencing. Zwier gave a whistle when she came outside in her hotpants. He'd never have dreamt of doing so if Ootje could still hear him. They go behind the shippon together, put the posts in, and stretch polytape from post to post. They check the electric fencing on the pastureland and replace it where necessary. Zwier starts with the section closest to the farmhouse. Trijn goes to the east of the pasture.

As Femke comes out onto the land, she stops and stands still a moment, gazing at Trijn in her cropped jeans and loose camisole top. She looks like a young girl instead of a forty-two-year-old woman – her mother, who is always so afraid of what people will think of her, and who is so narrow-minded when it comes to change. Femke prefers to wear overalls, because she thinks her legs are too long and white, her arms spindly, and her breasts too big.

She swiftly goes round, checking the electric wire. Then she hears a hawking sound, almost animal-like. It's coming from the other side of the maar, from the tumble-down old field barn, with the broken roof.

It's a former sheep barn, which the villagers call Siepke's Sleepstead, and it has long been a place of ill-omen. Its remote location, deep in the farmlands, without even a path leading to it, makes it very suitable for shady goings-on. One day at the start of the previous century, Siepke, the mother of nine children, was found in the barn, stone-dead. She'd managed to escape from the tie-stalls on her own farm, where her husband had chained her up with the cows and the cow-shit, because he thought she was having an affair with a young farmhand. A shepherd found her body weeks later, because he was wondering where all the flies were coming from. They never discovered the cause of her death. Her body was already too decomposed and no one really wanted to carry out further investigations, because, after all, an unfaithful woman was the cause of her own suffering. But over the years people whispered all kinds of stories about it. They said that one of her children had helped her escape from the stall, and that isn't unlikely. Perhaps the mother had specifically looked for a hiding-place that wasn't too far from her brood. Perhaps the father had beaten the truth out of a child, and Siepke's death was his revenge. Or perhaps she'd put an end to her own life, because they did find water hemlock in that little barn, when all's said and done.

As the years went by the tales about Siepke's Sleepstead went quiet. But in the past, on the farm of Schokland, Zwier did sometimes tell stories about it. Yet it became Femke's hideout where she liked to watch birds. Armed with binoculars, bird book and jotter, she noted how long the buzzard perched on its fencepost, where the marsh harrier built its nest in the reeds, how many wigeons gathered on the pool, and when the oystercatchers and godwits came back from Africa.

The hawking noises continue. She crosses the bridge, no more than a concrete slab, and hums softly as she approaches. She sees a dark, tattered, fingerless glove grasp at the edge of the half-rotted door and then Fokko stumbles out, slowly and clumsily, in his armour of old clothing. A rancid stench rises up from him. She stands by the side of the little barn, her hands in her pockets, and asks him what he's doing there.

'A guy has to sleep somewhere.'

'I thought you'd found somewhere to go.'

'That's probably what your mother fooled you all into thinking.'

Femke asks if he wants to come back and stay with them.

'No way!'

87

He nips back into the barn, grabs hold of an old army rucksack, stuffs some things inside it, and then shoves a plastic bag full of tealights, a sleeping bag, and an old pillow into the corner, everything as far away as possible from the hole in the roof. Then he emerges again.

'Just wait,' he says. It's not clear whether it's a threat or an invitation.

She asks if he needs anything and, without any hesitation, he says he could use an extra blanket, and a big sheet of plastic and some tape, to cover the roof.

'Okay,' she says and turns round. He puts his hand out to stop her, muttering in his gravelly voice: 'They say there's a big quake coming. No one knows when. No one knows how big. But it's definitely on the way.'

'Who says that?'

'Engineers, geographers, people who understand the ground better than they know their women. They're saying it. We'd better take them seriously.'

'I've never heard anything of the sort.'

'Then you should listen better.'

When she's almost at the bridge again he shouts: 'And a bite to eat every now and then.'

She raises her hand and then hurries back to the fencing.

The glorious day has lost some of its gleam. This lumbering man makes her remember that no one is ever safe.

Trijn, who has replaced the last piece of electric fencing wire, phones Femke while she's walking back over the bridge.

'Who was that?'

Femke doesn't answer.

'Who were you speaking to over there?'

'What do you mean?'

At that point Fokko comes out of the barn and strides towards the village.

'What's Fokko doing here?'

'That's the man from the muskrat control,' Femke says snappily.

'Yes, and I'm Miss Montreal. Come off it.'

'I'm going to start the current. Will you check the wire?'

Femke presses the screen and stops the call.

Trijn walks round the whole of the pasture again, holding the metal fence tester by its plastic knob. Every so often she puts the tester against the wire and hears the soft ticking sound that means there's current. She doesn't like Fokko tramping around here. His buzzard is ready for him now, and he hasn't yet come by to ask for it. Who knows? Perhaps he's dreaming up some kind of revenge. It worries her that Femke is denying that he's here. She should stay out of his way. Catastrophes are catching.

The current is running through all of the fencing. The cows can be let out, and Femke is happy. That's a start at any rate.

*

In the shippon Femke selects the cows that will be the first to go out. Trijn, Zwier and Brian are stationed at different places in the farmyard, prods in hand.

The oldest cows are coming through the doorway, the ones already familiar with the open land.

But they also need to be persuaded. After six months in the stall, the memory of the meadows has been ground down by their jaws and trickled away through their four stomachs. Once outside, the little group of cows sticks close to the shippon, one behind the other. The bellowing of the cows inside grows louder, as a sign of encouragement or indignation, or perhaps just from impatience.

The cow at the front, flaring her nostrils, is Trudy. She calmly and placidly sniffs fresh air into her lungs. Then she starts to walk, through the barricade tapes and into the meadow. As soon as she's there she flings up her back legs, as if she can only sense the air and space and the smell of fresh grass and the wind once she's kicked off the dust of all those long winter months inside the stalls, like a bull in a rodeo having to buck off a cowboy. And the cows behind her mimic her high spirits: they buck and leap and bellow and sniff and run across the land on their spindly legs, udders swaying, a herd on an open prairie stampeding wildly, enthusiastically, right into the meadowland, across the vast wide plain, quicker and quicker, like flying machines trying to build up sufficient speed to take off.

The herd changes direction without dropping speed, and thunders back to the familiar shippon; a savage horde on the point of storming the farmyard, not intimidated by the electric fencing, which is ridiculously puny in comparison to the massive bodies and madcap wildness. But the fierce yelling of the people in the yard, wildly waving their long sticks at them, makes the herd change course again.

They furiously trot further into the pastureland, like a many-headed monster, until eventually the sense of liberation settles down, like swirls of dust, and the bucking, running, and racing slowly dies away. Then the calm strolling begins, the smelling of the fresh grass, the grazing with grinding teeth. But the yearlings, feeling what it's like to be outside for the first time in their lives, have to pit their strength against each other after the wild trot – head to head, horn stumps clashing – because new circumstances require a reshuffle in the ranking.

When all the cows are outside, except the ones that are drying off, bellowing indignantly from the empty shippon, Femke looks at her mother and sees that even she is smiling. Femke goes and stands beside her.

'It's beautiful, isn't it?'

'Of course,' her mother says. 'Really beautiful. Like broom. That's beautiful too. And Ootje's gold pendant is beautiful. And cherries on a cake. But they're not necessary. Don't ever forget that.'

Femke swallows her reply and walks away from her mother.

*

When Femke wakes up in the morning and checks her phone to see what's happening with the milking robot, she sees the text message.

Hey, Blondie! Pick u up tonight, 7:30 sharp. B ready! (Kissy face). *D. xx*

Blondie. She stares at the message. It's the first time in her life someone has asked her to go out with them. And she's clearly in for a surprise, because Danielle hasn't said where they're going. What could she be planning? Bowling? The cinema? Does Danielle really fancy her? Her hand trembles. Her heart thuds, as if she's been running a really long distance. She has to get on with her work.

After sweeping up and cleaning the robots, and making a check on the dried-off cows, she gets the quadbike and drives onto the land.

It's very windy. Dark clouds are scudding across the meadow. Someone once told her that clouds don't float but fall, like a heavy blanket.

At the front of the quad, packed inside a sheet of agricultural plastic big enough to put over the roof of the little barn, is the parcel she's made up for Fokko: tape, a horse blanket, pink fondant cakes, a bunch of bananas, a bottle of water, a thermos flask filled with tea, cheese and salami sandwiches, a torch with new batteries, and a Lucky Luke comic. She's tied the hammer and the wooden posts to the back of the quad.

She races along the bank of the maar, her thick ponytail fluttering behind her like a wind vane. The quad bounces across the lumps of clay, the wind blows the clouds apart, and the clear blue sky appears, and an occasional bright beam of sunlight.

Suddenly she sees the marsh harrier with its black-tipped, speckled white wings, flying about two metres above the reedbeds. She stops the quad and follows the bird with her binoculars. The harrier, a male, is holding its wings in a graceful V and floats in the air, like a boat on the sea, swinging from left to right on the wind. It lands in the reeds and then immediately rises up again, higher now, with a long string of reeds in its talons, flapping behind him like the quivering tail of a kite. She feels really jubilant because it looks as if he's going to nest in the reedbeds again. Now she can also spot the female, bigger and browner. She's gliding high up in the air and wheeling. The male swoops down into the reeds with his nesting material.

Femke accelerates. At Siepke's Sleepstead she turns the engine off. Fokko is peering sleepily out of the doorway. She tips the package off the quad and he beckons her to come and bring it in, as if she's a delivery service. She puts it down in the middle of the sheep barn. In the corner there's a makeshift bed of pallets and straw, and an army sleeping bag. Fokko flops down on it and opens the plastic package, going through everything with delight, and muttering approvingly when he sees the bananas, sandwiches, and pink cakes. He tears off the wrapper and bites into a cake. She asks him what he's intending to do now. He can't carry on staying here, surely?

'I've got an appointment this afternoon,' he says with his mouth full. 'At the riggers' office.'

'So there's still hope,' she says. He nods.

She wishes him success, jumps onto the quad, and rides back into the fields, where she hammers in some fencing posts, a job that demands full muscular force. Hammering posts is the best way of getting rid of excess energy.

After two posts she straightens herself up a moment, and wipes the sweat drops off her forehead with her arm.

The male harrier skims swiftly above the reedbeds chasing off three crows that have just attacked the chosen nesting site. The crows return. The female harrier rises up out of the reeds, then lands onto the clay, and the three crows come down immediately in front of her. The female stays where she is, apparently indifferent to them, while the black birds swagger back and forth. The battle for territory is in full swing. The female harrier doesn't move an inch.

Then a kestrel races to help her. It plummets straight down from high in the air, aiming directly at the crows. At the last moment it swerves and lands right behind the bullies, flies up again, and then hovers above them, wings beating swiftly. Could it really be helping the harrier? Is something like this possible in the animal world?

The crows fly away, cawing loudly.

The kestrel vanishes and the harrier preens her wing feathers, like a woman fixing her hair between the rounds of a boxing match.

Crows are the ruffians of the bird world, Femke thinks, always ganging up together against a single bird. Nasty and merciless. She shudders a moment, then bangs the next post into the ground. Another two and she'll be ready. Then her phone gives a bright little ping.

Hey Blondie, or don't you answer to that name? Time and place tonight ok?

She's startled. She hadn't even thought about reacting. She answers quickly: *Everything's ok, the name too.*

Then an immediate ping. Two emojis: a wink and a kiss.

She bashes the last two fenceposts into the ground, quicker than ever. Then she rushes back home.

*

The dishwasher's on and the tv too. Zwier and Trijn are sitting on the sofa, drinking coffee. Femke walks in and nonchalantly says that Petra might be going to calve tonight and Betty as well, that she's going out, and can Trijn perhaps keep an eye on them?

'Where are you going?' Her mother looks up.

'Nowhere special,' she says. 'Can you keep an eye on them, Mam?'

'If you give me a proper answer, maybe. Where are you going?'

Femke tugs at the elastic band in her ponytail.

'Nowhere special,' she says annoyed. 'Just out with Danielle.'

'Since when is that not special?' Trijn asks. 'And can you let me know where you two are going?'

'No,' Femke says. And then swiftly: 'I don't know either.'

'That's strange,' Trijn concludes.

'You should be pleased. You're always wanting me to go out with people of my own age.' She mimics Trijn's tone for that last phrase.

'How late will you be back?'

'Mam, I'm twenty-one.'

Trijn says thinly that she'll keep an eye on the cows and tells her not to drink if she's driving.

Femke goes into the farmyard. She's in plenty of time, although she's changed her clothes three times. It's difficult to know what to wear if you don't know what you're going to do. And there's always the usual dilemma: macho or girly. Farming women dress macho, because of the work they do. No one ever finds that strange. But that means it's even more important to emphasise one's femininity. Facebook is full of photos posted by young women farmers, working in overalls, on their tractors, shovelling shit, delivering calves, but those pictures are carefully balanced with just as many where they're wearing short skirts or skinny jeans, with provocative t-shirts and carefully applied make-up. Most farming women are scared to death of being seen as butch.

She paces back and forth across the yard, her phone in her hand. Klaske pads along with her and tries to leap up, but she pushes the dog off, she doesn't want any dirt on her clothing. You don't want people in the city to identify you from the stench of the cowshed.

The setting sun is glowing in the west. A few bright rays of light appear below the thick layer of clouds, turning the sky and the land to a blaze of red.

It's twenty-five to eight, and then twenty to. Did she make a mistake about the time, or the day? How long are you meant to wait before ringing to see if anything's gone wrong? Or was it all a joke?

She bites her nails.

The wind has broken up the thick layer of clouds. The sun is sitting above the clean line of the horizon like a golden-red ball and turning the scattered clouds into a billowing sea of red, purple and golden-yellow, before it disappears behind the horizon after one last flare of light.

It's a quarter to eight. In the last bright ray of sunlight an estate car races along the concrete track, and not much later Danielle comes to a halt in front of her. Femke opens the door.

'Sorry,' Danielle says. 'One of the cows was on the point of calving.'

They tear off.

'We're late.'

'Is it far?' Femke asks.

'Course not. It's right here, in your village hall.'

Femke goes quiet. The village hall. That doesn't sound very exciting. It's the place for bingo, the brass band, and the drama club. Going to the village hall means it's bound to be busy, there's bound to be a throng.

'What's going on then, in the village hall?'

Danielle gives her a swift sidelong glance: 'Did I forget to say in my text where we're going? Why didn't you ask?'

Femke shrugs her shoulders.

'There's a meeting about the earthquakes. And all kinds of specialists will be there. That seemed like something important for you, I thought.'

'But not for you, then?'

'Not yet. But they say the quakes will eventually affect the dykes. If they do collapse, then I'll be the first to drown. Me and my girls.'

She points to the glove compartment, where the programme for the evening is.

A cold laugh echoes inside Femke. Lamppost. Bat Ears. Horse Face. How could she have imagined for even a second that Danielle would really be interested in her? She looks at the flyer out of politeness, but not a single letter of the text gets through to her.

Danielle glances sideways again. 'Did I make a mistake about it?'

Femke shakes her head. 'Oh no. It's very interesting.'

'Good,' Danielle says. 'Anyway, I think it's more fun if we both go.'

It's busy in the hall. Mainly old folk. She knows some of them, the parents and grandparents of children she once went to school with. Farmers in checked shirts and corduroy jackets, men with kippered faces, like Grampa. She wishes she hadn't put her glittery party-blouse on and she decides not to take off her denim jacket, even though she feels the heat fall over her, like a blanket.

On the stage there's a woman with her grey hair cut in the typical country woman's practical hairstyle. Danielle gives her a wave.

'I'll get the beers,' Danielle says. 'Can you look for somewhere to sit?'

And off she goes.

Femke struggles through the tightly packed bodies. A hundred voices are echoing around the room. Her breath catches and she breaks out in a sweat. She squeezes through to the side of the room and puts her hands over her ears. There are still one or two free seats here and there, but she hasn't got the courage to push herself forward. She moves towards two seats further back in the hall, half hidden behind a pillar. Danielle is at the bar, chatting to a bald chap, and then she starts to make her way through the crowd, holding the beers half in the air.

'Well,' she says, a little mockingly, 'you've managed to find the best seats here.'

She gives Femke her beer and is off again, briefly saying hi to someone as she goes. Then Femke sees her by the stage, greeting the practical-hair woman. And then there's an announcement telling people to sit. Danielle tries to get to the back of the hall again, but she gets stuck in the crowd, so she eventually squeezes herself into one of the rows, heading straight for an empty seat, then she turns round a moment, makes an I-can't-do-anything-about-it kind of gesture, and sits down.

Femke looks at the mop of curls, so far away from her, and is sorry she didn't have the confidence to press further forward. But after a short word of welcome a man with a shiny head steps onto the stage and speaks about tiltmeters, which can measure what's happening on the ground but which haven't been placed on the land. 'And,' the man says, 'you can guess why they'd rather not set up those kinds of meters here.'

A geologist with bushy grey hair gives a passionate account about *knipklei*, the old marine clays they have here, and about groundwater management, irregular ground movement, reduction of pressure, liquefaction, and drift. He talks about the faults that run under the land. About the risks of any kind of energy-related extraction in this kind of ground. 'The day will come,' he says, 'when there'll be a gigantic earthquake. I don't know when. I don't know how bad. I don't know how much damage it will cause. I don't know how many deaths there'll be. But that it will come is as certain as the fact that the sun will rise tomorrow.'

A shudder goes through the room.

An architect describes in a calm voice how old and distinctive buildings could be saved, as soon as people start accepting that restoration and strengthening costs more than demolition and new builds.

Femke remembers the grapple that demolished the Wide World, as if history had no value at all. The architect shows slides of a head-neck-rump farmhouse that has been restored and reinforced, and Femke is overcome by a feeling of immense excitement. It *is* possible!

After the architect the audience is given the chance to speak. A microphone is passed round.

A woman tells, in a choking voice, how she's had to give up her calf-rearing business because the animals were in danger, and now she's heavily in debt because there's no provision for compensating businesses and she has to pay off the mortgage. Now all she eats is bread and peanut butter.

A man shouts out that his slurry store is leaking, that the groundwater level on his land has risen, but that the riggers don't want to look at what's happening below the surface.

There's a woman who says there's a difference between being in the right and being proved to be right, and after three years she's given in and has agreed to the demolition of their old and characteristic farmhouse, because she no longer wants the fight for justice to dominate her life and her family's life.

And then there's the sound of a familiar gravelly voice and

Femke sees Fokko. He growls into the mike the story about his demolished house, the minimal compensation they gave him, and that he's homeless and still in debt.

People are shaking their heads and there's a suppressed muttering in the hall. The man Danielle was speaking to earlier picks up the microphone. He's in his thirties and is wearing a leather jacket. His shaven head gleams under the lights and there's a dark dragon's-head tattoo crawling up his neck.

'Didn't you think of taking them to court?' he asks, pointing at Fokko with the beer glass in his hand.

Fokko stammers that he doesn't have the money for that.

'You should never have gone along with their proposal,' the bald guy says.

A hum of voices in the room. A few of the farmers look angrily at him. Fokko comes onto the mike again and shouts: 'Have you got quake damage?'

'That's nothing to do with it,' the bald chap answers. 'You really should've taken legal action.'

'Have you got damage?' Fokko repeats with annoyance. 'Who exactly are you?'

'I'm Lieuwe Baartman, a lawyer,' the bald man says, and that makes a lot of people laugh, but he carries on speaking regardless, about how the victims need to band together to take legal action, so the companies can't evade the issue. The power of the masses, he calls it.

A long-faced farmer takes the mike.

'It's not as simple as that,' he says. 'It's easy enough to say you shouldn't accept an offer. But when the ground keeps quaking and your house becomes uninhabitable, when your business is about to collapse, and the bank is breathing down your neck, and your night's rest has gone to hell because of worries and bad nerves, then there's little room left for manoeuvre. Anyway, not everyone can muddle along for years.'

Fokko nods vehemently and there's applause. The bald man says he's willing to support people who want to take on the battle. The evening ends in chaos.

People start pushing their way to the exit. Femke stands by the pillar waiting while the stream of people shuffles out, till Danielle comes past and takes her by the hand. Femke lets herself be carried along till they come to a stop in the clear night air. The people flow past them. They're still holding onto each other and Femke looks up and sees thousands of stars.

Danielle suggests going for a little walk. They walk in silence, still hand in hand, past the pretty little red-brick houses of the village, which after sunset give the impression of being completely deserted.

They go past the canal with the stately mansion house where once upon a time, Danielle says, a gentleman farmer made his wealth on the backs of his labourers, and they sit down on a bench, looking onto the house in its park-like garden.

Femke asks who the bald chap at the meeting was.

'Someone I knew in the past,' Danielle says, 'when I was studying and used to live in a squat now and then.'

They sit shoulder to shoulder. Femke feels Danielle's warmth and sometimes Danielle briefly touches her in passing, a hand on her leg or shoulder, and then she feels the spot glowing for quite some time.

Femke tells Danielle that she saw Fokko's Wide World being razed to the ground and how astonishing it was to see this ancient farmhouse, so close to their own Schokland, being destroyed in the blink of an eye.

'Then it's all very close to you,' Danielle says, 'but Lieuwe is still right. That Fokko guy hasn't got a leg to stand on, because he signed an agreement and he got cash for it. Make sure you don't do that. You should hire a lawyer, and take them to court. You'll be proved right.'

Femke thinks about the woman who said she'd given up the fight. Because there's a difference between being right and being proved to be right. And it all depends on someone's resilience whether it's the one or the other. She sighs.

'Poor Femke,' Danielle says, putting an arm around her. Femke instinctively puts her head on Danielle's shoulder. They sit like this a while, almost without movement. Femke thinks to herself that she's never been so close to anyone else before. It's as if she's crying inside. And that's new for her too. That you can cry without making a noise. And that it's nothing at all to do with unhappiness.

Suddenly Danielle leaps up. 'Come on,' she says, 'let's get going.'

She pulls Femke up and they run to the car hand in hand, their footsteps echoing through the silent streets. They drive out of the village, to a concrete farm track where there aren't any houses. Danielle steps on the pedal and races down the bumpy track at 120 kilometres per hour. Femke is screaming and laughing, holding tightly onto the dashboard, and at the end of the track Danielle makes a hair-tight turn and races back. Then she brakes abruptly and says: 'Now you.'

Femke pushes the speed of the car up: 120, 130, and deliberately slings it around a bit. When Femke brakes at the very last moment, just in front of the metal gate that gives entry to the farmland, Danielle screams even louder than Femke did.

'Let's do some star gazing,' Danielle suggests, getting an old horse blanket and a plastic bag out of the boot. They climb over the gate and spread the blanket out.

'What's in the bag?'

'Emergency rations.'

'And what in particular?'

Danielle teasingly holds the bag up. Femke grabs at it, tries to stay upright, but loses her balance and falls over. Then there's a tickling bout, which changes into a trial of strength. Danielle grabs hold of Femke. Femke pushes her off and presses her onto the ground, pinning her arms down with her knees, until Danielle screams for mercy. Finally they lie together side by side on the blanket, panting for breath, their arms carelessly touching each other.

'So what's in the bag, then?'

Danielle sits up a bit and takes out a hip flask.

'Whisky,' she says. 'That's what makes little girls grow into big girls.'

She swigs greedily from the flask and then pours some of it into the top. Femke also sits up and takes a few sips. The stuff burns her throat and gullet and makes her whole body tingle. Danielle takes out a packet of cigarettes.

'Do you smoke, then?' Femke says astonished.

'Sometimes,' is the answer. 'We can't always be good girls.'

She thrusts a burning cigarette between Femke's lips, and then lights one for herself.

Femke coughs and laughs and her head swims. She lies down and cautiously puts her head on Danielle's lap, and that's how she smokes her first-ever cigarette. She looks at the stars and feels Danielle's hand on her hair. It crosses her mind that it is perhaps possible for a Koridon to be with someone.

Above her, as far as she can see, the firmament, jet-black and immense.

She points to the pole star.

'That's the brightest star of all,' she says.

But Danielle answers that this is just a fable, a story people keep on repeating to each other, until everyone believes it, as if that can make it true. 'People like echoing what others say,' she concludes.

'Not me,' Femke says, closing her eyes.

'Hey, Blondie,' Danielle muses languidly, her hand gently

stroking Femke's hair. 'How much longer will your mother and grandad be on the farm with you?'

'What do you mean?' Femke opens her eyes.

'It's your farm, isn't it?'

'No, not yet. It's a partnership.'

'But when will it be yours, then?'

The hand stops its stroking.

'I think when my Grampa and mother are dead.'

'Only then,' Danielle says indignantly. 'And you won't be able to do what you want till then?'

Femke sits up. They look into each other's eyes. Danielle gazes, as if she's trying to see something that's almost invisible. Suddenly something has faltered.

'You should be able to build up your own business, right? Like you want it to be,' Danielle says, stubbing her cigarette on the ground.

'So what would you do?'

Danielle grins. 'Care home?'

Femke shakes her head.

'My Grampa belongs to Schokland. He'd die in one of those care homes. And my mother isn't even forty-five.'

'Ah well,' Danielle says, 'so she's not ready for that yet. Perhaps as a care worker, then?'

But Femke doesn't find this funny and simply plucks at the blanket a little. Suddenly she can feel how cold it is.

Danielle stands up abruptly and says in a business-like voice: 'Come on then. Our girls will be waiting for us early tomorrow morning.'

They drive to Schokland, at top speed, with the music on loud, so that any roe deer that might think about crossing the road will be driven back to the fields.

And only after Danielle has come into the shippon with her to see if Petra has already calved and they've looked at her together, this cow in labour who seems to have no more strength left, and Femke decides that the cow needs help and ties the rope to the calf's forelegs and gives it to Danielle, and she herself massages the vulva where the threads of slime are hanging out and the hooves are already visible, and they wordlessly start tugging the rope together, guided by the rhythms of the strong contractions, and the silence is only broken now and again by the heavy puffing breath of the cow, and at each shudder of the cow's body they give the rope a firm tug and so pull the calf bit by bit a little further into the world, and finally the head comes out and Femke tears open the amniotic sac and the calf slides out of the cow, and they put it in front of Petra, and together they look at the mother licking her calf clean, with their arms round each other's shoulders, and Danielle says, 'We made a good job of that, Blondie', only then is there suddenly that closeness again. The miraculous awareness that it is possible to feel at home with someone else.

May 2017

TONIGHT IS THE NIGHT when April changes to May. Buds bursting open, a profusion of blossoms, birds chirruping, and hares boxing. A cruel season. Autumn suits Trijn far better.

She can't sleep. Femke has never been out gallivanting so late before.

In the past, on a clear moonlit night, when Trijn would race home on her bike up the concrete track, much later than she should have been, she sometimes saw a chink in the curtains of her parents' room and a shadow peering through it. Then she knew that Ootje was sitting on her upright wooden chair at the window again, her buttocks billowing over the seat, the white cotton material of her nightdress tight around her body, buttoned to halfway up her throat so that Zwier, who was lying in bed behind her, the sheets pulled over his head, wouldn't get any funny ideas if the slightest scrap of naked flesh was visible. As Trijn crept up the stairs on her stockinged feet, Ootje always came out onto the landing to hiss at her about decency, debauchery, and honour. She never asked her if she'd had a nice evening. Not even when she came home on time. But Trijn couldn't blame Ootje for that. She could never forget that she was the cause of the greatest sorrow her mother ever had to bear. Even though she was only twelve when the Accident happened. That was no excuse.

Zwier and Jort had been outside using the compressor to pump up the tyres of the big tractor and she was in the byre. It was her job during the school holidays to give out the feed to the few cows that were indoors, drying off.

She was opening up a feed bale with a pitchfork, and then she noticed a strange smell, a filthy rotting stench, not the usual smell of sour milk and manure. It was coming from Allie. And Allie was putting only the tip of her back-left hoof on the ground, as if she was walking on high heels. Stinking and stumbling. Trijn knew what that meant.

She dropped the pitchfork and hurried out, to the other side of the farmyard, where Zwier and Jort were standing next to the big tractor, their eyes on the compressor meter. The engine was throbbing. The air was hissing. She couldn't make herself heard above all the racket. She ran up to Zwier and tapped his arm. It was only then that he looked up, raising his chin in question.

'You've got to come,' she yelled impatiently, tugging at his hand. He shook his head, and gestured to her to wait a moment, but her impatience was too strong. For once she'd noticed something important, before he and Jort had. She kept tugging at him. He must have thought it was something very urgent. Jort was standing there, eyes fixed to the compressor meter, keeping a careful watch on the amount of air being pumped into the tyre. Zwier let himself be tugged away with her. But what did she know about overpressure?

In the byre Trijn pointed to Allie and proudly said *foul-foot*. Then there was a deafening boom, the kind of blast you might hear in a war. The explosion of the tractor tyre was so powerful that big strong Jort, who weighed ninety-four kilos and was a mass of muscle, was flung off like a rag. He fell to earth ten metres away. Everything that can break in a human being was broken.

For years on end, night after night, she'd imagine herself having the chance to redo that moment. How much difference a little patience would have made. If Zwier had stayed by the compressor, he might have noticed that the relief valve wasn't working properly. After all, he had much more experience than his son. Then her brother would still have been alive. There'd have been someone to take on the farm. Then the future existence of Schokland would have been guaranteed, and she wouldn't have caused Ootje such indescribable sorrow.

She'd started fantasising after moving in with Harm, when it soon became clear that life with him would be very different to what she'd thought. Even Harm couldn't stop her wishing for another life. Perhaps she could have been a skipper's wife, sailing in a barge with him along the rivers of Europe. She'd be at the wheel, skilfully manoeuvring the boat, her skipper next to her, an arm around her shoulder, all lovey-dovey. Or she'd be a master taxidermist, better than Jort had ever been, and she'd become an artist's muse, and he would set her up with her own studio in Paris. There she'd prepare specimens of the rarest birds, the kind she only knew from Jort's books: a Southern Bald Ibis, a Gentoo Penguin, a Himalayan Monal, a New Zealand kakariki.

These fantasy lives contrasted sharply with her real life in the grey little city flat. Harm was terrifyingly unpredictable. He was often driven by a malignant fury, which she never understood, but which she certainly seemed to provoke. His rage was her punishment.

Whenever the need to humiliate someone flared up in him, he'd take control of her body. It was always unexpected and she never learned how to prevent it. It started with a fierce look in his eyes, which he fixed on her. His jaw would thrust forward. A muscle in his cheek started trembling, a detail that always made her break out in panic. Then his cold hand, grasping her neck, holding her in an iron grip, thrusting her face down into the pillow, or onto the cold granite worktop, or against the rough bricks of an alley wall. Always with such force that she'd have to gasp for breath, while he'd be hammering away inside her, as if everything had to be broken.

She soon stopped perceiving her body as her own, so she wasn't even surprised when a baby nestled itself inside her, like a cuckoo's egg in the nest of a strange bird. She only became aware of it when it was too late to be sucked out.

As the years have passed, these memories have turned into tight scars. She's proud of the fact that she's never bothered anyone with them. And she brought Femke to the only place in the world where the child could be safe. She did what a mother is meant to do. But all those words in women's magazines that go with motherhood seem strange to her. Walking on air. Gratitude. Joy.

Calves are separated from their mothers as soon as they're born. It's not nice, for either of them, but you learn from experience that after a quick separation the suffering is soon forgotten, and then the cow can go back to best doing what it's here to do: producing milk.

Sometimes a thought wells up in her, which she'll never say aloud, because she doesn't want people to brand her as an unnatural mother. But secretly she does sometimes think it would be good for mothers and daughters to be swiftly and permanently separated. Not because mothers don't love their daughters, but because they love them too much.

Trijn keeps peeking through a sly chink in the curtain. She sees a sea of stars and a thin crescent moon, mute and unmoving, high up in the heavens. The concrete track cuts dark and straight through the farmland, until after the emptiness of the Wide World it dissolves into thick darkness. The ghostly silhouettes of three roe deer move cautiously across the field, foraging in the winter wheat.

She's wondering where her daughter is, on this Monday evening. It's almost two in the morning. The new day has already started.

Then she sees an estate car driving towards the farm, much too fast. The deer glide off into the dark night. Heavy bass thumping. The car goes past the byre, along the drive. Trijn slips out of her room and creeps through the attic lumber room to the front of the byre, from where she can see the farmyard through the wrought-iron rosette window with its little glass panes.

The engine is switched off. The headlights go out. The music drones on. Trijn sees a flame flicker. The face with its dark curls is lit up. Danielle takes a drag from the cigarette and then gives it to Femke. In the glowing light she sees her child, who doesn't like people and doesn't smoke, take the cigarette, hold it between her fingers and puff at it greedily. Meanwhile that lass lights a second cigarette, and when the flame has gone out all she can see in the darkness are two glowing points of light and vague shadows.

And Trijn stands there peeping through the rosette window like a surreptitious Quasimodo, till both the car doors open simultaneously and the girls go towards the shippon. The security light clicks on and she sees Femke take hold of the hand that Danielle reaches out to her.

She rushes back across the attic, bangs her knee hard against a jutting-out joist, suppresses a scream, stumbles, then hobbles back to her room. In bed she senses her knee swelling up. A sharp pain. That'll be hinkie-legs tomorrow. She lies still, her eyes wide open, like a nocturnal creature living in a zoo.

It's a long time before she hears the sound of the car driving away over the concrete track, and then the creaking of the stairs, the door to the attic, and the soft sighing of the attic floorboards under Femke's stealthy stockinged feet. Trijn's heart is thudding, just like her knee.

*

The next morning Trijn hobbles into the headquarters, leaning on Ootje's old walking stick. Her face is pale and her mouth is tight.

Femke asks what happened to her. She answers that she bumped her knee in the bathroom. And immediately after that: 'You were late last night.'

'I was just on time,' Femke snaps. 'Petra really needed help. I pulled the calf out.'

Zwier is sitting in his usual spot, with some of his little tins and a heap of nails, screws, bolts, nuts, and ring clamps in front of him. On the floor beside him there's a couple of old planks with nails in them. There's a hammer on the table.

'Do you know what they called it?' he asks, chuckling.

Trijn shakes her head.

'Tuesday,' Femke says proudly.

'Tuesday?' Trijn asks. 'What kind of a name is that?'

'In Africa children are named after the day they're born.'

'What's that got to do with us?'

'The harriers go to Africa for the winter.'

'Ah, that explains everything,' Trijn mocks. 'So where did you go then?'

'Yes, I had a nice evening, thanks.'

Then Femke tells them about the meeting in the village hall, and about all the people who are going through the same sort of thing as they are, and about the architect who can renovate old farmhouses, keeping the original features and making sure they'll be able to withstand quakes in the future.

'Did he produce an invoice?' Zwier asks sarcastically. 'It'll cost an arm and a leg, you know. Who'll pay for that?'

He sounds almost angry, but then he stands up and says: 'Well, I'm going to see if the gents have finally written their report. Those six weeks are long gone, damn it.'

They watch him leave, see him walk through the open door of the byre, that stocky figure with his crooked back, his bowed legs in green wellies, his uneven, tottering steps. He hobbles to the post box every day along the lonning, and every day he comes back emptyhanded.

If Femke has learned anything from yesterday's meeting, it's that many people are made to wait. A long time. Until they're broken. Only then, according to what people said yesterday, do they make an offer.

Once again in her mind's eye she sees the woman who said that there's a difference between being right and being proved to be right. A powerful, well-educated person. She'd battled with them for three long years, but eventually she'd given in. If even a woman like that couldn't win, what kind of future is in store for them?

She sets off, onto the land, to fence off another plot.

*

Zwier comes back laden with advertising flyers, the free local paper, and the cooperative newsletter. He's out of breath. Trijn hobbles her way through the headquarters, leaning on her stick, pours the coffee, and looks with concern at his purple-red cheeks.

'Shouldn't you go and see the doctor?'

'Why?'

'You've only got one heart.'

He shakes his head abruptly and fiercely.

'You're the one who needs a doctor,' he says, pointing at her knee. 'Nothing's amiss with me.'

'What if we go together? Me for my knee, you for your heart.'

He searches through the heaps on the table for nails of equal length and clatters them into a tin.

'I don't need a doctor,' he insists. 'I know exactly what that old sawbones will say.' And in an affected voice: 'You really should stop smoking, sir. And nibble lettuce leaves. And no more drinking. That's what he'll say. Right enough.'

'There are pills,' Trijn mutters.

'I don't want pills. I want certainty.'

'Is it worrying you so much?'

A risky question. A Koridon would rather dig deep into the ground than dig into himself. He doesn't answer but rummages even faster through the nails. His broad grit-grey fingers are amazingly quick.

'You need a bit of faith,' she says gently.

He stops scrabbling around.

'A bit of faith?' He looks up at her, mockingly. 'Faith in those tailor-made suits, who come here at a cost of hundreds of euros per person to tell me I haven't looked after my farm properly?'

He jabs a nail in her direction, and gasps for breath.

'And in the meantime,' he continues, and his voice grows louder, 'the ground quakes more and more. Every day the cracks get bigger. And deeper. The walls are more and more out of true. Like with flat-cut wood.'

His cheeks flame. Trijn answers calmly.

'But they have to check things out, Dad. After all, there are cheats.' She hesitates a moment and then continues: 'I heard about people who bought a car with their compensation and then started complaining again. People like that do exist. You do understand that, don't you?'

'That's not my business,' he says and picks up his tobacco pouch.

'No, but it is theirs.'

'I've heard people say,' he murmurs, 'that there's a big quake coming. No one knows when, no one knows how big, but there'll definitely be one.'

'I've heard that too.'

'If it comes,' he continues, 'before things have been put right here...' He falls silent. The only thing you can hear is his laboured breathing. And the rattling of the feed fence, further up in the shippon.

Then he rummages around on the table for a piece of paper, draws a bumpy line on it with a pencil, and with an angry gesture writes SANDSTONE beside it. Above that he makes a swift circle and writes RIGGERS' GOLD in its centre. Then in a fierce staccato he uses the pencil to make little dots above the circle, with an arrow pointing to it: SALT DEPOSITS. And above all that he draws a bubbly surface. CLAY.

Then he looks at her, as if his drawing has said all there is to say.

'Yes?' she asks.

'That was the situation,' he says. 'That's our land. You surely don't have to be very learned to realise that if you take this away,' he taps his pencil angrily at the circle, 'the whole lot will sink. That's just logical, isn't it? A child knows that much.'

She nods.

'They started pumping it up immediately, without giving any thought to the consequences. And that's why Fokko is a down-and-out now. What did he do to deserve that?'

He stops his hammering and looks at her as if Fokko's misfortune is her fault.

'Fokko,' she says with light scorn in her voice, 'always maintained things badly. Some of those cracks were there years ago, before anyone said anything at all about quaking ground.'

Zwier shakes his head and screws up his eyes. He glares at her from beneath his bushy eyebrows. But Trijn continues, with some fierceness: 'Cracks have always happened, Dad. Not all those folks ringing up and complaining have looked after their houses properly. You can't imagine how many people are lodging complaints, when they're the ones who've let things go to rack and ruin.'

The hammer slams down onto the wooden plaque. The table shakes. She jumps with shock and he rages: 'You can't blame me for not doing many repairs these past five years. Investing in things when the place is done for? No one with any sense does that. How dare you say I haven't looked after Schokland properly! That I haven't done everything in my power to…'

The blood rises to her cheeks. She stammers out that she didn't mean it like that, that she wasn't talking about Schokland, that it was just her way of saying it, and then she goes quiet.

Zwier flops down on his chair again. Silence fills the head-quarters. Only the laboured rasp of his breathing can be heard, like an echo of the wind sweeping around the shippon.

Then he picks up a pair of pincers and an old plank and starts pulling a nail out from it, like a vet working a rotten tooth out of a cow's jaw. And Trijn shuffles out. She gently closes the door of the headquarters behind her and, leaning on her stick, hobbles across to the Dead Bird Museum where she goes and sits on her stool. But no, she thinks. It's still Jort's stool, just as the Dead Bird Museum will always be his. Schokland has never been hers. She never felt like its heir, let alone its steward, although she has always loved that word.

She's nothing more than a farmhand, someone who's toler-ated, someone it would be indecent to kick out now, because they've been there so long.

*

The grass by the maar has grown high, with a universe of dan-delions inside it, all gone to seed now, white starry balls of fluff. The bank of the maar is strewn with buttercups, their petals wide open. Fen ragwort, forget-me-nots, and the purple marsh foxtail, all popping open.

A pheasant is scratching for food at the edge of the potato field. The sunlight shines on his bright red, mask-like face with its quivering wattles. Two dark-purple little ears peek up from its head, tufty and angular like those of a long-eared owl. Its bronze body is gleaming in the light, and its tail sweeps over the ground. Femke often thinks that such an eccentric-looking crea-ture doesn't seem at home here on the clay farmlands. Every now and then the bird spreads its wings out, shifting itself forward with some difficulty, moving just a few metres. Not enough to flap into another world.

Sometimes, late at night, she hears its harsh cries, as if it's hoping to attract company. She has never seen a female pheasant here at all.

She texted Danielle yesterday to ask her if she knew anything about managing the land for birds and making marsh pools, and the answer came in the form of an invitation to drop by this evening, with a row of emojis after the words: a little sun, lips, a wine glass and an exploding volcano. She did text back this time, and this morning she finished her work at top speed so she could go into the reedbeds as quickly as possible.

The air is sweet with flowering cow parsley. Yellow wagtails are dashing about on the clay farmland, and swallows are rushing high in the air, swooping down recklessly, skimming along the clay.

When she reaches the reedbeds it's as if she has landed in a concert hall. Along with the deafening noise of croaking frogs, there's a cacophony of bird calls. Delicate and soft, loud and shrill, cheeping, quacking, buzzing, grunting. Melodious little tunes, hoarse cries, imploring peeps, hooting honks – it's teeming with life and tenderness, and cries of hunger and territorial drive.

Small brown, black-headed reed buntings are clinging onto the reed stems like acrobats and fighting each other to defend their little piece of reed. There's a booming noise, the dark steamboat sound of a hidden bittern. A Canada goose is swimming in the middle of the pool, alone and majestically, with enviable ease.

Femke often used to come here with Zwier in the past. While they were walking along the maar he'd give her tasks to do: 'Bring me a stalk of Tall Oat-grass and of Reed Sweet-grass, some Marsh St. John's-wort, a Woolly Burdock, Shepherd's Purse and some Spike-rush.' Together they'd slit open the stems and examine the petals and stamens. Or he'd stop her abruptly and point to a bird in the air, or to a fox with a crow in its jaws, slinking out of the maize field. She loved sitting with him at the edge of the pool, in silence, ears pricked, and then spotting a reed warbler, a bearded tit, or a bluethroat on a reed stem, a gadwall, a wigeon, or a merganser on the pool, or dragonflies with their paper-thin, transparent wings and colourful little bodies. Skilful, graceful little flying machines zooming right above the water, without her ears being able to hear that zooming, and yet they did make a zooming sound because, as Zwier said: 'We can't always see or hear everything that's there.'

She sits down on the damp grass on the bank of the maar. In the water an enormous frog is lying on some slimy strands of algae, its warty skin gleaming. It lies there, inert and at full length, like a tipsy Frog King. Its back legs, stretched out behind it, look like two snakes growing out of its body, and its virulent green head, with its bulging eyes, floats on the water.

She never understood those fairy-tale princesses who could bring themselves to kiss the reptilian mouth of a creature like that, hoping it would transform into a prince. She was always more attracted to the princesses, but even when she was still very young she understood this was something she'd better keep quiet about. Perhaps it's different in the city, but this is where she belongs, here in Schokland. She'd be like a pheasant on the clay farmland, there in the city.

As she's walking back along the maar she hears her name being called. She can see Fokko's tall form some distance away, by Siepke's Sleepstead. He beckons to her. She reluctantly walks towards him. He heads straight for her.

'So,' he calls to her from a distance, 'what did you make of it?'

She only answers when she's so close to him that she doesn't have to yell.

'What do you mean?'

'That evening in the village hall, of course.'

'Oh, I picked up a lot from it. What about you?'

'Plenty of drivel, but not many deeds.'

'Did your visit to the riggers get you anywhere?'

He shakes his head and then: 'Do you think you could treat me again? With some of those pink cakes and tea and so on.'

'Okay, give me the thermos. Anything else? A Lucky Luke?'

'How come you knew they're my favourite comics?'

'So, who did you want to be? Lucky Luke, right?'

'No,' he says. 'They always used to call me Averell. But I didn't really mind. He was pretty dumb, that's true, but he was never alone, like Lucky Luke.'

'Lucky Luke isn't alone,' she says. 'He's got Jolly Jumper and Rataplan.'

He asks if Trijn has finished the buzzard yet.

'Probably,' she says. 'Do you want to come and fetch it? Or should I bring it to you?'

He shakes his head. 'As long as she looks after him for me. As long as she doesn't get rid of him, out of spite.'

'She won't do that.'

He turns round and lumbers back to Siepke's Sleepstead.

*

When Femke drives into the yard, Danielle is standing by the open door, and she welcomes her with a broad grin, widespread arms, a hug, a hand ruffling Femke's hair, a kiss on the cheek.

In the big living-kitchen there's a full pot of coffee on the warmer, a plate of biscuits on the table, and a bottle of wine and a packet of peanuts on the worktop.

Danielle stands at the stove, heating up the milk, and she urges Femke to sit down. But Femke lingers, looking around her, and then breaks the silence by asking Danielle if she's ever seen skylarks in her alfalfa fields. And when Danielle answers yes, she fires the next question at her. 'And have you got experience with field margins too?'

Without turning round, Danielle says: 'Are you in a hurry or something? I'll come and sit down in a minute.'

Femke stands hesitantly by the table, using one hand to support herself, as if she might lose her balance. And then suddenly, as if a small animal has broken free inside her, she goes to Danielle, stands behind her a moment with hesitant arms, and then clasps her arms around her with a sigh and presses herself against the strong back. Without a word.

Danielle bursts out laughing, turns, and puts her arms round Femke. Femke has to look down at her. She'd like to be smaller, would like to shrink herself, like caterpillars do when they're touched.

She looks into the dark-brown eyes that suddenly seem so shockingly close and Danielle searches for her lips. A long kiss. Eager fingers wriggle under the t-shirts like little snakes.

Danielle frees herself much too swiftly and whispers, laughing: 'Hey, Blondie, calm down a bit. We're getting a visitor soon.' She says it in the kind of tone that means it's a nice surprise.

Femke gives her head a little shake. 'I don't want any visitors,' she says softly, trying in vain to take hold of Danielle's hand.

'I'm getting a lodger.'

Femke stays silent.

'Lieuwe's coming to stay. The dragon-man. You saw him in the village hall. In fact, it's good that he'll be here. You could really use some advice.'

'But he isn't a farmer, is he?'

'No silly, he's a lawyer.'

'So why's he coming to stay here?'

It's difficult for her to ask the question. It's as if she has lost her voice.

'He's going to build up a practice here in the north and he doesn't have a house yet.'

'Why here?'

'Why not?'

Femke is still tingling, as if she's just stepped out of an ice-bath, but it looks as if the kiss of a few moments back had absolutely no effect on Danielle. Or that she's already forgotten it.

'So, what about us then?'

'We've got plenty of time for that,' Danielle says, pulling her fiercely towards her, and giving her a kiss, right on the mouth.

*

When Trijn enters the headquarters, Zwier is sitting in his usual place, with a wooden plaque in front of him, on which he has drawn five absolutely straight lines in pencil. He's putting nails on them, in order: big and little, thick and thin.

Trijn limps towards the desk, leaning on Ootje's stick. Her knee is still shapeless and painful, and when she looks at it all kinds of associations loom up of old women's legs, like her mother's: bandages, support stockings, calves with varicose veins, fungus nails. She shudders.

'I was in the village this morning,' Zwier says, 'to get some cement. Have you heard what happened to Spierstra?' He moves his hand sharply across his throat. She nods.

'In the barn. His wife found him there. And you must've been hoping it wouldn't reach my ears,' he says. 'They say he's the first death,' he continues. He dabs at a nail with the superglue nozzle and sticks it next to two other nails. "And what about my wife then?" I asked them. He looks up at Trijn. 'Do you know what they said?'

She doesn't answer.

'That she died of a heart attack. And that that's very different.'

'But it's true, isn't it?' she says, carefully. 'Ootje didn't want to die, did she?'

'No. But she couldn't live like this anymore.'

'I feel sorry for Spierstra's wife,' Trijn says. 'How can you carry on after something like that?'

'Well. You just carry on. There's nothing else you can do. Draaisma's slurry stores are leaking. Piet's house has been declared unfit for human habitation. Braaksman's shippon has collapsed, and Berendse's wife has left him, because she doesn't dare live in their ramshackle house any longer. And he's refusing to give up the fight… There'll be plenty more deaths, that's for sure.'

Femke comes in, her eyes glued to her smartphone, from which you can hear an ominous buzzing noise, sounding like a swarm of bluebottles. Above the buzzing there are high-pitched little beeps, one after the other, in ever swifter tempo. Without taking her eyes off the screen, Femke lets her mother look at it too. A dark map of the province can be made out, on which all the rigging locations and flare stacks are drawn. A red circle flashes up at every beep, leaving its imprint behind. Very swiftly, the region changes colour, to red for danger. The years flash by at the bottom of the screen: 2014, 2015, 2016, 2017. Angry little beeps, and every now and then the loud ring of a bell, as if someone's won a prize, although the ringing actually means loss.

'What's this?'

Femke explains that every beep is an earthquake. The bell indicates an earthquake above a certain magnitude.

'A what?'

'The strength of the earthquake.'

'And how did you find this?'

'On Facebook. Danielle posted it.'

Trijn sighs.

'Oh,' says Femke, 'and that means it can't be right. Right?'

'I didn't say that. But it doesn't do any harm to take things with a pinch of salt, especially information from a source like that.'

'What do you mean?'

'She seems to have quite outspoken opinions. She probably searches for information that fits her own ideas.'

Femke looks up in irritation.

'But don't we all do that?'

Zwier also wants to see the animation and she starts it again.

'Is every beep an earthquake?'

Femke nods. The first bell rings at 1990.

'Has this been going on so bloody long then?'

'Yes,' Femke says. 'At the time the only man who warned this could happen was treated like a village idiot.' And she rattles on indignantly: 'In Norway when they started drilling for oil they set up a fund to compensate for any future damage. They should've done that here too.'

Zwier's cheeks go red again.

'Things will turn out okay,' Trijn says soothingly. 'We just need a bit of patience. And there are people who've been properly compensated. People who cooperated with them.'

'You mean,' Zwier says, 'they sat around like tame sheep waiting to see what they'd kindly give them.'

'So what do you suggest then, Dad? Do we have to drive our tractors to the Hague? That's happened already. It didn't do any good. Riots at the village hall? That's been done too. It just cost the council more money, and smashed windows and torn-up street paving. We won't get anywhere with that.'

Then Femke interrupts.

'Some people want to start a class action.'

'Those aren't your words,' Trijn says reproachfully. 'That kind of idea can only come from people who aren't from round here. Watch out for offcomers. They always know so bloody well how we should do things. But hasn't it struck you that these people never have a stake in it themselves? That flibbertigibbet of yours, she hasn't got any damage at all, has she?'

'That doesn't mean she's not right.'

'You've got no idea what you're talking about,' Trijn fumes. 'That gas extraction, there's an immense amount of money involved in it, really important interests, international contracts, delivery terms, and obligations both to businesses and countries. We can't match that lot. The best you can do is make sure they're well-disposed towards you. Cooperate a bit.'

Zwier looks up mockingly at her.

'Cooperating means having to wait and see. Being humble. And in the meantime they tell you you're not taking good care of your farm. After a lifetime of toil.'

'But first you've got to prove that it's quake damage,' Trijn says.

'We shouldn't talk about quake damage, Mam, but gas extraction damage.'

'And if we call it that, does it suddenly solve everything?'

Something wild has got into Femke, Trijn thinks. She's been stirred up by offcomers. People who don't come from the claylands, not even the peatlands, or the sandlands, people who grew up on concrete. Who've never learned what it means to roll up your sleeves. People who think words solve everything. As if calling something by a different name changes anything at all about the cracks, the subsidence, the long wait.

And then Femke says in a clear voice: 'We should set a lawyer onto it.'

Trijn gives a mocking laugh.

'We shouldn't hold out a hand, but clench a fist,' Femke continues.

'That,' says Trijn, pointing Ootje's stick at Femke, 'has got to be another of your friend-by-the sea-dyke's ideas. Right?'

Femke nods.

Then Trijn bursts out about so-called free advice, about the hourly rates that lawyers charge, folk who don't sweat out their guts for a pittance. And how you just make things easy for the riggers if you start a lawsuit. They don't have to do anything at all, except string you along until the courts have rid you of all your money.

Femke shrugs her shoulders and walks out of the headquarters. Trijn picks up her phone to send a text message. A rain front will arrive in four days' time. The grass will have to be mowed before then. It promises to be a good first cut. Meanwhile she asks herself how she can convince Femke and Zwier that they're fighting a dangerous battle. That it could be dangerous to antagonise people from the companies they're opposing. The most important thing is to keep Schokland from going under. For Femke perhaps most of all. Because without Schokland, what would become of her daughter? What would happen if she had to live a normal bourgeois sort of life in a fast-paced world where you're only successful if you can network with any Tom, Dick or Harry? A world where you can jabber out any kind of unthinking assumption, because you're not held back by actual knowledge. A world where you can always put people down and have to sell yourself, as if you're a sales-rep. Where you've got to be tough and self-assured, or at least able to fake it. How could Femke survive in a society in which successful people all resemble each other, and sensitive, vulnerable people are perceived as failures?

Trijn is determined to do everything she can to keep Schokland going. Because of their ancestors, because they have a duty of stewardship, but most of all for Femke's future.

June 2017

Intermezzo

The cow parsley grows tall in the verges. The tufts of winter wheat are changing into knee-high shoots almost as you watch, and every now and then you can see the translucent ears of a hare popping up, the tips looking as if they've been dipped in ink. The grass looks promising, strong and well-grown. The weather forecasts are good. It seems it will be a fine first cut.

But if our hero Giuseppe Mercalli were still alive and if he visited the clay country to interview the inhabitants about the state of the land, the buildings, animals and people, he'd not only hear that there are more and more cracks in the houses and farm buildings because of the quakes, and the ground is subsiding further, and the groundwater level is rising, but that the people are also gradually becoming infected, as if they've been exposed for too long to toxic air.

The neglect, the lack of recognition, the increasing feeling of insecurity and powerlessness are all festering in them like decay inside concrete. Mercalli would probably discover that a suppressed fury is increasing, in this part of the country where level-headedness has always prevailed. And there's plenty of material in the farm buildings to vent that anger: pitchforks, tractors, air rifles, and explosives.

It's easy enough to find ropes and roof beams here too. And almost every man or woman has long known how to tie a proper noose and kick away a ladder.

This cultural landscape might look very lovely this month, but appearances are deceptive. The Mercalli scale is rising.

IT'S A RAW JUNE DAY. There's music in the byre, from the local radio station. The chickens are perched on the collar beams, the kittens play in the straw, spiderwebs flutter in the wind, which roars like breakers on the seashore. Femke and Zwier are standing over the bull calf, born last night with mucus in its lungs. It can hardly breathe. Trijn comes along and watches what they're doing. Every breath the calf takes is a struggle. Femke tries to get the little creature to drink a bottle of beastings. The calf doesn't have the strength to fight and lets Femke squeeze the teat into its mouth, but it doesn't suckle, even when she strokes her fingers along its throat to try to encourage the sucking reflex. Femke makes soothing noises. And Trijn, who often announces, with a degree of pride, that she's as tough as nature itself, suddenly feels compassion. She watches with fascination, seeing how doggedly and patiently Femke is trying to get the calf to drink. She's murmuring in an almost animal-like language, as only Femke can. The calf has pricked up its ears, but it won't suck.

Eventually Zwier stands up, shaking his head, and then Femke stops trying.

The calf falls back into the straw, stiffly and woodenly. Its breathing is laboured, and it makes rasping noises. It seems exhausted.

'A pity,' Trijn concludes. 'It's not going to make it.'

'We don't know that yet, Mam. I'm going to try a stomach-tube.'

'You know what I think about that.'

'Yes,' Femke says, 'I know what you think.'

Trijn walks back to the headquarters, sits down at the desk and watches what's going on in the byre while waiting for the computer to download the papers for administering the various plots of land. Femke comes back with the tube and gives Zwier the bag of colostrum. She pulls the calf up, clamps it between her legs, takes its head in her hands, and squeezes her fingers into its mouth. With her other hand she gently pushes the tube down its throat, very carefully, so she won't damage the fragile gullet and windpipe.

And Trijn watches through the window and is amazed at the energy with which Femke pursues such a risky job as this. No one else can handle the animals as well as Femke. No one else has that enviable ease. Trijn sometimes thinks that the old stories about people who are half-animal, half-human were perhaps invented by the parents of children who were just as mysterious to them as Femke is for her.

*

The evening meal is finished. The coffee is ready. Trijn is sweeping the floor round the table. Zwier has gone down the lonning again, to the post box. This is a trip he makes a couple of times a day now. The waiting is difficult for him.

The door bursts open. Zwier comes in, agitatedly waving a letter and an envelope, which he throws onto the table. He sinks down onto his chair.

'Blooming blasted bloody damnation.'

'What does it say?' she asks, hesitantly.

Gazing at a dark knot of wood in the tabletop, he waves at the letter. 'Go on, read it.' Her eyes fly over the text. Then she also slumps onto a chair. A stillness fills the parlour, the kind of stillness that broods over the land after a sweltering hot summer's day, right before the storm breaks. And in the room that for almost two years now has had to make do as a kitchen the atmosphere is just as charged, because the stratum of earth below them has changed into the flattest volcano in the world, a volcano that rumbles and shudders and quakes. Femke comes in and looks questioningly first at one, then the other. Trijn hands her the letter. Femke reads it and, although she never raises her voice, she cries out: 'This can't be right!'

'Oh yes,' Trijn says in a flat voice. 'Just look. They can do whatever they want. We can't do anything about it.'

'Oh yes we can,' Femke says. 'I'll just take it with me a moment, okay?'

Trijn wants to know what she's intending to do. Femke answers that she wants to discuss the letter with someone.

'Definitely not,' Trijn says. 'That letter can't leave the house. We have a duty of confidentiality.'

But Femke mutters that they surely can't agree to this offer and walks out of the room. She returns a little later and puts the letter on the table. Trijn sees a photocopy sticking out of her coat pocket.

'I'm off for a while.' Femke goes to Zwier, who is still staring at the knot in the wood with tears in his eyes. She puts an arm around him.

'We're not going to leave it at that, Grampa. They haven't got rid of us yet.'

He gives her hand a gentle pat.

'Right enough,' he mumbles, but with less conviction than ever before. She gives him a kiss, gives Trijn a cool goodbye, takes out her smartphone, and leaves the room without shutting the door.

When Trijn gets up to shut it she hears Femke in the hall saying in an agitated tone of voice: 'Is that Lieuwe guy still staying with you? I'm coming to see you both. He's got to help us.'

*

Just a little longer and the new day will dawn in the east.

Femke parks the car in the farmyard and sees that the lights in the back of the barn are on. She finds Trijn at work in the Dead Bird Museum. Her mother doesn't look up when she hears the door open, but continues working, as if it's perfectly normal to be preparing a turtle dove at two o'clock in the morning.

Femke watches Trijn from the doorway, seeing how she sews up the dove's belly. She pushes the fine needle through the feathers and skin with small careful stabs.

'Couldn't you sleep?' Femke asks.

'Where have you been all this time? With that lass?'

'Her name's Danielle, Mam,' Femke says calmly. 'And I'm a whole lot wiser now.'

Trijn still doesn't look up from the white belly of the dove. She ties off the thread, cuts it, and then turns the dove in her hands: a small slim bird with orange-brown plumage and little black-and-white stripes on its neck. A real beauty, but dead as a doornail.

'It's pretty,' Femke says.

'So that kid knows everything about our report now.'

'Yes,' Femke says wearily. 'There's a lawyer staying with her.'

Trijn doesn't answer.

'I'm going to bed.' Femke turns round. 'I'll tell you about it tomorrow. Sleep well.'

She goes into the byre. She wants to make a quick check on the calf, but a light is on in the headquarters too, and Zwier's grey hair is visible through the window.

She opens the door. The table is covered with Zwier's nail tins. He looks up from his plaque and says: 'I thought I was the only one still up.'

'Well, you're wrong about that. Mam's still in her den.'

He takes the jenever bottle from floor and asks if she'd like a nightcap. There isn't a glass for her, so she gets a cup from the cupboard and holds it out.

'Where did you go?'

'Danielle's place.'

'You really like her, don't you?'

She nods, swallows, and swiftly takes a gulp of jenever.

Zwier uses a pencil and ruler to place two dots on either side of the wooden plaque, absolutely equidistant, and then draws a dead-straight line.

'And is it mutual?' he asks.

She shrugs.

He looks aside. Femke stares into her cup.

'Well,' he says, 'I'm not someone to advise you on this sort of business.'

He rummages around in his little tins.

She takes another sip and asks him hesitantly if he loved Ootje.

'I don't really know,' he says. 'I did at first. But later? It's just like with a plant.' He pauses a moment. 'It withers for lack of water.'

They sip their jenever and listen to the sounds in the shippon. A cow knocking against the feed rail with her horns. A sleepy moo now and again.

'I've spoken to a lawyer. He wants to help us.'

Zwier shakes his head. 'Your mother's right. Lawyers cost an arm and a leg.'

'He says not. Says if we win the riggers will have to pay us back. The legal costs too.'

'If,' he says. 'You don't know that for sure. And how long will something like that take?'

She drinks, watches him roll a fag, and asks if he can do one for her too.

'Since when have you smoked?'

'I don't smoke,' she says.

'Alright then.' He gives her a fag and holds his lighter to it. She breathes in deeply and then puffs out.

'This isn't your first,' he decides.

'No,' she says. 'And not the first from you either.'

'Aye. Right enough.'

They smoke and drink in silence, and then he asks: 'And why's he doing that then?'

'Who?'

'That lawyer.'

She quotes what he said in Danielle's kitchen, that it's high time we put a stop to the conspiracy of multinationals and political interests. That it's always about profit for those guys, not about people or quality of life. That they should destroy the old boys' network.

'Right. And that young man is going to sort that out, is he?'

'He wants to help the victims.' As she speaks the word she feels the same discomfort she did then, when the bald chap said it and looked at her as if she were some kind of endangered animal. Someone you pity. A loser.

'Victims? That's what we are?' Zwier shakes his head. 'People always need to make others feel smaller. So they can look bigger.'

'Yes,' Femke says, in surprise.

Lieuwe had insisted that the riggers were benefitting from sowing confusion. From dragging things out as long as possible, so their rigging could continue. That's why they kept coming up with new rules, and enquiries, and arbitrators, and advisors, and experts, and why they turned down more and more claims, why they made accusations of poor maintenance, and why they didn't want to check below the surface and hadn't put good quake monitors in the ground and spent their time setting people against each other, and that's why they were creating an inner and an outer circle and were forcing people to accept confidentiality clauses and working against everything as much as they could. And the government was letting it all happen, because the profits were enormous.

Femke understood that what he was saying was all true and that she should stay to hear out the lecture, because Schokland had to be saved. Up to this point, the Koridons had always fought their own battles, but perhaps they couldn't get through it alone anymore.

Lieuwe and a few other lawyers were going to hold their first surgery on the following day, and they were hoping to organise a mass action to force the riggers to pay up, reinforce buildings, compensate, and buy people out. And his ambition was to eventually stop the pumping. If necessary, he said, not without a degree of melodrama, he'd go as far as the Supreme Court, and if that wasn't enough, to the European Court of Justice.

And while he was speechifying Femke found it more and more difficult to concentrate on the content, because he was sitting next to Danielle and letting his arm lean on the arm of her chair. That arm of his was far too close and Danielle didn't even seem to feel uncomfortable about it. And Femke was sitting there, the victim, alone on the other side of the table, opposite those who were supposed to be rescuing her. An immense wooden tabletop between them, like a hectare of impassable land, dense with thistles.

The byre door slams and Trijn hobbles in. Femke is shocked. Her mother looks like an old woman. She leaps up, opens the door to the headquarters, and asks if Trijn wants a nightcap too, and when Trijn comes in Zwier pours her a cupful of jenever as well.

'Would you two like to hear what that lawyer said?'

'Indeed I would,' Zwier says carefully, 'but not now. Can't take it all in anymore.' He points at his head with the shot glass in his hand.

'Are you sozzled?' Femke says, chuckling.

'Sozzled? Ah well, what's sozzled?' He glances at Trijn, who throws back her jenever, and then holds out her cup again.

'Another fill-up?' He sounds surprised. The cups are filled again and sipped from in silence, and then after a while he muses: 'So am I sozzled?'

Femke giggles and Zwier says he can prove he isn't, by drawing a dead-straight line. He gets his pencil and Trijn asks why he actually makes those nail pictures.

'I've been doing that for more than a year now,' he says, 'and you've never asked me before.'

'That's right,' Trijn says. 'I've never wondered about it before either.'

'Why do you stuff those dead birds?'

'Because Jort did it,' she says softly.

'Right enough. But is that the only reason?'

Trijn thinks a bit. 'I started doing it because Jort did it, but I carried on doing it because it's a nice thing to do.'

She stares at the jenever in her cup, and gently swirls it round.

'Is that right?' Zwier asks.

'When I mount them, then they stay with us.'

'Aye. Right enough.'

'And now you'll answer me. Why do you make those nail pictures?'

'It's my farmer's cuneiform, written in nails.' He's slurring his words.

'What do you mean?'

'I can't quite say, and that's why I'm making a nail picture,' he says, laughing. And Trijn stands up, leans over the plaque and pretends it's a musical composition. She burbles a few notes.

'Everyone,' she calls, and Zwier sings along.

More jenever is poured and then Trijn tugs at Femke's sleeve and points to the plaque.

Femke looks at both of them and then at the nail picture. She thinks about what Zwier said about Ootje. She thinks of the withered plant, of her own shuddering when she was made out to be a victim. She thinks about the lawyer's arm on the arm of Danielle's chair and says, staring at the rusty score: 'I think it's a sad song. About a heart overflowing with sorrow. That's what

I think.'

'Aye. Right enough.'

'You phrased that nicely,' Trijn says and looks straight at Femke. 'I always thought you were better with animals than with words.'

'If only you knew all the things you don't know about me,' Femke blurts out.

'And I'd really like to know them.' Trijn gives her a serious look.

'I'd really like to know them,' she repeats.

Femke stands up.

'I'll just take a look at the calf.' She's about to walk out of the room, but Zwier grabs her arm. He wants a goodnight kiss. She kisses him on both cheeks.

'You too?' she asks her mother.

'Well, if it'll come off.'

Femke kisses Trijn and Trijn takes her daughter's head in her hands, looks straight at her, and says: 'You're my brave little girl.'

Femke quickly stands up.

'Good night,' she says and leaves.

She goes to the straw pen and the calf is lying there, dead-still, on its side, its front legs outstretched. It already has a film over its eyes and saliva runs from its mouth. It is lying completely still. A stillness that's only possible when there's no breath pumping, no blood streaming, no more beating of the heart. No more fighting for gasps of breath.

Femke drops down in the straw beside the dead calf, takes hold of its head, and gently strokes the favourite spot where calves so like being stroked, hard on the inside, soft on the out-side, and she weeps.

*

When Femke comes downstairs the following morning, a bit later than usual, she starts work without seeing anyone else at all.

She wheels the barrow to the straw pen and drags the stiff, cold bull calf over its rim. The rigid legs stick out, spindly white-red-and-brown flecked poles with smooth little hooves. She fetches a cloth from the lumber area and lays it over the corpse, and then speaks to the answer-machine of the carcass disposal firm. She gives the name of the farm and the code-number for a dead calf. Twenty-three.

Then she pushes the barrow down the lonning. The sweet, heavy scent of May blossom and cow parsley, the magenta-coloured clover flowers and purple foxtails, the great tits twittering in the poplars, the yellow wagtails on the fields, the meadow pipits yoyoing, the swallows skimming along the ground, the crows cawing, and the soft summer breeze all pass her by.

She puts the wheelbarrow next to the post box and walks back, imagining what it would be like to get rid of dead people in the same way. Just like that, in a wheelbarrow, by the side of the road, a cloth over the body, and then tapping in the code for 'other animals'.

She thinks back to yesterday evening, when she was at Danielle's, and the feeling of queasiness increases. Danielle and the bald lawyer, bending their heads together over the photocopy she'd given them. While they were reading it all she could see was that arm, pumped up with weights and perhaps even with steroids, straying every now and then towards Danielle's shoulder, lingering there, and then sometimes the smooth manicured hand would glide over the dark curls. He and Danielle read the impersonally phrased text together. It said that the organisation did not consider itself to be responsible for the damage. That the Koridons would not be compensated, but would only receive a small indemnification, as a gesture of good will – a fine-sounding phrase, melodious even, as if using that would soften the callousness of the decision. Femke stared at Danielle's dark curly mop of hair beside that bald shiny head, so close together. The dragon head in his neck was sticking out its fiery red tongue at her. Lieuwe asked her an occasional question. How many reports had they had before this one? How many experts had visited as the years went by? And how had they managed to cope without a kitchen for the past two years?

'We just did,' she said, and he and Danielle gave her a look that turned her into a pathetic victim. Yet she still answered them as conscientiously as possible.

Danielle pushed a biro and jotter towards her. Lieuwe went on about the enemy's ruthlessness. He indignantly reminded her that the gas companies, with the government's consent, had dramatically increased gas extraction the year after the biggest earthquake, the one that had caused so much damage, that they'd even doubled its production. Of course she remembered that. The people from the village had spoken about it at the time, stoically, the same way you talk about drought or a deluge of rain, as something unavoidable.

Lieuwe was rattling on about setting up a mass legal action and while he was talking, Danielle stood up and went out of the kitchen.

Femke looked at the man's mouth moving, going on and on about justice, until without a word she stood up in the middle of what he was saying. He went silent a moment and then cried out: 'Hey, where are you going? I'm talking to you.'

She didn't answer but shut the door and went to the utility room, where Danielle was. She was crouching down, with her back to the door, and was just on the point of getting up, a couple of bottles in her hand. Femke ran towards her and threw her arms around her. Danielle tottered a little and a bottle fell and broke, making the beer splash up. Danielle swore, turned round, and put her arms around Femke. They stood like that a moment, close together, Femke's thudding heart against that wiry body.

The door of the room opened.

'What the fuck,' Femke heard him say, and she clamped herself tighter to Danielle, who said that Lieuwe should leave them alone a while, that they'd be back in a moment.

'Give me a beer then, at least,' he said. Danielle let go of Femke, gave him a bottle, and he shut the kitchen door as he left.

Femke gazed into Danielle's eyes, which were looking at her impassively.

'Why's he staying with you?'

Danielle took Femke's head in her hands.

Femke really wanted to say that she didn't want to be a victim. She tried to find the words to remind Danielle that they'd made some kind of promise to each other last time, mouths ablaze, fingers groping.

She said nothing at all.

'Listen, Blondie,' Danielle said harshly. 'I like seeing you, but I don't belong to you and you don't belong to me. I'm not the kind of person you can own.'

Then Danielle kissed her and Femke nuzzled into her again, but Danielle let go much too quickly and said: 'Here, you take the beers and I'll get some snacks. And don't forget what Lieuwe tells you. He's really good at his job.'

*

Zwier is sitting in the headquarters. She asks if he slept in, but he shakes his head.

'I went to the surgery.'

'To the doctor?' she asks in surprise.

'No, of course not.'

He pushes the free paper towards her. *Free Consultation in the Village Hall for Gas Victims.* And a paragraph about three lawyers who want to work on behalf of people with quake-damaged property.

She points to Lieuwe's name.

'That's him,' she says. 'The one I spoke to yesterday.'

Zwier nods.

'Why someone thinks it's necessary to have a snake tattooed on his neck is a mystery to me,' he says.

She smiles.

'Did he tell you how long it can take if you start a legal process?' he continues.

'A long time.'

'Exactly. Years,' he says. 'And in the meantime, everything falls apart even more.'

'If it gets dangerous, we'll have to raise the alarm.'

'And then?' her Grampa asks, narrowing his eyes. 'What do you think will happen then? I mean, what do *you* think? Not that bald feller.'

'Then they'll have to do even more shoring up. But if things get really risky, we'll have to leave the farm. And if it's too expensive to repair, it'll be knocked down. Like Fokko's.'

'Aye. Right enough. And I'm afraid that's exactly what they'd prefer to do. Restoration is more expensive than demolition. It's just like it was in the past. They cleared the whole island of Schokland because the government of the time, Willem III and his cronies, thought it was too expensive to put things right again. Most folk didn't want to leave their native ground, but they weren't consulted. I'm speaking about a hundred and sixty years ago now, but not a jot has changed.'

Femke nods.

'That kind of legal action will cost tons,' Zwier continues. 'And it'll take too long for me. The byre won't hold out. A strong storm, a new quake, and we'll have lost it.'

'So what do you want to do?' She asks the question cautiously. His forehead is deeply furrowed. His bushy eyebrows hang above his eyes like dark awnings.

'I just don't know, my lass.'

He taps a nail on the table. And then again, in a voice that changes to a sigh: 'I just don't know.'

He stares ahead.

'It's daft,' he continues. 'We've always had problems. When the roof blew off, when the harvest got drenched, with mad cow disease, the milk quota, hassle with the cattle, hassle with the land. There are always disasters, at all times.'

'Yes.'

'Yet I always managed to get through them.'

He goes silent, and then carries on: 'There was only one time I felt as bad as I do now.'

'That time with Ootje?'

He shakes his head.

'That time with Jort,' he says and his eyes, already glistening, turn red.

She puts her hand on his.

'I know this isn't my fault, and yet it feels as if it is.' His voice breaks.

'Grampa,' she says. 'We'll think of something. I promise you.'

He looks up at her.

'That's right, my lass. You keep up your spirits.'

'Just going out for a bit of a walk,' she says, and flees from the headquarters.

With her face into the wind she walks through the billowing grass, which moves like the sea, as if everything is completely normal.

*

Trijn's tongue feels like a piece of leather. She slowly gets up, hobbles to the bathroom, flings two paracetamols inside her, and sluggishly gets dressed. She makes herself a cup of tea in the parlour, she can't think about eating any bread just yet, and while she's sitting at the table, gathering up the strength to start the day, she asks herself what went wrong. How is it possible that hardworking, respectable people like herself and that big rigging business, a profitable and apparently respectable organisation with an impressive head office, can't come to an agreement with each other?

They've been patient for many years now, the Koridon family. They've shown understanding for the fact that the riggers had much more on their minds than their case. They've always been reasonable about the long periods of waiting, about the fact that they kept sending new people to check things over, and that they had to start from scratch every time. They've been reasonable when they were told they were in the right and they'd get compensation, but then this was undone by the next set of experts. Trijn has always remained friendly, decent and polite, and that's why she was convinced that they, unlike Fokko, would get a favourable outcome. Just like other people in the area, who've been properly compensated without too many problems.

The only thing that could have gone wrong, she thinks to herself, are Zwier's telephone calls. Perhaps the calls irritated them, perhaps she shouldn't have left him to do the contacting. She should go there and do something about it. The sooner that terrible decision is off the table, the better.

And so she drives to the riggers' headquarters. It's a building in the form of a glass and steel honeycomb, in a typical industrial zone: an area at the edge of a city, developed on the drawing board, in which businesses, a hospital, and a cemetery can be found one behind the other, like a sequence of logical steps in life.

She walks into the foyer, with its shiny, smooth marble floor. Behind a large counter, gleaming like their milk tank just before an inspection, there's a receptionist in a starched white blouse, with a puffed-up blue-and-white scarf, embellished with a gas-pump logo.

With professional friendliness, the young woman asks how she can be of help to madam.

Trijn answers that she wants to speak to the person responsible for dealing with the damage.

'What kind of damage?'

'Quake damage. Or rather, extraction damage.'

And who is she here to see?

'The person responsible for dealing with the gas extraction damage.'

The young woman says, in a patient tone of voice, that she needs a name, and Trijn answers in a similarly friendly voice that she must have some idea which people are concerned with the gas extraction damage. And that she'd like to speak to the top boss.

'People aren't meant to come here without making an appointment. Moreover,' the young woman adds, 'you're at the wrong address.'

'If I'm not mistaken,' Trijn answers, still with complete self-control, 'I'm at the head office of the gas rigging firm, right?'

'But has madam registered a damage claim?'

Trijn hauls an over-stuffed folder of correspondence out of her bag and places it on the counter. 'This isn't even half of it. We've been presenting our case for five years already.'

'If you'd paid attention,' the young woman says, in the kind of tone people use when they're giving patient instructions, a little like Trijn herself used when she was explaining to Brian how the milking robot worked, 'you'd know that damage claims are dealt with by a separate organisation. We no longer deal with those.'

The young woman, who in terms of age can't be much older than Femke, then looks at the correspondence address and continues: 'You could have saved yourself this whole journey, as this organisation is not very far away from you. The sensible thing would have been for you to have phoned your advisor. Everyone who has a registration number is allocated one.'

It sounds as if she's talking about a prize animal.

'We've had four different ones already. That's why I want to speak to someone higher up for once.'

The young woman clamps a pen between her thumb and index finger, which have something of chicken feet about them, what with the yellow varnish and the sharp points of her filed nails, and she writes a phone number on a piece of paper that she pushes towards Trijn.

'They won't receive you there, either,' she says, 'without an appointment. It's extremely busy.'

She advises Trijn to do the right thing and make an appointment. 'Because,' she says, in conclusion, 'that's how we do things in this country.'

She shouldn't have said that.

'Oh yes! That's how we do things in this country, is it? I can't remember anyone making an appointment before we were thrown out of our beds by an earthquake. Before our walls were torn apart, our windows shattered. Yes, they did make some kind of an appointment with us when a deadline was mentioned for when the report would be ready. That was all decently arranged. But the date passed without any kind of communication. And we waited, and waited, and waited. Much longer than the agreed date. And then we got a report saying the damage would be compensated. But the money never came. Just more months of waiting, and waiting, and waiting. And yes, then they made another appointment. And came to take another look. And then more waiting and waiting and waiting. Until a letter came that said the damage wouldn't be compensated after all. On further consideration. And meanwhile the whole place is cracking apart and the animals are in danger. And nothing's happening. Is that how we do things in this country?'

Trijn takes a furious step forward, as if she's about to drag the young lady with the scarf and chicken claws right across the counter.

The receptionist stays calm. She must have passed her communication skills unit *Dealing with Difficult and Aggressive Clients* with flying colours. Yes, she really does understand that it's all very frustrating, and that madam must be sick and tired of it, but...

Trijn isn't listening anymore and rushes off with an angry and powerless: 'I'm not going to leave it at this.'

*

It's the warmest June day ever recorded in the country. All week long experts on the TV and radio have been sketching out scenarios of doom. Global warming seems to be happening at a swifter pace than anyone had thought possible. The polar ice caps are melting at a furious rate. Images are shown of gigantic glaciers, walls of ice thundering violently into the sea and vanishing. Calculations demonstrate that the sea-level is rising far quicker than previously predicted. An expert draws the sombre conclusion that with this scenario there's the chance that more than half of the country, which after all is not much more than a dyked-in layer of silt and clay, will be swallowed up by the advancing sea.

The three of them are sitting in the parlour, all the windows propped open. Trijn is trying to cool down by fanning herself with a copy of *Tractor & Machinery*. Zwier is sitting in his chair with his white vest on, his face scarlet, and his feet in an ice-bath.

Femke is lying listlessly on the sofa, for once dressed in shorts and a loose sleeveless top.

There's a ping.

Coast clear. (Dragon emoji) *gone. Coming to visit?* A row of suns, red lips, two women's faces, a red chilli pepper, and an exploding volcano.

She quickly leaves the room, sits down on a pile of boxes in the tie-stall, and stares at the display. It's the first sign of life from Danielle since the night she asked for advice. Femke had been convinced that what had previously happened between them was for Danielle no more than a light-hearted little game, a joke even.

She texts a red question mark back.

This is immediately followed by a ping: *Miss you.*

The blood is thudding in her veins and she answers: *See you soon.* Then she jumps up and puts her head round the door.

'I'm off for a bit.'

'Where to?'

'To Danielle's.' It sounds triumphant.

'Be careful.' Zwier winks.

*

When Femke gets out of the car she smells the sweet, invigorating scent of freshly mown grass. Danielle is sitting up high on the sea dyke, where land, sea and sky so easily shift into each other, where the boundaries between earth and water and mirage are always blurred, where the bright evening light makes the clouds reflect on the glistening ground, where the air trembles and the rolling waves come and go. Danielle opens her arms, there on the sea dyke, and Femke enters her embrace like a wave tumbling into a bay, she feels the heat, and then there's no stopping it.

*

Afterwards they lie languidly on the sea dyke. Femke's skin is tingling. Their hands rest on each other's naked bellies. The evening turns to night without it becoming one jot cooler. The heat continues. But a half moon appears, a little sickle in the sky, like you get in films in which everything is perfect. And then Danielle asks, smiling sweetly: 'Which would you hate the most, drowning or being crushed to death?'

'Why should I choose between them?'

'Because.'

'I want to be here with you.'

Danielle grabs hold of Femke's long hair and pulls it back teasingly, not too hard, but so she can't escape.

'But if you have to choose.'

Femke cautiously shakes her head, just brief, tiny movements. Moving hurts. Danielle doesn't let go.

'I don't want to choose.'

Danielle pulls a little harder, forcing Femke to shift her head further back. 'You have to.'

Femke takes Danielle's hand in both her own hands, tries to free herself, and says very firmly: 'I won't choose.'

'Being drowned or being crushed to death,' Danielle insists.

'But why?'

'You have to choose. Now.' Her voice is stern.

'Then I want to drown, but only together.'

Danielle grins. Their mouths meet and the journey of discovery continues. When they've calmed down again, lying side by side, their faces close together, Danielle declares: 'That was your first time, right?'

Femke nods. And with more courage than she's ever had she says: 'I'm going to sleep with you tonight.' It's not a question, but a decision.

Danielle shakes her head. 'That's not possible, Blondie.'

'Why not?'

'The dragon will be back.'

Femke's breath catches. She retorts, though she has to squeeze the words out: 'Then he can sleep on the sofa.'

Danielle laughs. 'He won't put up with that.'

Then Femke feels her skin tighten and she shivers, in spite of the warmth.

*

June is the greenest month. It's the month of neon-bright ryegrass, of deep green stalks of wheat from which light green ears are fighting their way skywards, of dark green potato foliage. In the distance you can see the plumes of sandy-coloured reeds where waterfowl are busily raising their young, trying to stop them being polished off by foxes or harriers, who are also doing their best to raise their own offspring, at the expense of field mice and songbirds.

Femke is startled by the shrill screeching of magpies, the sharp distress calls of peewits, and the stuttering, high-pitched alarm call of the last bitterns still nesting on the land. Clouds of grass are being thrown up by the fierce rotating blades of the mowing machines. She hasn't gone across the farmland this year to put posts around the nests. She'd wanted to investigate whether it might be better to leave some plots of land entirely unmown, even though that would mean less yield. She'd wanted to discuss it with Trijn. She forgot to do so.

Trijn is wondering what happened at Danielle's. When Femke got home her mother noticed that she seemed very upset, but her daughter hasn't said anything at all about it. Femke has no idea how to put into words the euphoria, the feeling of being loved and desired, and her disenchantment afterwards. Ever since that evening on the sea dyke she's felt like a goldfish swimming round in a bowl, all alone. Every now and then a face appears.

Her mother's, or Zwier's, or Brian's. Answering them, having a normal conversation, costs her enormous effort. A fish in a bare bowl. Cold-blooded and voiceless.

*

Trijn has turned the grass and is driving the tractor back through the fields. Zwier and Femke have their hands full with the torrent of calves born last night. They're not only busy with the young animals, but the heifers learning to use the milking robot for the first time also need their attention and firm guidance. The most stubborn ones are the heifers from Femke's breeding experiments. But Trijn is keeping that to herself. Femke has become more or less unreachable recently, even without reprimands. Why, Trijn asks herself, is it so difficult for a daughter to properly appreciate her mother's interest in her? Why is the love between a mother and her daughter met with irritation, and regarded as interference? Why is concern seen as disapproval? What is needed to understand each other better? Getting closer? Or increasing the distance?

As Trijn drives the tractor into the farmyard she sees Fokko sitting on the bench, a big refuse sack in front of him.

'Well,' she says, as she jumps off the tractor, 'long time no see.'

'That was what you wanted, right?'

She nods.

'I've got something for you.' He hands her the dustbin bag.

'What do you mean?' A mistrustful look.

'Have a look,' he urges. 'I'm not pulling your leg.'

She hesitantly takes the bag from him.

It's not heavy, but there's something big inside. A mass of feathers, black, white and bluey-grey, a long thin neck, some red, naked flesh. She peels back the plastic from the monster, and the more the bird becomes visible, the more her excitement grows, because what she's seeing she has only seen before as a transient, flying high overhead. Sometimes in the early spring, when they're working on the land and hear a gurgling sound, they look up and see a flock of cranes flying at a great height above them, their long legs stretched out behind them like divers.

This specimen is completely intact. It has an untidy plumage, gigantic wings, and a bill like a dagger. It's a beautiful, tall bird, the biggest she's ever held.

'Where did you get this?' she asks enthusiastically.

'I did some odd jobs for a few days for a farmer in the peatlands. It was lying there, in the fields.'

'What a find,' she says. 'I've never seen a crane down on the land here. Do you want me to mount it for you?'

'No,' he says. 'It's a gift. You can do whatever you like with it.'

She thanks him. For a while it's silent.

'I still have your buzzard,' she says. 'Do you want to see it?'

They walk into the barn. She clears a space for the crane in the dead-bird freezer.

'Have you got a new house yet?' she asks.

He shakes his head.

'But it can't go on like that, can it?'

'Just you wait,' he says.

She takes the buzzard down from the ceiling, where she's hung it up with string, its wings outspread, its head pointing down.

Fokko swallows.

'You've made a good job of that.'

'Yes,' she says. 'It turned out well.'

He takes the bird from her. 'That's him. My Wide World buddy.' Then he puts the bird on his head. 'How does that look?'

'How does that look?'

He nods. 'I've got a plan,' he says. 'I want to fix him onto my head.' He pulls a woolly hat out of his inside pocket, the kind with ear flaps and cords you can tie under your chin. 'We'll have to come up with some sort of way he can stay on top of my head. And I thought it might work with this kind of hat.'

'Why does it have to go on your head?'

'Because I've got a plan.'

'And are you going to tell me what your plan is?'

'No. The only thing I'll say is that I've got to be a birdman.'

'A birdman?'

He doesn't answer.

'So, you want to fix it onto this hat,' she concludes.

'Yes,' he says, 'but perhaps it's too floppy.'

'I think so too. You need it to be stiffer. Especially if you want to walk around with it on. And do you want to wear it outside?'

He nods.

'It'll catch the wind.'

'Well, I was thinking,' he says, 'that if we put a foam base in here, that stuff you use for bird bodies, and then make little holes in the hat and fix his feet with wire into the polystyrene, that might do it.'

'That's possible. If we have two wires coming up from the feet, then it'll be steady. But I'll have to open it up again.'

'I can do it myself.'

'Not at all. I'll do it for you.'

'Great. When will he be ready?'

'Come and ask in three days or so.'

He gives her a thumbs-up and then dashes out of the barn.

She stands looking at him, hesitates a while, and then calls out: 'Fokko, if you want you can take a shower here.'

He stands still and nods, surprised.

'Come on then,' she says. 'I've got some clean work clothes as well. Then I can put those filthy things of yours in the wash.'

'How come, suddenly?' he asks, as they walk into the byre. 'You didn't want me around.'

'Because you stink.'

Upstairs she gives him a towel and only then completes her sentence: 'And because I was wrong.' She rocks back and forth a little on her stockinged feet and says: 'Because it's not your fault.'

He looks questioningly at her. 'What's not my fault?'

'That you lost the Wide World.'

His face clouds. 'Of course that's not my fault. Did you think it was?'

She nods.

'And why do you think differently now?'

'Progressive insight.'

'You haven't bloody well signed, have you?' he says with alarm. 'That's what they want, they want you to sign, and at a certain point you think, what the hell, let's just do it, I want to stop all this bother. But I should never have done it. Don't do it,' he says emphatically. 'Don't sign.'

'It's not that difficult,' she says hesitantly, 'to work out what you shouldn't do, but much harder to decide what you should.'

'Just you wait,' he says. 'I've got a plan.'

She gives a pitying laugh.

'Go and take a shower. I'll sort some clothes out for you.'

In the parlour she makes tea and butters some bread. As he's tucking into the sandwiches, wearing a clean t-shirt and an old but clean pair of corduroy trousers that belonged to a former farmhand, she tells him how things went on the afternoon she was sent away from the riggers' head office and then drove on to the place they'd conjured up to deal with the damage claims, where eventually they did agree to talk to her. The interview was granted, after she'd stood at the front desk for an hour, patiently repeating, without raising her voice, that she would only leave after she'd spoken to her new case manager, or client advisor, or whatever the chap was now called. It was a minor victory for her that she was eventually allowed to talk to someone, a man who once again informed her that if she didn't agree to the offer, she'd be placed in the complex case file.

'What do you mean, complex?' she'd asked. 'You lot have wrecked our farm with that gas rig-up of yours and it has to be repaired, and quickly too, otherwise the whole place will collapse. That seems pretty simple to me.'

He smiled and said it really wasn't all that simple. Moreover, the whole procedure for awarding damages was being scrutinised at present and it would be some time before things could proceed. Especially for complex cases. He put a lot of emphasis on these last words. Then he stood up, wished her good luck, and went up the stairs again to his shiny office.

Fokko listens to her while he bolts down one sandwich after another. When Trijn has finished speaking, he says: 'Just you wait and see. I've got a plan. Nobody fucks with Fokko.'

As if he, the very person who lost the Wide World, could be Schokland's saviour. Trijn smiles. It's a friendly smile, but not one of hope and confidence.

July 2017

WHENEVER FEMKE HAS GATHERED enough courage to send a text, usually at the start of the evening, the answer is always the same. It doesn't make any difference if she asks: *Shall I drop by?* or *Have you got time for me?* or even if she announces: *I'll come now.* Whatever text she sends, it's always answered with a stop sign and a dragon.

She slowly comes to realise that a complicated game is being played, and that she barely understands its rules. A game that very occasionally seems to be about closeness, warmth and desire, but immediately afterwards only offers icy coldness. It's a game, as she comes more and more to realise, that not two but at least three people are playing. And only one person decides the rules. A game of singular intensity. A game in which she feels imprisoned in a bare goldfish bowl. The taunts flung at her when she was younger often echo through her head. Lamppost. Bat Ears. Horse Face.

Koridons are always alone. A Koridon is a good farmer, but Koridons understand very little about intimacy. Even in the school playground, when she tried to make herself invisible, she understood that she'd have to manage alone. She's not the kind of person that people love. Only her grandfather loves her, but he does that from habit.

She sometimes consoles herself by thinking back to the one night they spent together in Danielle's bed.

It started with a text message: *Coast clear.* (Dragon emoji) *in Wild West tonight.* Their union was fierce and intense and painful and wonderful, over and over again, as if with every eruption they were kindling more energy. And Femke seemed a new version of herself, a version who could be loved. A version that glowed. She knew what she had to do, what she could do, and what she wanted to do. Everything seemed perfect, a whole night long.

At half past five she got out of bed, went into the kitchen as if she was completely at home there, and came back with a tray loaded with coffee, bread and orange juice. Danielle clapped her hands.

'I've never had breakfast in bed before!'

'I'll bring you breakfast in bed every day,' Femke promised, but Danielle shook her head.

'The dragon will return,' she said, pronouncing the words slowly. She took a sip of orange juice and laid her hand on Femke's leg.

Femke took hold of the hand and asked, as neutrally as possible, as if she wasn't actually being eaten up by jealousy: 'Why do you want him?'

'Because I don't want to choose. Because I can love lots of people at the same time. I've just got a big heart,' was Danielle's answer, and Femke was howling inside. She looked down, at the crumpled bedsheet, strewn with breadcrumbs. Danielle grabbed her hair, then gently pulled her head back and whispered: 'But it's not like this with anyone else, sexy.' And after that it was impossible to avoid the next eruption.

'When will I see you again?' she dared to ask, when she was sitting in the car an hour later and Danielle was leaning on the door and still talking, telling her something about a diseased ash tree on the point of dying.

'We'll see, Blondie,' she said, leaning over for a last kiss.

'Shall I...' she started to say, but Danielle covered her lips with her hand and said: 'Shhh.'

A forced smile, a subdued goodbye, and she drove away, over the flat landscape, past a field full of shining, absinthe-green barley, billowing like a velvet sea. And yet all she could think of was lava. A glowing hot stream of it, bright orange and blood red, bubbling out of a volcano. A savage stream covering everything alive and scorching it and changing it into a hard, black stone. Impenetrable.

*

It's been raining for hours already and nothing in the thick, solid greyness of the blanket of clouds creates the impression that it will soon be over. After a dry June all that water is good for the land, but it's enough of a reason for Trijn to sigh that she really doesn't fancy checking out the pasture fencing. Femke offers to do it. As if she's redeeming something by doing so.

She walks across the land dressed in waterproofs, with her hood up and a full denim tool apron, carrying a roll of electric fencing wire over her shoulders. There's not a bird to be seen. Yet she enjoys walking in the pouring rain, in the squelchy wetness, under those immense clouds, from which raindrops are clattering with infernal force, like bullets from a machine gun.

As she's walking from one piece of wire to the next, she sees something strange poking out above the green foliage of the potato field. She peers through her binoculars.

There are birds that do belong here. Every now and then there's a vagrant, and there are increasingly more of them as climate change intensifies. There are birds she recognises from books, TV programmes, or from the Lucky Luke strip cartoons. Birds you know about, that live on the prairies, in the high mountain ranges, but not here, on the flattest, wettest land in existence. You don't get carrion birds here. And yet there is one, standing in the pouring rain, in the middle of the potato foliage, on this flat clay soil, all huddled up, its neck tucked into the feathers of its hunched shoulders. Its bald head is lowered, in a vain attempt to protect itself against the streaming water.

She's never seen a griffon vulture in real life before. It's a bird that belongs to the cliffsides of the high crags of Spain and the Caucasus. It must be hopelessly lost in this summer rain, in the chilly sea winds. And it's standing there all alone in a field of seed potatoes, although it's a gregarious bird, a supremely sociable creature. How did it end up here? Was it a lack of food that drove it northwards on a south-westerly wind? Didn't it know that every dead calf in this cultural landscape is immediately cleared away by the carcass disposal service? In this utterly mercantile country even death is a source of money-making.

The vulture is a captive in the potato field. The pouring rain has changed his plumage into a heavy, leaden coat.

The little roe buck, which has its scrape in the wetlands and grazes every morning at the edge of the potato field, comes up towards the giant bird, full of curiosity, much braver than when it notices a human being. It sniffs, lifting its muzzle up in the air. How does such a creature know that the vulture is a scavenger, that it won't attack him with its sharp beak? What kind of intuition do animals have to tell them who you can approach and who'd you better avoid?

She watches them with fascination, wondering how hungry a vulture would have to be to attack the buck after all, to turn that warm, soft creature into a piece of carrion. The difference between one and the other is no more than a well-judged stab of the dagger-like beak.

She walks through the drenched meadow, checking and replacing the wire. The vulture is still sitting in the same spot. It seems even more hunched up, beaten down by the rain. But eventually the rain stops. She sees the bird spread its gigantic wings as if it's mimicking a cormorant. A prehistoric bird among the potato plants.

The roe buck vanishes. The vulture sits there with outspread wings for at least half an hour before it takes off. She sees it spiralling higher and higher, and then spots a buzzard racing towards it, tiny in comparison to the gigantic creature, but that doesn't stop it from making a fierce dive at the stranger. It doesn't seem to bother the vulture. It carries on flying while the buzzard circles higher and higher and then makes its next attack on the bald neck. A second buzzard comes to its aid. And as always when she sees a single animal attacked by several others, she feels compassion for the loner. She watches the creature till it can no longer be seen.

Once she's back in the byre she hangs the soaked waterproofs on a peg and then goes through to the headquarters. Her mobile pings. She wipes the raindrops from her eyes with her arm, presses on the icon, and looks with astonishment at the photo that Danielle has sent her. Under a plastic awning she sees a man-sized bird's nest, made of branches and straw, and sitting up straight inside it, like an imperturbable Red Indian: Fokko. He's wearing a kind of dark-brown habit and has a woolly hat tied tightly to his chin, with a buzzard towering up from it, its wings outspread. There's a banner hanging from the front of the nest, but she can't read the text.

Your neighbour protesting. Come and join him.

She texts back: *Where?*

An immediate answer: *The riggers' head office.* (Three kissy mouths).

She dashes into the headquarters. Trijn and Zwier are standing there, bent over the local newspaper. She grabs the towel to dry her face and hair, but Trijn beckons her impatiently across and cries: 'Come here! Look! Our Fokko's on the front page!'

She reads out the headline: LOCAL VICTIM'S PLAYFUL PROTEST, and then the article which in a few short sentences explains Fokko's story and finishes with the observation that Mr F. Veenker is not planning to leave before his problem is solved.

'I fixed the buzzard on the hat,' Trijn says with pride.

'You did?' Zwier and Femke say together.

Trijn nods.

'How things change,' Zwier mutters.

'I'm going there now,' Femke says.

'Over there, you mean?'

Femke nods.

'We'll all go,' Trijn decides.

Before Femke can say anything in reply, Trijn rushes to the door, because she wants to get changed and she advises them to do the same.

'Nothing doing,' Zwier protests. 'I'm not going to make myself out to be something I'm not.'

'Then you two wait for me a moment. We'll go in your car.' Trijn nods at Femke.

'Well,' she says doubtfully, 'I really wanted to go now. I think it's better to take two cars.'

Trijn turns round, her hand on the door handle. 'That really is nonsense, and a stupid waste. And you're the one always going on about sustainability. And if for once we can actually go out together, then it's not right again.' And then she's gone.

Femke stares at her phone.

'Ah well,' Zwier says. 'Are you in a hurry?'

She nods.

'Aren't you being taken for a bit of a ride?'

She nods again.

'Aye, that's how it is, right enough,' he says. He takes the cover from his lighter, puts the nozzle of the lighter fluid can into the cotton and squeezes it.

'Well now,' he continues hesitantly. 'Anything's possible, nowadays. And your mother and I are perhaps not the best example for you...'

He waits till the cotton is drenched in petrol.

'They say it's possible, two men... or two women... but...'

He pushes the cover back over the lighter.

'I mean...,' he says, turning the wheel. A flame lights up. 'You can think you've found the right one, but you can be damned well mistaken...'

'But how do you know,' she says, 'if you're mistaken?'

'Well now,' he says, 'I can't say I really understand such matters. Some people find out too late.' He clicks his lighter shut and puts it inside his tobacco pouch. They hear the door of the byre closing.

'I'd still like to give it a chance,' she says, holding the door open for him.

'Do what you have to do,' he mutters, 'but if the happiness doesn't outweigh the misery, then –' He slashes his hand across his throat.

When she's at the wheel, with Zwier beside her and Trijn in the back chattering away excitedly about Fokko's protest action, Femke thinks about Zwier's words. How can you weigh happiness and misery against each other? Isn't happiness being on the newly mown sea dyke together, watching the birds? And the surprise of seeing in the other's eyes what you yourself desire? And is happiness only those rare moments spent together, or is their memory happiness too? And isn't even yearning, waiting until she's allowed to be there again, also a form of happiness? If that's the case, Femke concludes, then she doesn't have to break off with Danielle. She puts her foot on the pedal and even Trijn forgets to criticise her.

*

For the past few days Trijn seems to have turned into a heroine from the Harlequin Romance novels she loves reading: Trijn Koridon, Master Taxidermist.

All the people who've joined the Nest Protest come to Schokland to ask her for a bird hat. Her Dead Bird Museum has turned into the protest action's workshop. People come inside and are full of admiration for the birds, the snow-white carcasses and the vases full of feathers, and Trijn has all kinds of questions fired at her. Who taught her taxidermy? Isn't it rather gory work?

Where does she find the time for it? People are full of compliments and she often hears them say that her work deserves a wide audience. It's as if the taxidermy she did on all those winter evenings, when she was trying to drive away the monotony of her existence, was meant for this moment.

Fokko's one-man protest has woken up the region. People have suddenly realised that fear is prevalent well beyond their own wrecked walls. It's as if people needed the fury of that desolate birdman to recognise their own.

So many people join Fokko inside his nest that a second nest is built beside it, right there on the wide paving in front of the Centre from Here to Nowhere, as the locals call the building. A kind of campsite emerges, with little dome tents. People bring food and banners with slogans such as: ARE WE MEANT TO LIVE IN NESTS NOW? A NEST IS ALL WE'VE GOT LEFT. RIGGERS GOT US INTO THIS MESS. And when it rains messages are sent via the Nest Protest App asking for heavy-duty plastic sheeting and umbrellas.

It amazes Trijn that so many people from the area are coming to ask her for a bird hat, when they've always lived according to the adage: 'act normal, and that's crazy enough'. And that they're prepared to get into a nest wearing woolly hats with earflaps, with a great black-backed gull, a goshawk, a goosander, a gadwall, a golden plover or a goldcrest stuck on top of them, and then to spend the whole day and sometimes even the night in the nest.

All the spotlights are suddenly focused on them, and the victims – that damned word can't be avoided – are now being noticed by the rest of the country. All thanks to those strange bird-people, who are completely different to the stereotype of the northerner living near the inner dykes: those big-boned folks in sturdy jackets, people who never do anything that their forefathers didn't also do, who may have adopted the machinery of the modern era, but not the mentality, people without words and with claw-like hands, people who can't entirely be scrubbed clean of the reek of manure.

These people are here now, dressed in black and white robes, pieces of cloth with holes cut out for their heads and arms, to tell the grim history of events in this area where people are usually so silent. The disguise helps. It's easier to talk about humiliation when thanks to the bird on your head you can play the part of a non-existent creature. The bird-people tell the stories that ordinary farmers and citizens can't manage to speak about.

And because it's July, the month when journalists are news-hungry and politicians have all gone to faraway beaches, the Nest Protest is suddenly the centre of attention. Newspapers, radio bulletins and current affairs programmes are all full of stories about the crumbling lives of the northerners. Many journalists visit Schokland. They take photos of Zwier and Trijn posing in front of the timber props and the barriers hiding the kitchen from view. One camera team cut through the sealed fencing to take a photo of the inhabitants behind the bars. Symbolism is not avoided. They take shots of Trijn inside the increasingly empty Dead Bird Museum. The peacock showpiece is still on the cupboard and is a favourite item of background décor, just like the glass cases and their bleached bird heads, mussel shells, and bird beaks.

Femke isn't all that involved in the protest, as it's mainly being carried out by older people. Perhaps that's good too. The farm work just goes on. Swallow nests still have to be cleared from the milk tank site, spiderwebs have to brushed off, hooves have to be clawed out. There's grass cutting and turning to do, the hay has to be baled, and the drainage needs improving. Trijn is still working, but her phone rings more and more and there's yet another farmer or someone from civvy street or a journalist who wants to speak to her. Suddenly Trijn is the centre of the world's attention, which thanks to crazy Fokko has discovered her at last.

While she's fixing the birds on the hats, she listens to all the stories about the most long-winded disaster that has ever overcome this country. Like the one about the woman whose husband went to pieces because of all the haggling and then wasn't there to see his farm buildings being demolished or his wife being deported to a new-build house in the village. Or the one about the couple from the magnificent fortified manor house, now completely wrapped in scaffolding and under threat of demolition. The farmer who isn't allowed inside her own farmhouse anymore and is camping out in the byre, chooses a cuckoo for her hat, because, as she says: "The cuckoo lays its eggs in another bird's nest and I've been forced to part with my own nest". A great big man from the north, with a square head and an equally square body, chooses a ridiculously small bird, a swift, its sickle-shaped wings spread right out. The tiny little bird contrasts sharply with the man, but he chooses this one because swifts don't need shelter, they live in the air. The nests have been tolerated for ten days now at the entrance of the Centre from Here to Nowhere, and that's seen as a triumph. Nothing at all has been heard from the riggers for the time being.

And Fokko sits in his nest day and night, the progenitor of the protest. He towers above the hay, back straight and head held high, a proud victim. He's hammered out a solid story from his misfortune, and he tells it over and over again. It always ends with him pointing at the bird on his head and saying: '... and my best mate witnessed the destruction with his own eyes, and then crashed to death against the walls of our grief.' That sentence is repeated by all the media.

It's the evening of the tenth day of the protest. Trijn is sitting in the parlour, exhausted, when her phone rings. It's Fokko, who excitedly informs her that he's been phoned up by the public broadcasting people for their late-night programme and that they'll have to trot across there tomorrow night with the birds on their heads. Some of them will be allowed to tell their stories and they'll send a coach so all the others can sit in the audience.

'Everyone,' Fokko bellows, 'will have to wear a bird hat. You too.'

'But I don't have one.'

'But you've got some birds still, haven't you? One of the editors will ring you tomorrow morning. They want to know if you're a good talker. You've got to be able to tell your story in thirty seconds flat.'

Trijn shoots up.

'I've got to make another bird hat,' she gasps at her father, who is looking at her in amazement. 'Just one more.' She rushes out of the room.

*

Femke has been walking along the maar. It's been too busy at the farm for her these past days.

The ears of barley are golden yellow, and so are the ears of wheat. The cows are grazing in the bright green meadow. Along the maar it's bristling with herbs and wildflowers: the tender little flowerheads of the light violet sea aster, the scented spikes of sweet flag, the cylindrical meadow foxtails, and red clover. A little strip of wilderness in a cultivated landscape on which everything unplanned is drenched to death by enormous spraying contraptions.

'Product land,' Femke mutters as she walks past the potato field. She thinks about the tubers swelling underground. She sees the white and lilac flowers strewn across the field like bridal candies, and she knows that in a week or so these will have to be sprayed and killed off. The growth must be stopped, because seed potatoes have to conform to a standard. Deviations cost money.

On the land all around her the ryegrass is growing at a furious pace, but the only thing it's good for is to give a cow some protein, and it has to be supplemented with concentrates. Their small patch of alfalfa, which is much more nutritious and exhausts the soil less, was harvested under a month ago, and the new growth is already shooting up nicely. That gives her heart. She'd like to switch to organic farming, but the right moment to take the plunge hasn't come yet.

Swallows skim through the air, sharp as knives. A mallard forms its outstretched wings into two arcs, as if they're little parachutes, and then, with back rounded and legs forward, it lands in the reedbeds, right by the spot where the marsh harriers are bringing up their young.

She must check the cows. Trudy is on heat. The cow is bellowing and mounting other cows, and is being mounted. Got to get a sperm straw into her, as Zwier is wont to say. She finds old Patch-face in the pasture, sitting down like a dog, looking as worn-out as a slumped senior citizen. Femke speaks gently and soothingly to her, strokes her head and touches the ears, which feel cold. The cow needs an infusion, but she can't do it alone. And it won't work with Zwier either. He isn't strong enough now to force six hundred kilos of unwilling meat and muscle to toe the line.

First Trudy then, she thinks, and walks the cow back to the shippon. Meanwhile she wonders how she can give Patch-face an infusion. Trijn won't be able to help her. She'll be leaving soon for what Danielle is in the habit of calling the 'Wild West'. Since yesterday evening, when Trijn heard that she's going to take part in a live chat show, which will be broadcast on the nation's public service channel, as she keeps telling everyone, Schokland is bubbling over with her excitement.

Trijn has chosen to wear the cobalt blue dress she bought last year for the Farm Women's Union AGM, where she was giving a talk about farming women who do more on the farm than typical women's work. She bought a pair of shoes in town this morning, the same colour as the dress: court shoes with towering stiletto heels, the kind worn by news presenters, which Trijn always said weren't footwear but instruments of torture.

Once she was dressed and made up, she paced up and down the parlour, forcing herself to take little steps, holding in her hands a little piece of paper with her words on it, words that will present their farm drama in thirty seconds flat.

No, Trijn definitely won't be laying her weight on top of Patch-face. Femke hesitates, then gets her phone out and texts: *Milk fever in the house. Strong woman needed to control 600 kilos.* Three biceped arms as her sign-off.

When the three of them drove to the riggers' head office, less than two weeks ago, Danielle was there. She'd wanted to kiss her on the mouth, right in front of Trijn and Zwier. Femke just about managed to turn her cheek towards her, in the nick of time, and then Danielle whispered in her ear: 'Hey, Blondie. So when will you finally come out of your closet?'

She didn't answer, but in some ways she thinks it's a good sign that Danielle wanted to kiss her in public.

A text comes back immediately: *I'll come late afternoon.*

Femke answers: *Stay for dinner. My mother won't be here. Then we can watch the show tonight.*

The answer comes back straightaway: *Perhaps I'll stay the night...*

In the parlour Trijn's appearance surprises her. Tottering on high heels, in her cobalt blue dress, and wearing a hat that would look right for the Royal Ascot Ladies' Day. For a farmers' protest action, Femke thinks, her mother is rather overdressed.

Trijn wasn't keen on wearing a woolly hat with ear flaps. She was too vain for that. So she chose a wide-brimmed straw hat, which must once have belonged to Ootje. She glued a foam block inside it and carefully fixed the pièce de résistance of her Dead Bird Museum on top: Jort's peacock.

The cobalt blue of her dress and shoes are mirrored in the gleaming breast feathers of the gigantic creature bobbing on her head, peeking out proudly at the world with its black eyes and the sharp lines of its white eye stripes. The peacock's train, with its hundred and fifty spectacular iridescent feathers, is draped across her arms and shoulders, and the fine thin feathers glide down her arms like brushstrokes. It makes Femke think of the over-exuberance of that lonely pheasant on the clay.

She goes back to work again and brings Patch-face some fodder and water before starting the insemination process. It's crucial to choose exactly the right moment. She takes the straw from the nitrogen tank, filled with the semen of a Jersey bull, brings it up to temperature, places it in the gun and puts that inside her overalls, against her body, so it doesn't cool down. She gets a long plastic arm glove and the lubricant, gives Trudy a pat on the backside, and then with her hand deep inside the cow searches for the mouth of the cervix. Then she carefully inserts the sperm gun, making soft soothing noises while doing so, and gently pumps twelve million sperm cells into the animal. In six weeks' time the vet will confirm whether or not the attempt has been successful.

Towards evening, when the coach is tooting its horn across the farmyard, Trijn walks across the yard, flanked by Femke and Zwier, tottering on her high heels. The bus is full of protesters. The door opens. Fokko leaps out, almost loses his balance and falls against Trijn, who is caught in the nick of time by Femke and Zwier. Fokko apologises. His cheeks are gleaming and smoothly shaven, his hair is in a ponytail. He's wearing jeans and a black velvet jacket that's only a little worn-out at the elbows. Lieuwe, the bald lawyer, is sitting on the front seat, as if he's the tourist guide. He's wearing a fancy tie and a shiny pair of black, buckled, leather brogues. His outfit looks like the ones the quake experts wear. Femke thinks he also looks far too flashy for a protester.

The driver puts Trijn's peacock hat inside the luggage compartment, with all the other birds. As Trijn hoists herself up the steps of the coach, Fokko cries out that the Queen of the Protest Group has arrived. While everyone is cheering, the bus drives out of the farmyard. Femke and Zwier wave goodbye to them, and then Femke sees Danielle's estate car at the top of the concrete track drive onto the verge to let the bus go past.

'Well, who might that be?' Zwier asks and when Femke answers he says, chuckling: 'When the cat's away...'

Danielle gets out of the car, shakes Zwier's hand, spreads her arms and asks Femke teasingly: 'Closet open or closet closed?' and in reply Femke tugs Danielle towards her and kisses her full on the mouth. While they're kissing, Zwier steps back and watches them. When they let go, he says: 'Could the ladies please take some account of my poor old heart?' He shakes his head and walks towards the shippon.

'Where's the invalid then?' Danielle asks. Zwier stands still, turns round, and says she needn't be insulting.

'On the farmland,' Femke laughs.

'Maybe,' Zwier says, 'we ought to eat first. Dinner time's long past. No one seems to have thought of that. We don't have to chuck all our traditions onto the midden in one fell swoop.'

Femke is dismayed. No one has seen to the cooking.

'Well, what a good host you are,' Danielle says teasingly. They get a couple of pizzas from the freezer and there's some lettuce and tomatoes in the fridge. While they're eating, they talk about how successful this protest action has been, and what could happen as a result of it, and how this hopeless situation must surely come to a swift conclusion now. And while they're talking, a stockinged foot worms its way up into the warm space between two legs, and Femke finds out you can use the muscles of your thighs for caressing and stroking.

After the meal Femke suggests giving Patch-face her infusion. Zwier asks if he ought to come and help them. She shakes her head. They'll be fine without him.

'Well, you phone me then if madam throws you off,' he says. 'You doubtless think you don't need men for anything now.'

'That,' Danielle says, 'is more often the case than men would like to believe.'

Zwier looks at her silently, his eyes narrowed.

They go into the hallway and as soon as the door is shut, Danielle presses Femke against the wall.

'The cow will have to wait. Where's your room?' Danielle whispers and they stumble up the stairs without letting go of each other. The fire catches and sounds emerge from Femke's narrow bed that have never been heard in this house before, which even if they ever were roused by a solitary hand were immediately smothered in starched linen and the straitjackets of decency. And Zwier is sitting downstairs, playing deaf, his feelings of secret pleasure alternating with mortal alarm.

*

It's the dead of night. Trijn has kicked off her heels. Instruments of torture, right enough. The hat has been plonked on the table; the peacock train droops down. She is lying stretched out on the sofa, a glass of Zwier's jenever in her hand. The energy has drained from her, like blood from a butchered chicken. I'm really pleased, she thinks, that there wasn't a welcome committee waiting for me when the bus dropped me off. No father, no daughter, and thank god, no flibbertigibbet standing there waiting. She's gone and parked her estate car in the farmyard, Trijn notes, in full view of everyone. She didn't even try to hide from me that, on the one evening I'm not at home, she's thrust herself into my daughter's bed.

A fat lot of use, she thinks, being on national television. I don't want to be on telly ever again. As if she hadn't flung all chances of ever being anyone's spokesperson to the winds.

If you don't do something, she asks herself, because you've no idea at all that you're meant to do it, does that make you guilty? Has anyone ever been sentenced for not knowing the law?

I got on that bus, she thinks, just a few hours ago, and everyone was pleased to see me because, thanks to my bird hats, we'd be on national telly getting attention for our cause, and because I'd played an important part in the highest profile protest that the north of the country has ever seen. And a few hours later we're driving back, and I'm the laughing stock of the whole group. Never before, she thinks, has a queen toppled so swiftly off her pedestal. Now it's absolutely clear, once and for all, that she doesn't deserve anything other than a life here, in this tumbledown place called Schokland.

Madam Peacock, she thinks. That's how she was addressed, all kitted out in her spectacular outfit, which had drawn cries of admiration from the broadcasting house's porter and make-up girls. This bird protest was so creative, so original, so marvellous, they'd said. And she was the fairest of them all. The cobalt blue Peacock Queen, from the claylands up north. The enthusiastic young make-up artist declared that the eyeshadow she'd applied *absolutely* matched Trijn's sky-blue eyes. Then she gazed at her more intensely than anyone had ever done before and concluded that Trijn looked stunning. And although Trijn knew it was her job to give people these kinds of compliments, to help them get their nerves under control, it still did her good, because this was the first time anyone had ever said anything like that to her.

She remembers them all sitting round the table, ready to begin: she, Fokko, Siewert, and Lieuwe, with microphones pinned on, and the rest of the bird-protesters in the audience. A spectacular sight. The presenter rattled off what they could expect that evening and their item was introduced with Fokko's catchphrase: *a buzzard has crashed to death against a wall of grief, and in a moment you'll hear from the Northern Nest Protesters exactly what that means.* There was a countdown and during the counting someone else came and sat down at the table, an impeccably dressed man, someone she vaguely recognised, and Fokko whispered in her ear that he was the man in charge of the riggers. The ON AIR signs flashed and the programme began.

First, they interviewed a film director about his latest film, then a chef who made meals from ingredients past their best-before dates, and then it was their turn. They showed a film-clip, with images of their expansive landscape and their shored-up houses, and then the presenter asked Fokko to tell his story. Then it was Siewert's turn, and then Trijn. She was introduced as the bird-woman who'd made the hats and was asked how she prepared them, how long she'd been doing that, and how she'd got hold of the birds. She thought these were introductory questions, before she'd be allowed to tell her story about Schokland, but after just a couple of sentences she was thanked, and the presenter asked Lieuwe about his mass legal action. Then the presenter turned to the director of the rigging company, who'd been listening with a scornful look in his eyes and who started by commenting that the people here were far from representative. Most of the people affected, he claimed, had been given more than adequate compensation. There was booing in the audience. The presenter asked for silence. The director carried on speaking, unperturbed. He went on about complex cases, and falling between two stools, and ended by saying: 'No one can expect us to foot the bill for old, badly-maintained farms. We've got a business to run.'

The booing grew louder and Lieuwe started talking about profits and duty of care, about a complete lack of generosity and a government that was still failing to do anything about it. 'Your company,' he said, stabbing a finger at the director, 'must compensate for any damage caused by the extraction of gas. You're obliged by law to do so. And if you don't do it, the courts will force you.'

The director said, with a nasty smile, that he had just one little question. 'You're talking about legal obligations,' he said, and his voice sounded triumphant, 'but I have a strong suspicion that you yourselves are in breach of the law.'

'Demonstrating is a democratic right,' Lieuwe answered, and the man nodded and pointed at Trijn's peacock hat, at the buzzard on Fokko's head, at the swallow, and then with a sweeping gesture at all the birds in the audience.

'This lady has an exceptional collection of dead birds, isn't that so, Madam Peacock?'

He gave Trijn a piercing gaze, like a hawk that has spotted its prey. Trijn froze, although she still didn't understand his intention.

'Koridon,' she said. 'My name is Koridon.'

He gave her a sharp look.

It went silent in the studio. No one understood what the man was getting at. The camera zoomed in on the rigger's face and his bright blue eyes, a hawk striking at its prey. Then the camera swerved to Trijn, who couldn't prevent a muscle in the corner of her mouth from trembling.

'I can't see any tags on these birds,' the man said, and then went quiet, as if he'd made his point.

The presenter said, annoyed, that they were here because of the earthquake damage, not because of the birds, which were just a playful expression of a serious protest by people who'd been entirely abandoned to their fate.

'I've just been reminded,' the man continued, imperturbably, 'of my legal obligations. But these people are themselves in breach of the law. And apparently this lady, who's been a taxidermist for twenty years now, doesn't even know what I'm talking about. Right?'

Again, those piercing eyes that seemed to drill right through her. Trijn doubtfully shook her head. The man addressed the presenter.

'Dead birds have to be registered. Twice, in fact. When they come into your possession and when you prepare them. The specimens here tonight include protected species. This lady is clearly working commercially. She sells birds to the protesters and is looking for publicity, but she really doesn't know her business. I can see twenty criminal offences pinned on the heads of these people. I'm curious to know what the court will think of this.'

'That has nothing at all to do with the gas extraction,' Lieuwe said, while the camera crew zoomed in on Trijn's face. White as a corpse, draped with suddenly inappropriate cobalt blue and emerald green peacock eyes and gently quivering feathers. The gigantic peacock on her head, which all of a sudden had become an extravagant curiosity, bobbed gently, as if her humiliation was slowly bringing it back to life and it might flap up at any moment, clamouring loudly.

'You may reject this as being beside the point,' the man said, interrupting the presenter, who was again stressing that they were here about an entirely different matter, 'but this is to do with the legal protection of birds, to prevent their heedless slaughtering. It's a law that protects the vulnerable and is enforced with extreme strictness. That is something you should be discussing tonight, isn't it?' Now he was looking at the people in the audience.

'Okay,' the presenter responded. 'You've made your point. Back to the quake damage.'

'I didn't sell them,' Trijn said.

'And you didn't register them either,' the director bit back.

She swallowed and said nothing. No one had ever told her that you couldn't simply prepare dead birds without getting punished for it. She should have suspected that in this country, where even death is a source of profit, where every patch of ground has had some bureaucrat deciding what it's meant for, where you can't demolish a single farm building without checking that it hasn't got some kind of rare bat inside it, where not a single egg is sold without a quality mark to prove it contains only legal poisons, where you can sell plastic bags but you can't give them away for nothing, where you can only put manure on the soil if you have the right papers, and where you can't rent out a single shed without permission, such a collection of dead birds is impossible, without a civil servant registering them. Of course it's not allowed.

Meanwhile the presenter asked the director what he would be doing to indemnify these people. The man then ranted on about revised procedures, new protocols, A, B and C categories of damage, about a future in which everything would be sorted out quicker and with greater transparency, about needing just a little more patience.

Trijn was shivering in spite of the hot studio lights. She clamped her lips tight and waited for the final signature tune, and then gave the presenter a business-like shake of the hand. The woman thanked her and said she'd done a great job, and she shouldn't take it to heart. The bird protest was fantastic, and that lawsuit really wouldn't go ahead.

The director, gleaming with self-assurance, also shook her hand. 'Chin up, little lady. What you give, you must get.'

Lieuwe approached the man, wanting to argue with him, but the director cut him off with: 'See you in court.' Then he left the studio, flanked by his advisors, ignoring Fokko's abusive language.

The atmosphere on the way back home was resigned. Most of the demonstrators thought the director's indictment was simply a distraction strategy and found it a shame that they'd been thrown off balance by it. Some of them said to Trijn that she shouldn't take it too much to heart, after all they'd got the chance to air their case on national television.

But Trijn retreated to the back of the bus and closed her eyes, as if she was asleep. Meanwhile she listened to all the whispering. She was convinced everyone was blaming her for her ignorance, even though they didn't dare say that outright.

By the time she was dropped off at Schokland, most of them had dozed off. Only Fokko took her by the hand and told her not to let the bastards grind her down. She shook herself free and got out of the bus without saying a word.

Everything's gone wrong, she thinks.

She knocks back the last drop of jenever, then stands up to go to her room, those few square metres of space beside her parents' bedroom, the place where she's always licked her wounds.

August 2017

FEMKE IS WALKING ALONG the drainage channel by the side of the shaven farmland. The farmers are doing their level best to bring the grain in before they're hit by the advancing rain front. Everywhere clouds of dust are flying up from the gigantic machines that are threshing the grains off the stalks and separating the chaff from the wheat. Birds shoot up in panic. A roe deer leaps across the stubble field and vanishes into an as yet unthreshed plot of land. The dark tips of its ears peek up from the billowing wheat stalks like a U-boat's snorkel. A young harrier is on the stubble ground, plucking at the remains of its prey, looking dazed, staring shakily into the emptiness.

This morning Femke drove back from the house by the sea dyke, where she'd been invited yesterday evening. For Danielle, love needs to be as tenuous as air. As soon as dawn breaks, the chill kicks in again. The only commitment Danielle can live with is having no commitments.

There's a heron by the side of the channel, its neck tucked in, its back bent. The long greyish-white breast feathers flap like tattered bunting. The long-legged bird gazes into the distance. Then it stalks stiffly across the stubble field and stops, picks around in the soil, suddenly turns round, quick as a flash, and the next moment it has a mole in its beak. The creature hangs helplessly from the steely bill, its dark pelt standing out against the pinkish-yellow beak. A pink paw, meant for digging underground burrows, flails powerlessly in the air, and in one single movement the heron gulps it down. It shakes its head wildly a moment and then, as if nothing has happened, it resumes its gazing.

Femke wonders if Fokko is camping out in Siepke's Sleepstead again, since the inglorious end of the Nest Protest. From one moment to the next the quakes in the north are no longer of interest. There's more urgent news now: politicians are back from their holidays; presidents are talking about war; the European

Union is at the point of collapsing; and a fire has broken out in a factory farm, causing thousands of pigs to lose their lives. In short, the silly season is over and interest in their case is ebbing away, although nothing at all has been solved. The damage claims have not yet been settled. No new protocols have appeared. Fokko still doesn't have a house. Slurry stores are leaking. Siewert continues to live in a so-called suburb and has no rights to anything. And Lieuwe still hasn't managed to organise a class action. After all, people here aren't used to doing things together, and if they do happen to do so, then things don't work out well, as the television appearance clearly showed. There's a reason the farms are located miles away from each other. Neighbours have to travel long distances if they want to meet up. The only kind of people who live here are comfortable with that.

Dark rain clouds are gathering in the west and there's a competition in full swing at the boundaries of their land: will the arable farmers manage to harvest their grain before the rain soaks the earth?

Femke walks across the little bridge to Siepke's Sleepstead. If Fokko is camping out there, he perhaps needs some consolation in the form of tea and pink cakes. She hums to make her presence clear, but she can't hear any old man noises. She knocks on the wooden door, but there's no reaction, and she goes in. A faint blueish light is coming through the heavy-duty plastic stretched over the hole in the roof. In one of the corners there's Fokko's sleeping bag, some tea-lights, a couple of empty bottles, the thermos flask, and the Lucky Luke comics. She looks around. Nothing is left now of the former brick-built sheep barn, her secret little house, where the terrible stories of the past still seemed to fill the air; nothing but a neglected and tumbledown hovel.

The edge of a map is poking out from beneath the pile of comics. She pulls it out and opens it up. It's a topographic map of their own area. She spots the maar, a winding waterway through the green meadows and arable land, the little red squares that stand for the farms, the thin stripes that indicate small roads, and the straight yellow stripe of the provincial road running from west to east to the river delta. Scattered here and there across the whole area someone has sketched death's-heads. She counts them. There are nineteen. One of them is in the fields, not so far from Schokland. She knows the place. The skull marks a rig, the location of a gas drilling site. Just like all the other death's-heads. She folds the map up. She is about to put it back, but then she spots a well-thumbed little book: an English-language cookery book, with recipes. She leafs through the booklet, which is printed in typewriter script, and sees that the recipes aren't actually for dishes, but spell out how to make explosives: exploding tennis balls, bombs made from artificial fertiliser, and thermite-filled flowerpots, a substance that becomes extremely hot, as the text emphasises, and can't be extinguished once it's lit. Feeling nervous, she carefully puts the map and booklet back under the comics, and leaves the hut feeling troubled. She walks back along the maar and asks herself what she should do about this secret discovery. She wishes she hadn't nosed around in Fokko's stuff.

The bank of the maar is full of purple reed plumes and magenta-pink rosebay willowherb. The yellow umbels of the wild parsnip and the dark yellow of tansy shine out. She walks in the sunlight past the tender plumes of grass. If you ignore the dark threatening rainclouds in the west, everything looks lovely.

*

One by one, in the days following the television show, the protesters bring the birds back. It has clearly dawned on them that being in possession of an unregistered bird could make you the accessory of a criminal act. Trijn takes them back with a feeling of discomfort. They're not her birds anymore, but economic offences, and more than anything else they're symbols of failure. With some people she thinks she can spot a certain reserve and timid glances at the concrete track, as if they're scared the police could arrive at any point. No one says anything like this. They all have friendly words for her and deny that the show was a failure. All of them thank her. Siewert accepts a cup of coffee and she can't stop herself saying that it must have been her illegal birds that destroyed the impact of their appearance. He disagrees. According to him the media were just using their suffering as a form of entertainment, a nice item of news in the silly season.

That ten-day high of mutual solidarity is over. Even for Trijn her feelings of forlornness were less strong then. Now everyone keeps themselves to themselves again. Every bird pressed back into her hands confirms the fact that there's no longer any feeling of unity. She sits in her Dead Bird Museum, among the birds propped on their wobbly hats, scattered around on the work-bench and the floor, and she wonders when and how they'll be confiscated from her. Will the police come? Will she be summoned and asked to report somewhere? The thought that all those years and years of work will be confiscated causes a tearing pain inside her, like a stockbreeder must feel when a whole barnful of chickens, or pigs, or beef cattle is lost. Preparing her birds was something that had no other purpose except the pleasure she got from it, in contrast with almost everything else at Schokland. It was the only thing she did that didn't have its origins in guilt. Every well-mounted bird signified a conquering of the daily grind. A promise to herself. Just as once upon a time the yellowing newspaper article, still pinned to the board above the worktop, had also been.

And she chides herself, because she, who has always placed so much importance on thinking things through, on doing things lawfully, who always made sure she did things as they should be done, has unintentionally, but truly, become a crook. Someone with fifty-seven economic criminal offences on her conscience. Trijn Koridon, the lawbreaker. She'll have to appear in court and she'll get a criminal record. It's a good job Ootje isn't here to see this.

When she says something to Zwier about her being worried there'll be a police raid, he bursts out: 'All that drivel about the birds is just something those smooth-cheeks have come up with as a red herring.' He gestures round, at the coloured stickers on the walls. 'That's what they should be concerned about. Even that bloody Centre for I-Don't-Know-What earns pots of money from our misery. If one of those shiny-shoes ever comes to our farm to bother you about those birds, I'll drag him into the byre and shove his nose inside a crack till he snorts up the debris. Let him sort that out first, before pestering you because you've dared mount a few dead birds.'

Then he leans over his nail plaque, rummages in the tins, and searches for a few nails of the same size, before hammering them into a metal circle.

Trijn considers making a phone call herself, to the provincial bureaucrats, the police, or the government Department for Entrepreneurship in the Netherlands. Perhaps that would be better than simply waiting. Hello. You're speaking to that stupid farming woman who's been mounting dead birds for twenty years now. Yes, even birds on the Red List. That woman with a barn full of larks and wagtails and golden plovers and cuckoos and corncrakes and snipes and pintails. That silly cow who cheerfully appears on television with all those illegally acquired birds, on prime-time television no less, and, ah well, I'd really like you to punish me now for that.

They'll see you coming.

Trijn has no idea what to do next. She has slowly come to agree with the riggers: they've become a bloody complex case.

*

Swallows skim across the land, their little seep-seep cries sounding through the air. Swallows, Femke thinks, are always enthusiastic. No swallow will ever make you think: that one sounds down-hearted. Marsh harriers, that's another matter. However graceful a harrier might be, there's something a bit wrong about them. A short-sighted raptor, one that needs its ears to catch its prey. That's why they fly so low against the wind, that's why they look less spectacular than a buzzard spiralling up, riding the thermals, mewing loudly. That's a creature that knows how to get noticed.

For the third day in a row she spots the young harrier on the farmland. Its egg-yellow head is twitching back and forth. It plucks at its feathers with its beak, not with any real conviction, but as a way of passing time, while it's waiting for its mother to bring him a bite to eat. A needy, lonely little creature, there in the stubble field. You'd think that during all those hours of waiting it could try to get something itself, is what crosses her mind. How else can you learn to do it, that hunting? Isn't such a creature sometimes afraid that one day its mother won't come back and it will have to manage all by itself?

Trijn is entrenched in her Dead Bird Museum. For three days now Femke has been urging her mother to phone the muck-spreader man. Thirty cubic metres has to be spread across the land before the new month begins and they won't be allowed to spread any more slurry until the spring. The slurry store has to be emptied. Every day Trijn vaguely answers that she'll do it, but nothing comes of it. Every now and then she stands in the yard looking towards the concrete track and when Femke asks her what she's waiting for, she says in a thin voice: 'Oh, nothing.' And then she goes back into her Dead Bird Museum.

Of course, Femke could ring up the slurry spreader too. But she can't believe that Trijn is no longer focused on the farm work. And Zwier is also becoming less active. It looks as if she's the only one still dealing with their hundred cows, their land and their future.

The organic farming advisor has been again and has warned them that for eco-farms the most essential thing is prevention. Organic farmers have to steer clear of problems much more quickly than conventional dairy farmers, because the consequences of a mistake are far bigger than for normal farmers, since a conventional farmer can just give the animals extra antibiotics. An organic farmer, he instructed them, has to know which animals are right for breeding. The best breeders, he said, using the well-known farming mantra, are the biggest killers. They were sitting around the big table in the headquarters and it looked as if she was the only one who was actually listening to him. Trijn and Zwier just sat on their chairs, mute and unmoving.

*

Yesterday, after dinner, Femke got a text message and she rushed straight to the sea dyke, where Danielle was sitting waiting with a thermos flask of coffee and two mugs. They watched a flock of golden plovers through their binoculars: finely drawn, speckled, golden-brown works of art on legs, with black bellies, and curving white bands going up via the neck and ending in stripes by the eyes. Their plumage was gleaming in the late sunlight. The little bird-balls were running about among each other, almost floating, picking worms out of the wet glistening sand, which reflected the glow of blue and purple-red clouds.

Danielle poured out the coffee and Femke said she was worried about her mother.

'You should feel happy about it,' Danielle said, handing her a mug. 'This is a chance to do things your own way. Make the switch. Now.'

Femke put both her hands round the mug and asked: 'Aren't you ever scared?'

'Scared? What should I be scared of?'

'You know. Things going wrong.'

'No,' Danielle said. 'That doesn't ever scare me. What could go wrong?'

'Everything. The milk yield plummets, the harvest fails, there's an outbreak of BSE, the roof blows off, everything goes up in flames, or collapses. Everything can go wrong. Always.'

'What terrible nightmares you've got in that head of yours. If things go wrong, there'll be plenty of time then to get wound up about it.'

Femke didn't answer. The golden plovers kept piping away. A melancholic background choir.

'Are you really scared of all those things?' Danielle asked.

'Sometimes,' she said vaguely.

Danielle shook her head. 'Fear,' she said firmly, 'is a useless relic, left over from the past. When we still had to fight or flee.'

'Not many people would agree with you. You can't choose. Either you're scared or you're not scared.'

'No. Really. Fear is a choice. Just like happiness.'

'So, if someone's unhappy, or ill, or poor, that's their own choice, is it? The place you're born, the parents you have, whether or not you get ill, they're all your own choices?'

'No, they're not. But you can choose how to deal with them.'

Femke looked at the sun peeping out from below a mountain range of clouds, an orange-purple-red glowing ball, a last flickering-up of bright light, after which darkness would blanket the earth. The thought came into her head that when Danielle and she were talking, the distance between them increased. And she thought of something else too. She knew there was one thing, in fact, that Danielle was scared of. So scared that she couldn't even feel her own fear. But she took care not to speak about it.

She asked herself if it was bad that they never really understood each other when they were talking. Was that something important? Or was the fire enough? She wished she knew more about these kinds of things. She had no idea if it was a bad thing to only be allowed to turn up when Danielle wanted it. What was the name for what she and Danielle have?

'Maybe,' she said hesitantly, 'I've never properly imagined what it'll be like when I'm alone in Schokland. One day, when Zwier is no longer there, and Trijn perhaps starts doing something else. Then I'll be left alone there. Just like you.'

'Yes,' Danielle said. 'Welcome to the club of independent farming women.'

'But,' Femke said doubtfully, 'aren't you ever lonely, then?'

'Sometimes. But then I send a text.' Danielle grinned. Femke swallowed.

'But before me?'

'Then there were others.' Danielle went silent, before teasingly adding: 'Perhaps there still are.'

'Lieuwe,' Femke remarked. Lieuwe hadn't recently been mentioned as being at the farm anymore and Femke had drawn the conclusion that they were no longer together. That Danielle had perhaps put him out of the house. Danielle took the mug from her hands, pushed Femke back onto the grass, lay on top of her, and with her mouth close to Femke's murmured: 'You'd really like to know that, wouldn't you? If you're the only one?'

'Yes,' Femke said.

Danielle stroked her hair.

'You're perhaps the dearest I've ever had. And the yummiest too.'

A caress, a hand on her face, a warm palm on a cool cheek.

'But you're not the only one.'

A sack full of bones and a bleeding heart.

'All I want is you,' Femke said softly.

Danielle tugged her up. 'Come on, sexy,' she said. 'I want you too.'

They walked to the house, arms around each other, pressed closely together, and Danielle whispered to her, like a snake, that she didn't believe in exclusive relationships, just as little as she believed in fear. But she did believe in causing eruptions. Shock after shock after shock.

And Femke let herself be carried along, and only much later, when she was in her car again, and it had grown dark already, and a miserable little crescent moon was shining, and she was driving along the sea dyke, did she realise that all the time she was with Danielle, on that bed, skin against skin, heart against heart, she had in fact been in a goldfish bowl. Even when they were having sex together, she'd been alone.

*

Fokko is on the land, in front of Siepke's Sleepstead. He raises his hand and stumps hastily across the bridge. Femke goes to meet him. He looks uncared for again, as he used to do. He calls to her from a distance, as if he's picking up the thread of an old conversation: 'I wanted to ask you, have you lot got any artificial fertiliser?'

She waits till she's closer. 'No,' she answers curtly. 'And good afternoon to you too, Fokko.'

'Aye.'

'The artificial fertiliser's finished, and we're not going to order any more. I want to switch to organic,' she says. Then she asks how he's doing. He gets his packet of shag tobacco from his back pocket, starts rolling a fag, and shrugs his shoulders. Then he licks the paper with his rasping tongue, that reminds her of a cow's tongue, and seals the cigarette.

'Crap,' he says. 'I did actually hope they'd give me a house.

Have the police been yet?' he continues in the same breath.

'No, of course not,' she says, annoyed. 'They're really not going to waste their time on a few dead birds.'

'They bloody will,' he says. 'No way they'll let it drop. But they're not going to get my buzzard. Never.'

'Have you given up on the Centre, then?'

He nods, lights his fag, inhales, and says in a wheedling tone: 'But Fem, you can order it.'

'What?'

'Artificial fertiliser.'

She bites her lip. She remembers the map with all its skull and crossbones.

'What do you need artificial fertiliser for?'

He shrugs his shoulders. 'It's not a big deal, is it? Ordering a bit of fertiliser for me?'

'No, I won't,' she says, trying not to think about the cook-book. She hopes he won't notice her nervousness. 'From now on I only want to use our own manure. I'm changing to soil-based agriculture. I'm not allowed to have any artificial fertiliser in my paperwork.' And then she immediately follows this with: 'I'm in a bit of a hurry, Fokko. I'm buckling under the work.'

She slowly starts walking away.

'Never mind,' he says. 'I'll ask that mother of yours then.'

'You leave her alone,' she snarls. 'She's got enough on her plate now and she's done enough too.'

Fokko calls back: 'Oh yeah. She's done that, alright. Just a shame she didn't get those bloody things registered.'

'Did you warn her? Of course not, you bloody pig.'

She sticks her middle finger up at him and is shocked at her action.

'Well done, lass,' he shouts. 'Sticking up for your ma. That's right. Toodle loo!'

He waves goodbye and traipses off.

A curlew flies overhead. The long, curved beak points forward. Its shrill cries carry far across the fields.

'He's none too happy either,' Fokko shouts.

She walks grimly back to her Schokland.

*

Brian flings open the door to the Dead Bird Museum. The church tower clock has just struck twelve. The lad stands in the doorway and yells: 'Frikandels, Trijn. I can't find any.' He sounds panicky. She smiles.

She automatically reaches her hand out to him and lets herself be tugged along, through the barn, across the yard, to the back of the byre, to the freezer. The lid is open. Boxes of pizza, lumps of meat, and frozen bread are scattered on the ground. She dives into the chest freezer, looking for frikandels. She's forgotten to buy new stock.

'No frikandels today,' she says brusquely and puts the food on the ground back into the freezer.

'Frikandels, frikandels, frikandels.' He's stamping his feet and flapping his hands about.

'We'll have fried eggs today,' Trijn says and shuts the lid. The lad is yelling for frikandels. She tells him to be quiet, but in vain. Brian stamps, flaps and screams. Klaske is barking. She sees Zwier's head pop out from behind the headquarters' door.

'Stop it, Brian,' she snaps at him. She takes him by the shoulders and gives him a good shake. The screaming gets worse. Zwier angrily comes up to them and pushes Trijn aside. His broad, veined hand, with its ossified greyish nails, swings through the air and lands with a smack onto Brian's always rosy cheek. He immediately goes quiet. Klaske is still barking. The cows drying out from lactation in the byre moo anxiously. The lad stands there motionless and then he starts whining, softly but carefully, like a dog sometimes does. He falls to the ground with his head on his knees. Klaske gives a sharp bark and vanishes behind the low brick wall. The cows keep on mooing. Zwier crosses his arms, gazing with irritation at the whimpering boy. Femke comes in, and looks questioningly at Trijn, who grumpily mutters: 'Frikandels.' Femke squats down beside Brian, puts her hands on his arms and asks: 'Shall we go and get them, Brian?'

His whimpering stops immediately. He leaps up, grabs her hand and pulls her along with him. Trijn opens her mouth to say that this is going too far, that they really could have something other than frikandels sometimes, that the lad doesn't always have to have his own way, but then there's an overwhelmingly loud boom.

From a dark crater deep beneath the stone, the sand, the salt, the clay, from the flat volcano, from the inmost parts of the earth from which year after year tonnes of gas have been pumped out, a thundering sound rises like the sound of an out-of-control truck intent on creating as much destruction as possible, its engines blaring as it tears up from the cavernous depths. And above the ground beams crack, walls split, glass shatters, metal fencing clatters, and the cows bellow. Destruction makes an infernal din, and the Koridons and Brian are spinning around on their legs, grasping out with their arms to get a grip onto something, the freezer, or the heaving walls, or each other. Zwier tries to hold onto Trijn, but he misses and crashes down onto the rolling concrete. Trijn loses her balance and falls over him. The noise is deafening. And then, like an abruptly stopped film, it's all over.

There's a soft dripping sound coming from the milking pen, and a pattering of debris, and in the other byre the panicky bellowing of a cow in the throes of death and the frightened mooing in answer from the few other cows that are not on the land. Trijn pushes herself up. Zwier is lying still with his eyes shut and his leg strangely twisted.

'Dad!' He doesn't move. 'Dad, Dad,' she repeats, crouching down on her knees, her hand on his old face, two fingers on his neck. She's checking. A sigh of relief. There's a soft pulse inside.

'He's alive,' she says, and she hears Femke on her mobile asking for an ambulance. Femke is deathly pale and is standing with her arm around Brian, who has pressed himself against her. She bends over, without letting go of Brian. He bends with her, as if he's her rag doll, and she gently strokes her Grampa's cheek.

Then she straightens up, her lips pressed tightly together. The bellowing of the cow in the old byre chills her to the marrow. Trijn nods towards it. Femke hesitates.

'Go on,' Trijn says, and Femke runs with Brian into the youngstock byre.

Trijn hastily gets up, fetches a pair of overalls from the coat hook and lays them under her father's head as a pillow, putting a coat over him for a blanket. She takes his hand, pats his cheek, and keeps calling, softly and repeatedly, as if by doing so she can stop him ebbing away, as if she's throwing her voice to him like a lifebelt he can clamp onto. And then, it seems like hours later, but it must be minutes, because the debris is still pattering down and the cow is bellowing in panic, he opens his eyes, looks at her, and says: 'I'm still here.'

'Yes,' she says, and her tears fall onto his cheeks.

'Can you get off my leg?' His voice is weak.

'I'm not on your leg, Dad. An ambulance is coming. They'll be here in a jiffy.'

He closes his eyes again and groans softly.

In the byre the heifer calf that Femke and Danielle brought into the world is lying under a beam that has broken like a matchstick, the back of its body shattered, its head in the air like an enraged bull, bellowing with pain. Femke and Brian use all their strength to pull the beam off the calf.

Trijn has left Zwier alone and she rushes in.

'I'll have to phone the vet,' Femke says. 'She won't make it.'

'Do you need any help here,' Trijn asks, 'or can I stay with Dad?'

Femke nods. 'Of course,' she says. 'I'm not alone. Brian is helping me. Right?'

The lad looks pale, but he gives a brave nod.

'I'm your man,' he says in a trembling voice.

'Exactly,' Femke says. 'Stay here with Tuesday. I'll fetch the tractor.'

Femke takes a moment to kneel down by Zwier. She briefly strokes his cheek and asks: 'Come home again quickly, won't you?'

'I'll do my best,' he says, hoarsely, and then immediately says: 'What's up over there?'

'A beam's fallen on Tuesday,' she says.

'Is it bad?'

She nods.

'Will the roof hold?'

'I don't know. I'll get the youngstock out of there in a moment. I'll put them outside.'

'Will you manage?'

She nods again. 'Don't you worry about that.'

She stands up. She's about to walk out of the byre but Trijn pulls her towards her. 'Look after yourself.'

Outside the barn is still standing, the feed silo is sagging down at a strange angle, one of its legs has given up, and there's a crack all the way through the concrete of the yard. In the fields the cows are grazing as if nothing at all has happened.

Trijn breathes a sigh of relief when she hears the sirens coming closer. As he's hoisted onto the stretcher, Zwier opens his eyes and says: 'So you got your way.'

'Yes,' she says. 'Quite a lot needs to happen to get you to the doctor. But I got my way.'

'Aye. Right enough.'

She gives a bitter smile. He closes his eyes again and for the first time in his life he is carried out of the byre.

*

With the help of the tractor, they lift the beam off Tuesday. The back of her body is completely shattered. Her hip bone is sticking out. There's blood everywhere. Femke is about to sit down with Tuesday while they're waiting for the vet, but Brian is shrieking and pointing at something a little further back in the byre, behind where the little brick wall once stood. There, in her former hiding place, the safest spot in the farmhouse, is Klaske, buried under the collapsed bricks. She quietly walks to the dog, closes her eyes, and wipes the grit off her lifeless body, her chestnut-brown pelt and her soft fluffy ears. She swallows and then stands up.

She goes with Brian to sit with Tuesday. The heifer is making gurgling sounds and snorting painful breaths. Her bulging pupils seem to be bobbing in the gleaming whites of her eyes. Femke strokes her and makes shushing noises, monotonous and constant, until the creature grows more restful and the snorting calms down.

A vehicle drives into the yard. A door slams. Brian's mother comes into the byre wearing a tight-fitting light-beige raincoat, her handbag clamped rigidly against her. When she sees Tuesday's shattered body, with the bone sticking out, and the blood-red straw, she claps her hand to her mouth. 'You could've been killed, all of you,' she says, and it sounds like an accusation. She wards off the unrelenting fear with a continuous stream of words, because she was scared they were all dead, because Brian didn't answer his phone and Femke and Trijn hadn't either. She's heard on the car radio that the quake was almost as powerful as the one from five years back and that there's been a lot of damage. Nothing has been said yet about mortalities, but that doesn't mean there haven't been any.

'Come with me,' she says in a commanding tone, and then, turning to Femke: 'He can't take this sort of thing.'

Femke tries to find an answer, but before she manages to say anything Brian starts howling and says he has to stay with Tuesday till the vet comes. The mother tugs at him. Femke goes up to him and whispers in his ear that she'll look after Tuesday and that his mother needs him more now. He gives in and follows his mother out of the byre.

Finally, the vet arrives. He releases the heifer from her suffering and then walks across the land with Femke. There doesn't seem to be anything wrong with the rest of the cattle. They check the roof. The broken collar beam is hanging down at an angle. That has to be taken away and the roof will have to be swiftly propped up. They spot fresh cracks in the old tie-stall byre and in the yard. Only the milking parlour seems undamaged.

She asks him if this was the big earthquake everyone's been whispering about for months now. He shrugs and says: 'I don't think so.'

'So, things will get worse then,' she concludes.

'No one knows for sure,' he says, and asks if he can go inside with her, to inspect the farmhouse.

'Just go in,' she says. 'I'll be fine, thanks.'

The farmhouse can wait. There are more urgent things to do. She gets her tool apron from the barn, which is still standing, with perhaps a little more subsidence. She has to set off a plot of land where she can put the youngstock. Fortunately, it's summertime. She walks onto the land and images flash through her mind: Klaske dead. She wonders whether she should bury her, or if she should leave her corpse by the side of the road, like with a calf. She sees her grandfather lying on the concrete again.

Tuesday's wide-open panicky eyes. And then she suddenly hears that tremendous din once more, and where there was simply a feeling of incredulity then, as if the spinning around on the undulating ground was simply a dream, she now starts panicking. Her breathing quickens, blood pumps through her veins. She falls onto the ground, curls up her back, pulls in her legs, puts her arms around them. She folds herself up into the smallest possible ball and presses herself as deeply as possible into the grass, like a snipe, her body tense as a saw blade.

Then she feels the earth trembling, not like before, but a familiar tremor, made by the hooves of trotting cows. She straightens herself and sees the herd trotting towards her, then gets up quickly, resting her hands on her knees. She takes deep breaths, in and out. As if she's pumping herself up. She hears familiar snorting, and warm breath is blown out across her. Trudy rubs her body against hers. The animal remains there, right in front of her, and Femke, whose legs are trembling, and who can hardly remain upright, turns to the cow for comfort and leans against the colossal body, half across it. The rest of the herd stands in a circle around them. Leaning over the quivering, warm pelt of the cow, Femke's eyes fill with tears.

The cows stand there, quietly looking at her, their big eyes bulging out from their long black and white eyelashes. They sniff at her with their rosy, snorting muzzles. Their ears move back and forth. Then Femke stands up, wipes her face clean with the sleeve of her overalls, looks at the pastel-blue sky, where there are high cloud formations, cloud-ripples, cloud-frills. As if it's a beautiful summer's day.

She picks up the electric fencing wire and sets to work.

September 2017

Intermezzo

'Our wonderful country,' as Giuseppe Mercalli used to say about Italy, at the start of the twentieth century, 'is a shaky country.' He was convinced that to understand an earthquake a thorough seismological knowledge of the specific area was needed. Only then would people be able to predict where the earth would quake and how intense the tremors would be. Then the only remaining uncertainty was when an earthquake would occur. Mercalli urged his government to act on the results of his research and thereby prevent or limit damage in earthquake-prone areas. His work was ground-breaking in the development of modern measures to protect the population. But people seldom listen to pioneers, no matter how well-founded and scientific their predictions might be.

'My warnings,' Mercalli concluded with bitterness, after twenty years of publishing his findings, 'have fallen on deaf ears.'

But his own brave spirit wasn't to blame. He calmly stood on the crater rim of Stromboli, which habitually flung volcanic bombs high into the air, and on the edge of his beloved Vesuvius as it spewed out red-hot lava. Yet he still managed to maintain a balance between his scientific curiosity and his survival instinct. An unsteady balance, because his desire to describe the disastrous effects of earthquakes was greater than his fear. He made a meticulous study of everything that moved, shifted, fell down and broke whenever there were volcanic eruptions or earthquakes. After the great earthquake of 1884, he hastened to the disaster-stricken region of Andalusia, and went to Liguria in 1887, without any fear of possible aftershocks. He established that when an earthquake happens the first real problems can be categorised at Level IV, when windows start to rattle in their frames. At Level VI furniture falls over and plaster cracks; at VII chimneys tumble down; at IX cracks appear in the

*ground and there is general panic; and at XII the destruction is
total.*

*Giuseppe Mercalli knew that clear insight is the key to improving
human destiny. That if we are to avoid disasters, we need scientists
with the determination to build up knowledge, politicians with the
courage to draw the right conclusions from their work, and indus-
trialists prepared to be guided by ethics. History teaches us that such
people are always lacking.*

*And so the Italian government of that time also failed. It chose
not to listen to Mercalli. Morality doesn't make money, when all's
said and done. Ignorance is much cheaper. The result of this ostrich-
like policy was that the victims were robbed not only of their houses
and those dear to them, and of their sense of security and independ-
ence and pride, but that they were expected to wait quietly, like
stranded ships, until the state managed to find the time, money and
willingness to set them afloat again: into a future where no claims
could be made. A future in which they were expected to be humble
and grateful – and poor.*

*Mercalli devoted himself to prevention. He mapped out what
people could expect from earthquakes. But he wasn't able to carry
out research on the post-earthquake situation, or on how a victim
can return to a normal human existence. Perhaps he did still want
to carry out such an investigation. But he burned to death before he
could do so, carbonised in a conflagration caused by an overturned
paraffin lamp. Yet there were also rumours that the deadly fire was
deliberate, that it had been started by criminals.*

THE ONCE WELCOMING PARLOUR, built from big cloister bricks and smaller nineteenth-century bricks, from the brick factories once situated on the banks of the maars and rivers, can no longer be called a parlour. Nor an emergency kitchen. A mine drift, that's what it looks like, a place for creeping and crawling through metal poles set on metal beams. Steel clamps hold the walls together, and on some of the windows there are crossed planks of wood, making the room dim even on clear days. Outside a criss-cross of timber stops the walls from collapsing. The furniture is all higgledy-piggledy, as it has to be fitted around the many props. The way the room is arranged has nothing to do with comfort anymore. The farm of Schokland looks more and more like a half-drowned island in a sea of clay. It's a good job, Trijn and Femke often think, that Ootje doesn't have to go through this anymore. They've considered having their meals in the head-quarters in future, but remain faithful to the parlour, because they're afraid that everything you abandon will be lost forever.

There hasn't been an official decision yet about Schokland's fate. But in both Trijn and Femke the fear is growing that for so-called humanitarian reasons they'll soon be evicted from their farm. One hundred and sixty years ago, with complete confidence, the inhabitants of the island of Schokland were the ones waiting for the state to help them, unlike the young Koridon lad, who had decided to leave and go it alone. But after twenty years of suffocating poverty the island-dwellers were forced to leave, and then all that the island was good for was to be a breakwater and a port of refuge for ships in distress.

The Koridons are scared they'll be deported and made to live in a nice little through-lounge house, in a new-build neighbour-hood in a declining village, with a cow-shaped post box and a paltry pay-out to console them. They certainly know that the riggers' aim is to have Schokland demolished. After all, a dairy farmer no longer has the right to exist. Phosphate rights, the nitrate scare, the nitrogen crisis, plummeting milk prices, climate change. One less Head-Neck-Rump farmhouse: ah well, it might be cultural heritage, but it's not as if it's The Night Watch.

No one says this directly, of course. Words of compassion cost nothing. But Trijn and Femke are absolutely convinced that this is what people think, and not only in those shiny office bunkers; that the majority of the country believes this too, because they're not silly season news anymore now, because the national feelings of compassion are lavished on other tragedies again.

At night they lie awake and images of doom flash by, for both mother and daughter. They can picture the herd being taken for slaughter, in spite of their protests, because what can you do with a hundred dairy cows in Venus Avenue or Comet Street? Night after night they hear each other stumble across the landing, but they'd rather not speak about what is keeping them awake.

They're sitting opposite each other at the big table, acting as if it's completely normal for the two of them to be there alone. Trijn watches Femke fishing the meat balls from the vermicelli soup and throwing them back in the pan. Normally she'd transfer them surreptitiously to Zwier's soup plate.

'You can take the balls out of the soup, if you like, but it's made with beef stock, you know.'

Femke looks up briefly at Trijn.

'I know that, Mam.'

'Sorry,' Trijn says. 'That wasn't nice of me. I do try and take account of all this veggie bother, but I keep forgetting. Sorry. Really.'

They eat in silence until Femke asks: 'Have you noticed that Siepke's Sleepstead has fallen down?'

'Yes, but it didn't need a lot for that to happen.'

'I wonder where Fokko is now?'

'He'll have found somewhere.'

Without looking up from her plate, Femke asks: 'How was

Grampa today?'

'Still really angry.'

'Can he come home soon?'

'That's the question. His leg isn't actually the problem, though of course it will be quite a thing, with that leg in plaster in this mine shaft.'

'What is it, then?'

'He puts up with the physiotherapy, surprisingly enough. That physio lass knows how to win him over. It's his heart that's the problem. They've sorted out the medication, but now he's being trained by a life coach.' She pronounces the title with some exaggeration.

'A what?' Femke asks, laughing.

'Are you still bringing him tobacco?'

Trijn gives Femke a searching look.

'He has to stop that smoking of his. But he seems to have hidden shag all over the place. With other patients, in the cleaning cupboard, under the mattress, under his neighbour's mattress, everywhere. Or he hobbles outside on his sticks and scrounges from passers-by for just as long as it takes for him to build up his stock again. He's incorrigible.'

Femke concentrates on her soup but can't suppress a smile.

Trijn narrows her eyes.

'I thought so,' she says. 'You've got to stop that, Fem.' She sounds very stern.

'He's been smoking for fifty-two years now,' Femke says. 'No one will cure him of the habit.'

'Then it'll kill him.'

'But if he chooses that himself?'

'Don't meddle in this, Femke,' Trijn says fiercely. 'You really don't want to find yourself feeling guilty about his death before too long. And you will, if you're his supplier.'

'He's an adult, Mam.'

'He's addicted, and not just a little bit either.'

'Yes,' Femke says, 'but if he wanted to quit, he'd make it happen.'

'But that's exactly the problem,' Trijn replies. 'Addicts can't do that.'

'Perhaps you should accept, for once, that people sometimes make choices you don't agree with.'

She stands up and lifts the soup pan from the table, clears the soup plates, and looks inside the casserole, where two beef and pork slavinks are braising.

'I'll fry myself an egg,' she says.

Trijn puts the pans on the table, with more noise than necessary.

'You do that,' she snaps, more unpleasantly than she really wants, and yet she can't stop herself. 'Everyone here does exactly what they want anyway.'

She serves herself some potatoes and a slavink. Then she tilts up the pan to get the gravy.

'Perhaps,' Femke says, as she's breaking an egg on the rim of the frying pan, 'it's time for you to start doing that too.'

The egg sizzles in the hot butter.

Trijn looks up as if a hornet has stung her.

'And what's that? According to you?'

Femke manoeuvres the spatula under the egg, shakes the pan back and forth to loosen the egg, and answers: 'I don't know. But perhaps there's something you'd really enjoy doing.'

She slides the fried egg onto the plate, ladles herself some potatoes and green beans, and then focuses on mashing up the potatoes.

Trijn asks icily: 'What makes you think I don't enjoy what I'm doing here?'

'But you don't, do you, Mam?'

Trijn doesn't answer.

They carry on eating in silence. Then suddenly, and it seems to come out of nowhere, Femke says, softly but firmly: 'Do you know what I think, Mam? I think one of us should rent rooms somewhere.' She's silent a moment. And then, like the blow of a sledgehammer: 'And not me.'

A crackling silence. Then Trijn bursts out. Who does she think she is? They're in a partnership, a third of the farm is hers, how could she get it into her head to speak so bluntly to her mother, without any kind of courtesy at all? Getting rid of her, at this point too, now everything they possess hangs from a thread. Where does she get the cheek?

Femke doesn't even blink. She isn't looking down, isn't shrugging her shoulders, and doesn't flinch.

Since the day the earth quaked and the ground heaved and she thought their last hour had come, since Zwier has been forced to go into a care home and let himself be nannied there, since Klaske was crushed under her hiding-place wall and Tuesday met her horrifying end, since that day something has changed in her. As if she can no longer allow herself to be driven by fears that seem rather trivial, now that their entire existence is reeling.

She calmly stands up, puts her cutlery on her plate, takes it to the sideboard, zig-zagging through the props and poles, and says: 'That's what mothers and daughters do.'

'What do mothers and daughters do?'

'Let go of each other.'

Trijn narrows her eyes, like a cat on the point of tearing its prey apart, a little shrew or some other puny creature.

'Yes in-deed,' she says, enunciating the phrase syllable by syllable, 'but it's not normal for a mother to rent rooms. It's usually the daughter who leaves.'

Femke nods calmly. 'Look at the state of things here.' She waves her arm around the room. 'This means we're going to have to fight, otherwise we'll lose everything. They want to wash their hands of us.'

'And you're going to stop them all by yourself?'

It's the familiar mocking tone, but Femke stands firm.

'I want to do everything I can to save Schokland. I want to carry on farming here, but in my own way.'

'And you can't use me for that?' Trijn jumps up, walks angrily through the mine drift, squirming her way through to the only window without a wooden cross, and gazes out across their land and their cows: in one plot the dairy cattle, in the other the youngstock, because the old byre has turned into a No-Entry-Danger-of-Collapse-Zone. It won't be long before it'll be too cold outside for them.

Femke looks at her mother's back. She thinks about how Trijn was described in one of the articles this summer. *An energetic woman in the bloom of her life, nothing like the clichéd image of the dour northerner.*

It's good, Femke thinks, for people to acknowledge that we're not a stereotype, but that doesn't mean that the cliché isn't sometimes true. She stays by the sideboard, a fork clenched in her fist. She stabs it into the palm of her hand and sees little white dots appear in the skin.

'I don't want any more opposition.'

Trijn doesn't react. Femke carries on. The pricking of the fork is hurting her.

'Those riggers, Mam. They want to get rid of us. That's the easiest and cheapest solution for them. Buying us out for almost nothing, because of so-called poor maintenance, and then cutting the whole business short.'

'Like they did to Fokko.'

'Exactly. And that mustn't happen.'

Trijn turns round. She sinks onto the wooden window-seat and sits framed by the window and the light streaming in, a sad-looking woman set against the background of a vast, cloudless landscape.

'No,' she says, 'that mustn't happen.'

'I'll definitely need help, Mam, but I can't stand any more opposition. You've spent your whole life doing penance.'

'Is that so? And if that is the case, what's it to you?'

Femke stabs herself harder with the fork.

'What do you think?'

'I have no idea. I've never wanted to burden you with anything.'

Femke hesitates a moment and then mutters: 'But that doesn't mean you haven't.'

They look directly at each other, as if by looking really carefully they might be able to see something in each other that has been invisible till now.

'What in God's name have I burdened you with?' Although Trijn doesn't intend it, it still sounds like an accusation.

Femke looks at her fist. She's jabbing her hand with the fork more and more fiercely.

'Stop doing that,' Trijn says brusquely, nodding at the fork insistently.

A hole in Femke's palm begins to bleed.

'Now stop that!'

Femke puts the fork on the sideboard with the washing-up, wipes her hand on her trousers, and sits back against the wooden worktop. Trijn is still sitting in the window-frame, a little slumped. She picks at the dirt under her nails.

'If I hadn't been born, you wouldn't have had to come back here.'

Trijn shakes her head.

'Perhaps,' she says cautiously, 'you actually saved me. Perhaps I'd never have got the courage to leave him otherwise.'

'That sounds nice, but that's not what you've been thinking all these years.'

Trijn is amazed at Femke's firmness in discussing things with her.

'I've sometimes wondered,' Femke continues, 'what you'd have become, if I hadn't existed.'

Trijn shrugs her shoulders.

'Not a farmer, anyway,' Femke concludes, and gives a little laugh.

'Anyway, isn't this a totally impossible moment to suggest this? Me renting a place somewhere? How do you see that working out? The herd, the land, the administration. And all this –' She gestures around her. 'You'd never manage. And what about Zwier then? Are you going to put him in a retirement home, or have you written him off already?'

'Of course not,' Femke answers fiercely. 'He'll stay here. I'll always look after him.'

Then there's a painful silence.

Femke stares at a thick metal bolt fixing one of the props into the floor, a substitute for the windows of the stove and the warm flames flickering behind them. Flaking wood varnish, orange-coloured lead paint to protect the metal from rust.

'I hope,' she says, 'we can build something out of this awful state of affairs. I think we'll only survive if we start doing things completely differently. And then you can't always be stamping on the brakes.'

'Am I such a bother to you?' It sounds sorrowful.

Femke goes to Trijn, squats down beside her, and takes hold of her hands.

'I think we're a bother to each other.'

She looks up at her mother.

'You're not a bother to me,' Trijn says firmly. She looks at Femke with sadness in her eyes.

'So how do you see it then? Are we supposed to carry on like this for the next thirty years? Farming together, because that's the way things are meant to be? Because a mother only leaves the farm when she moves into sheltered accommodation?'

Trijn shrugs her shoulders.

'I'm not only saying this for me, but for you too,' Femke says, with more gentleness in her voice. 'Wouldn't it be good if you finally started doing what you really enjoy?'

Trijn straightens her back. 'And you think you'll manage in this mess all by yourself?'

Femke stands up and then sits down on the window seat next to her mother.

'I don't know, but I'd like to try.'

'Is that your own idea, or is it something you've got from that flibbertigibbet?'

'Danielle, Mam. You don't ever seem to get it, but I really am grown-up now. I've been doing this work since I started walking. I know where I want to take things. And that has nothing to do with Danielle. I haven't seen her at all since the day of the earthquake.' She grimaces, as if she has cut herself with a sharp knife. And although Trijn now gives her a searching look, hoping for an explanation, Femke doesn't respond.

'I'm not going to make you leave, Mam,' Femke says. 'I wouldn't even be able to. You're right about that. But perhaps you need to think it over. You've got your own dreams as well, haven't you?'

'Dreams?' Trijn gives a pitying shake of the head. 'Dreams don't exist for people like us.'

It's silent again. Femke looks over her shoulder, at the sky in which a few evening clouds are floating into view.

'The swallows have gone, did you know that?'

Trijn gives her a questioning look. 'And what do you mean by that?'

Femke raises her shoulders.

'It's just something I noticed. They've suddenly vanished.'

And then she continues: 'Wouldn't you like to do something with those dead birds of yours?'

Trijn laughs sneeringly.

'How considerate of you to remind me of that. There's still a court case hanging over me, yes.'

She stands up, slaloms across to the table, rummages in drawers.

'What are you looking for?'

'Zwier's shag.'

Femke laughs.

'Are you starting the boycott already? Before he's even home?'

'No. I'm just dying for a fag. I suddenly need a smoke.'

There's a broad grin on Femke's face. She digs a packet of cigarettes from her trouser pocket and offers one to her mother.

'For once I won't stamp on the brakes then,' Trijn says. She draws fire into the cigarette from the flame Femke offers her and says: 'Come along.'

She walks to the one window that hasn't been reinforced with wood, pushes it open, jumps out, and extends her hand. They sit down on the little bench that always stood against the house but has now been shifted forward so there's room for the struts. It's almost dark. The clouds turn purple and orange and yellow. The cold of night comes on. A blackbird is singing. The drumming sound of a woodpecker rings out, as if it's spring.

'I miss Klaske,' Femke says. Trijn nods. Femke is annoyed to find herself thinking about Danielle and she remembers the night of the day when the whole province was shaken by one of the biggest earthquakes they'd ever had, till now. A quake with its epicentre under Schokland, causing a huge amount of damage, but fortunately no deaths, according to what was reported. An earthquake that on the Richter scale counted as being not very substantial, which meant that people who wanted to ignore it could imagine there'd been very little impact, while for the people who lived in the clay country it had once again emphasised what had been their daily reality for more than five years. Relatively light tremors taking place at a shallow depth have enormous acceleration at ground level, with a huge impact on houses and farm buildings, which can't withstand this kind of violence. The clay ground transmits tremors as if it's blancmange. The Richter scale has nothing to say about that.

Femke heard nothing at all from Danielle, the whole day, and she only realised this when she was sitting on the edge of her bed that night, when everything that could be saved at that point had been saved. She felt very worried. Perhaps Danielle's farm was in a very bad state. She sent her a text: *Are you okay? And the girls?*

She waited a while for an answer, but nothing came, so she texted her again: *Please, answer me. I'm very worried!*

Minutes passed. Half an hour. An hour. Then she stood up, rushed to the car, and drove to the sea dyke, passing a collapsed barn. Her heart was in her mouth. She could see the farm in the distance. It seemed to be intact. She drove down the narrow road along the dyke and saw that there were three cars parked in the farmyard. She stopped the car at some distance from the house, wondering what to do. From the car she studied the buildings. The door to the shippon was open. Everything seemed normal.

A young woman with long, messy hair came out of the house. She was wearing tight, brand-new, ripped jeans.

The lamp outside the house made a circle of light in which the woman stood, leaning against the open door of the shippon. Femke saw her take a packet of cigarettes from the breast pocket of her denim jacket. A figure came out of the shippon and walked into the circle of light. It was Lieuwe, carrying two bottles of beer in his hands. He handed the woman one of them and she gave him a cigarette. He leaned his arm against the shippon door and bent down towards her. Femke heard a door slam and laughter. Three figures ran out. Danielle appeared in the circle of light, with two men behind her. Danielle gave Lieuwe a shove, making him fall against the woman, and she ran away, across the dark farmyard. One of the men followed her. They vanished into the darkness. Femke heard the familiar laugh. She started the car, turned the headlights on and stepped on the pedal. At that moment she heard a shriek.

When she got home there was a text: *I saw you! Why did you drive off?*

Femke texted back: *Grampa* (ambulance emoji). *Klaske* (coffin). *Tuesday* (coffin).

She lay in bed waiting for a very long time, but Danielle didn't answer. Eventually she fell asleep. When she woke up the following morning, there was an answer: *Bad luck. Got visitors. Take care. Till later!* A thumbs-up.

That was when Femke decided to stop being her beck-and-call girl.

A few days later she got a text: *Everything ok? Time for fireworks?* A whole row of the familiar emojis. She put her phone away and didn't answer, even when another text came a little later: *Anyone at home?*

October 2017

ZWIER IS SITTING with his crutches beside him on a bench in front of the care home, with a bagful of medicines, leaflets containing advice on exercise and diet, and a list of check-up appointments. He is sitting right below a No Smoking sign, a fag dangling from his lips. He has something of the air of an old soldier come home from war, Trijn thinks as she steers the car down the drive. He hasn't lost his stubbornness in the care home. He refuses to go inside with her to thank the staff and hand over the cake she has bought in his name. On the way home she prepares him for the situation. They hadn't dared to tell him the whole of it, given that any kind of excitement, according to the doctors, might have proved fatal. The farmhand's room has been made ready for him. It's more convenient to be there while his leg is still in plaster. Trijn doesn't tell him they've been advised that it's safer not to go into the part of the house where his bedroom is, and she also hasn't told him about the advice to be inside the house and farm buildings as little as possible anyway. As if it's a question of choice. She does tell him that the old byre has become too dangerous and that the youngstock are lodged at a farm some distance away, for the time being. And that they've come to a temporary arrangement with the bank, to give them some respite. Whether they'll be able to manage with that until the riggers make a settlement with them, if the riggers ever do settle, that's the question.

As they drive into the farmyard, Femke comes to meet them. Zwier gets out of the car and looks down as usual, but there's no bouncy, chestnut-brown cloud jumping up at him.

'Oh,' he says. 'I'd completely forgotten that.'

He points one of his crutches at the crack in the concrete in front of the byres, then at the crippled feed silo, and one by one at the new cracks in the byre walls and at the wooden props, still a light blonde. Nothing escapes him. Trijn urges him to go inside. There's coffee and cake in the headquarters. 'To celebrate your homecoming,' she says.

'I haven't got the impression,' is his slow and careful answer, 'that there's much to celebrate here.'

They show him the undamaged shippon, hoping that will cheer him up.

'For as long as it stays like that,' he says sombrely, but as he hobbles through the shippon, where for the past two days they've housed the herd again, because the nights are too cold and the ground is too wet to let the cows stay outside any longer, they see him relax. Every so often he stands still by one of the cows, stroking it, patting it, and his sombre look makes way for a light smile.

'I'm home again.' He sounds contented.

They get back to work. Femke cleans the milking robots.

Trijn makes a start on the administration, registering the phosphate rights and medications. She can hear Zwier's muttered curses as he checks the recent correspondence with the bank and the riggers and every now and then she just has to smile.

Through the windows of the headquarters Trijn sees a man in a suit entering the shippon. He isn't the flashy kind that the riggers usually send, but an old-fashioned sort of man in a respectable dark blue suit, an ageless person, with a sharp nose and smooth-shaven cheeks, a dark brown leather briefcase in his hand, the kind she used to have at school, with big silver-coloured clasps and a thick leather handle. The kind of old-fashioned, indestructible bag she really hated.

She opens the door of the headquarters and the man introduces himself as Hessel Sjoerdsma, special officer for the Food and Consumer Products Safety Authority, in the Control and Enforcement Department. He checks the form in his hand and asks if she is Ms Koridon. The blood drains from her face.

Zwier examines the man from head to toe and asks: 'Rigger?'

'Excuse me?' the man asks, and Trijn says nervously: 'No,

Dad. I'm expecting this gentleman. Please come with me.' She walks outside quickly, before Zwier can carry out the threat he'd made, that he'd force such a bureaucrat to snort up the debris. She takes him into the now-chaotic Dead Bird Museum and waits stoically. The man whistles through his teeth.

'Not bad at all,' he says.

She stays silent.

'How many birds do you have in your possession?'

She asks him if he would like coffee or tea. He thanks her, but says no, and walks along the birds, scattered around messily, still fixed to their hats. He picks up a redshank, examines the bird very carefully and concludes that it hasn't been at all badly done. Trijn can't help smiling. He takes hold of the golden plover, the swallow, and a couple of other birds. Then he looks at the peacock, which she has put back on top of the cupboard, still on the wide-brimmed hat.

'That one,' she says, 'was done by my brother. Years ago.'

'It's clearly a talent that runs in the family.'

He asks her again how many birds she has.

'Fifty-seven.'

'Are you sure of that?'

She nods. He sits down on Jort's stool, his briefcase on his lap. He uses the bag as a support for the form on which he is making notes.

'Are all the animals in your possession here in this room?'

She nods again.

'Nothing in the living room? Nothing stored in a cellar or a freezer? People sometimes forget those.'

She starts. The freezer. There must still be birds inside it.

He suggests taking an immediate look.

As she's opening the freezer lid, she remembers Fokko's gift. The first thing the bureaucrat grabs hold of is the refuse sack and he gives her a questioning look.

'A common crane,' she says, embarrassed.

He opens the bag, takes the bird half out, carefully examines it, and asks how she acquired it.

'I was given it.'

'By whom?' he asks in a business-like manner.

'I'd rather not say.'

'Why not?'

'So I don't cause him problems. He hasn't done anything illegal. He found the bird in the peatlands. A few months ago.'

'Ms Koridon,' he replies, 'if I were to believe everyone who told me they had found a bird that was simply lying around somewhere, then birds would be falling from the sky all day long like drops of rain. Otherwise, there's no way it could happen.'

He regards her sternly. She looks back undaunted.

'It's really true,' she insists.

'That,' he says with a sour smile, 'is what they all say.'

He carries on rummaging through the freezer and notes down a robin, a great tit, and a glaucous gull.

'Any more corpses in the cupboard?'

He chortles at his own joke.

'No,' she says. She wants to put the crane back in the freezer, but then hesitates. 'Or are you going to take everything away with you?'

He shakes his head.

They go back into the Dead Bird Museum.

'Ms Koridon,' he says. 'I've checked the background of this case a little before coming here and I have to say, although I'm not someone who is particularly impressed by protests and uproar, yet,' and he pauses a little, 'there are very few people who can do something like that with such flair.' He points to the peacock hat. 'Hats off to you.' He chortles again. 'Now, tell me honestly, you're a farming woman, you've spent your whole life dealing with a state that wants you to register everything.

You can't shift a cow, or sell a litre of milk, or get rid of a single bucket of slurry without having to justify it. Are you really trying to tell me that you've never thought, in the twenty years you've been practising taxidermy, that you should register these birds, whether they crashed against your newly-washed windows, or gave up the ghost on your midden, or were given to you as a gift?'

She looks straight at him. 'No,' she says firmly. 'Truly.'

'That's rather strange,' he insists. 'You strike me as being an intelligent woman. I presume you play an important role in the administration of this business. Women always do the admin. After all, they're much cleverer.' He carries on in a conspiratorial tone: 'So, you've never heard about registration? Certification? Madam, I find that very hard to believe.'

'It's really silly of me,' she answers. 'I think so too. But my taxidermy was separate from all my other work. When I came inside my Dead Bird Museum,' he smiles when she says that phrase and jots something down, 'then it had nothing at all to do with the rest of it. I only prepared birds for my own pleasure.'

He gives her a very searching look. She starts feeling a bit uncomfortable with it.

'You say you do this for your own pleasure. Let me tell you, I've seen plenty of mounted creatures already and among them some terrible failures. I don't know any amateurs at all who can do this work with such craftsmanship. Are you qualified? Who taught you how to do this?'

'My brother used to do it. He died young and then I took it up. My first birds really were terrible failures. The very first one was completely lopsided. I've probably still got it somewhere.'

'Ah,' he says, sticking his fountain pen in the air, 'yet more birds?'

She starts.

'Yes, the box of freaks is right here, in the cupboard.'

She gets it from the bottom shelf and takes out her very first skylark, that odd creature, with a neck that's too short, and legs set too far back so it tips forward when you put it down, and lumpy wings, and squinty eyes, all of which give it a ridiculous look.

'This was my first.' Even she has to smile about it.

'You've certainly learned a lot since then,' he observes drily, and then: 'A moment or two ago you called this your Dead Bird Museum. Do you mean to say that it's also open to the public?'

She shakes her head. 'No one ever comes here, except for the protest action. They did then.'

'And have you ever sold any birds?'

'No.'

He writes. She leans against the worktop, looking down at the neatly combed dark brown hair, the dead straight parting. He has long, spotless fingers. The golden tip of his fountain pen scratches over the paper.

'There's cake,' she says. 'My father has just come back from the nursing home. Why don't I get a cup of coffee for you after all, with a piece of cake?'

He looks up and grins. 'Well,' he says, 'on further consideration that seems a very good idea. It'll still take us some time. I have to register all the birds. The more that are on the red list, the more serious the situation, as you'll understand.'

'Yes,' she says, 'of course.' But in one way or another his tone doesn't worry her so much now.

His eye falls on the yellowing article on the pinboard, with the photo of the Parisian taxidermy shop, where death is transformed into a luxury item.

'You've been there,' he observes.

She shakes her head. 'No, that was the plan once, but nothing came of it.'

He sings the praises of Paris, the Louvre, the Sacré-Coeur,

Notre Dame. And then he mentions Deyrolle, the legendary shop. He points to the yellowed photo and says: 'That shop is almost more beautiful than all the other gems of the city. A woman with a hobby like yours,' he concludes, with a degree of solemnity, 'should really make a trip there some day.'

She gulps. She suddenly feels all nerves.

'What do you take in your coffee?' she asks, before taking to her heels as swiftly as possible.

*

The land is completely drenched. The leaves on the trees are a tired green. Zwier is sitting in his old place in the warm head-quarters, working at a square nail picture. In front of him there are little piles of nails sorted by size. He has used diagonal lines to work out the centre of the board and has tapped in a bright, smoothly scoured nail there. Then, with mathematical precision, he hammers the nails into a fanned-out spiral shape.

Femke is reading an interview with a dairy farmer and asks Zwier if he knows the man.

'Pruiksma, Pruiksma,' he says pensively. 'I've heard of him. Somewhere in the west? One of the big chaps, right?'

'Yes,' she says, 'really big. In the past. He was one of the top ten dairy farmers.' She reads out loud: 'I understood exactly how to get the cows to give plenty of milk.'

'Aye. Right enough.'

'Did you know he's switched?'

'Is that so?'

'Do you know when that man made the switch?'

He shakes his head.

'When he saw an ad from his own milk cooperative, saying they needed to buy calf milk.'

'How come?'

'They were selling milk replacer for calves. Then he realised that the milk he himself was producing was so lacking in nutrients and contained so much rubbish, that it wasn't even good enough for calves. He thought about his two young children and their future.'

'And then what?'

'And then he switched to organic.'

'And they all lived happily ever after.'

Zwier is sorting out a new set of nails.

'So we won't, then,' she says, sulkily. Why do people always feel attacked when they hear that someone's doing things differently? It makes her feel curious. Particularly because this was such a successful dairy farmer, someone who had the courage to ask himself if what he was actually doing was ruining the future of his children, his animals, and his soil. Someone who dared to question his own routines. In the interview with him the man says it was like waking up with a shock from a stupor that had affected him, and his father, and all the teachers at agricultural college, and all his colleagues too. He realised they'd been blind to the long-term consequences of intensive dairy farming.

'Do you know,' she continues, not able to prevent herself, 'why artificial fertilisers were promoted so much after the Second World War?'

'No more hunger, that was the slogan.' Zwier declaims the words with the poignancy they must once have had.

'No,' she says. 'That was the sales talk. That's the way they convinced the public. That was how they justified intensive farming. But the real reason, this farmer says, was that after the war the American explosives manufacturers were looking for a market for their new product, when there was less need for explosives. Peace was a disaster for the armaments industry.'

'If that's right, then I understand at last why that artificial fertiliser was so cheap at the time. My father never grasped how they managed it.'

'And that's how they got you lot addicted to it,' she says.

'Well, well,' he replies, 'it's "you lot" now. Aren't you part of it anymore?'

She carries on reading out the article. Switching to organic, it says, is mainly a question of letting things be. Doing less. Letting nature get on with her own work.

'That's all well and good,' he says, 'but it's not as easy as it sounds. You have to arrange the whole farming business round it. And given the present state of affairs, that seems pretty ambitious at the moment. We've got enough to worry about.'

'But that's really not the case,' she says fiercely. 'Everything has to be overhauled. The whole place needs to be restored and reinforced, perhaps even re-built in part. This is exactly the right time to do things differently. And that's what I'm going to do, Grampa.'

'Right,' he says. 'And do we still figure in that story?'

'It's my future.'

'But my legacy.'

For a moment they're silent. As if they're trying to work out which should carry the most weight.

Then Zwier continues: 'You shouldn't underestimate it. It's not just a question of getting rid of the fertilisers, not using antibiotics anymore, and turning the cows out to pasture. It takes years to build up a strong herd. If you're going to switch to organic, then you have to start working on genetic potential. Not all cows are fit to be organic cows. You want a strong breed for that. A Holstein cow needs a large amount of feed and it's got a fairly quick passage rate. And then you have to add minerals to the feed. You're not meant to do that if you're organic.'

'So what do you think I've been doing with the inseminations?'

She gives a wide grin.

He frowns. Then he points his hammer at her: 'You'd better know what you're doing. Don't make random experiments.'

'I damn well do know what I'm doing. For quite some time now.'

He chuckles. 'A coup. That's what it is. You're carrying out a secret coup in Schokland.' And then, with glistening eyes: 'So what do you think? Blaarkop? Frisian-Dutch?'

'No,' she says. 'I think we should go for Montbéliardes. Or Brown-Swiss.'

'They're not pure dairy cows.'

'That's right. Milk and meat. I want dual purpose cows. No more waste.'

His eyes narrow. He stares at her, chewing his lips.

'Then you're really making big changes.'

She nods.

He stands up and gets his crutches.

'I'll just go and make my physio happy. A little stroll every half hour, that's what she's prescribed.'

He'd rather please the bloody physio than have a proper discussion about going organic, Femke thinks. He shuffles out of the headquarters and into the yard. She follows a little later, gets the wheelbarrow, and goes to the feed silo, an upside-down rocket with a botched leg. One day, she thinks, I won't need this stuff anymore. Then my cows will only get good grass to eat – a proper salad buffet, with chicory and plantain and yarrow, dandelions and clover. She pushes the flap open and the pellets clatter into the barrow. Clouds of dust fly up.

She walks back across the yard with the loaded wheelbarrow and sees a flight of geese, like an open zip against the grey-blue blanket of clouds, honking loudly on their way to the mouth of the river. Geese always sound as if they've been deeply wronged, she thinks. They're the most aggrieved of all creatures.

When she goes back inside the shippon she hears a hopeless

wailing above the usual noises. She lets go of the wheelbarrow and runs to the steps going downstairs. Zwier is sitting on the top step. He's crying. She bends over him and asks where it's hurting. He shakes his head and points his crutch down into the cellar. A brown ooze is dripping in a small but steady stream through a crack in the wall meant to keep this space clear of tonnes of cow shit. Behind the wall is the underground slurry store. A dark pile of muck steams on the ground.

She sits down on the step beside him, puts an arm over his shoulders, and doesn't say a word. Every form of hope seems frivolous now it's clear that even their shippon, built six years ago with a king's ransom borrowed from the bank, can't withstand the tremors.

She strokes his shuddering back.

We Koridons, she thinks, have always been go-getters. That was something we were proud of. We didn't wait to see what happened to the sea-battered island. We used our initiative. They couldn't grind us down. But the time comes when it's over and done with. Then you're just prey for a falcon, like everyone else. We're being gobbled up: head, heart and breast. They won't leave anything of us behind.

'Come on,' she says, and helps Zwier stand. He lets her lead him away, flops down on his chair in the headquarters, and drinks the glass of water she gives him.

'I'm going to report it,' she says flatly, though she knows there won't be any point. And she'll have to inform the contractor. The cellar wall will have to be shored up. The fight for emergency payments and all the other stuff will be added to the long list of things to do with their case, lying around somewhere in some bunker of an office building, on some smooth-faced administrator's desk, who is too busy pumping the gas supplies dry to deal with their problems, even though this has been going on for five years now.

When she picks up her smartphone she sees the text message.

Hey, Blondie. I'm not far away. Time for a coffee? Kisses, a heart, a little volcano.

As she looks up she sees Danielle walk into the shed at that very moment. Her heart starts thumping, she swears softly. Zwier silently follows her glance. She rushes out of the headquarters to meet Danielle, who open her arms for a hug.

Femke keeps her distance and stays where she is, with her hands in her pockets, and gives her a cool 'hi'.

'Hey, Frosty,' Danielle says, 'what's up with you? You never answer.'

'Come with me,' Femke says and walks ahead of her out of the shippon. She sees it's dry, for the first time in days and probably only for a while anyway – the next shower is already looming over the land. She walks behind the shippon and sits on the gate, her hands firmly clasped around the metal bars. Danielle stands opposite, staring at her with an amused grin.

'What's up, Blondie?'

'I don't have any time.'

'No time to answer my texts?'

'No.'

'How come?'

'Well, we've got a lot of problems here.'

'You always had a lot of problems here. That didn't get in the way before.'

Femke clasps her hands more firmly round the steel bars.

'I miss you,' Danielle says in a pleading tone, and it feels as if a hand is stroking Femke's cheek. Her breath falters.

Danielle's eyes shift away from her, across the farmland. She kicks some gravel out of the way, and then gazes into the distance. In the silence it briefly seems that everything is possible. But then there's Danielle's voice again, more business-like now.

'A lot of damage?'

Femke gives a brusque nod.

'But your Grampa's back again.'

Silence. And then: 'The slurry stores are leaking.'

That wasn't something she wanted to say.

Danielle whistles through her teeth. 'Then you've turned into an even more complex case.'

'Yes.'

'Isn't it time to take them to court now?'

'Ah,' Femke observes, 'so Lieuwe is still around.' And then, in a cool tone of voice: 'No thank you. We'll do it our own way.'

Danielle looks straight at her.

'And that is?'

'I'm still working that out.'

'And I won't be part of it?'

Femke swallows. 'I can't do it,' she says.

'What can't you do?'

'Be your beck-and-call girl.'

'My what?'

Femke looks across Danielle at a crack in the wall of the byre. An old crack, which has been there so long she's almost used to it. She can't imagine anymore what it was like to be in a house and a byre without cracks. On a farm where everything is stable, and familiar, and unchangeable.

'Hey, Fem,' Danielle says, as she comes closer and tries to put an arm round her. Femke fiercely shakes her off.

Danielle tries to catch her eye. And suddenly Femke does look straight at her.

'Do you remember,' Femke says, 'us talking about fear?'

Danielle nods.

'Not long ago I was walking by the maar and a group of tufted ducks were swimming in front of me. Every time I got closer they flapped up, flew a bit further on, and then landed in the water again. They kept flying and swimming in the same direction as

231

me. That meant I bothered them for half an hour. But if they'd turned round and gone straight towards me, I'd have walked past them and they'd have been rid of me.'

Danielle stares blankly at her.

'It's like that with fear too,' Femke concludes.

'Your fear?'

'No,' Femke says. 'Yours.'

Danielle says coolly: 'I'm not afraid of anything.'

Femke doesn't answer. A little breeze is blowing across the land. She lifts her hand to brush some hair back from her eyes.

'Well,' Danielle says, a bit uneasily, 'are you going to explain it to me?'

Femke slowly shakes her head.

They look at each other. Femke can feel her face burning. She turns her gaze away.

'Let's just say that I don't want it to be like this.'

'But how then?'

Femke shrugs.

'You'll have to turn round to find that out, just like the ducks.'

Heavy drops of rain begin to fall from the leaden sky.

'Well,' Danielle says, giving Femke a last look, who carries on staring at the grey clods of clay on the concrete, 'I'll be off then. Bye!'

She hurries off, with forced cheerfulness in her voice, and strides out. Femke watches her leave, blinking her eyes.

As she's walking back through the shippon she sees the estate car tearing down the lonning, and she bumps into her mother, who is watching the car.

'What was she doing here?' she asks.

'Nothing,' Femke says. She says that there's yet another problem. She leads her mother down the steps into the underground slurry store and shows her the crack through which the cow muck is gently but steadily dripping into the passageway.

*

On the other side of the world islands are being swept by one hurricane after another, and after an exceptionally hot and dry summer here in the flat clay country, rain has been falling for weeks from a charcoal grey sky. The meadows are flooded. There are deep pools of standing water on the blue clay soil. The farm-yard is drenched. Moisture is rising into the shippon, the house, the headquarters. You can't get rid of this damp with any kind of heating. And they're still having to wait. The life of the farm remains at a standstill. Whenever Femke gets in touch with the various organisations she has to contend with well-trained switchboard operators and receptionists who've been coached to let the victims' anger slide off them and to fob off the complain-ants. All the bigwigs of the rigging businesses have been meeting up for months now, to sort out new protocols and other regula-tions, and all the various commissions, and dialogue tables, and feedback groups previously set up are being evaluated. And the victims are expected to quietly carry on waiting, after all the years of reporting on the quake damage they've suffered, all the forms they've filled in, all the experts they've welcomed into their homes, the information they've provided, the old building plans they've searched out, and the appeals they've written. And well-paid advisors and case managers and politicians talk themselves hoarse about it, but there are still no proper measures in place, let alone compensation, repairs, or reinforcement.

Two things go steadily on: the crumbling-down of the houses and farms, and the gas extraction. And in Schokland they're beginning to realise that it's a mistake to assume that the state protects its population. For Trijn that's the biggest shock of all, to be forced to realise that the government is still not on the peo-ple's side, just as it wasn't when that island in the Zuiderzee bled to death. A hundred and sixty years after evacuating the island of Schokland, the state still has other priorities: it has to stay on good terms with the multinationals, and the country enjoys the benefits. And as a consequence, the suffering of the people in the clay country is perceived as nothing more than unavoidable, incidental damage. Here in the clay country a picture of how the world works has been totally destroyed.

But in Schokland Femke is refusing to yield to a scenario of doom that as the days pass looks increasingly like reality. With greater single-mindedness than ever, with a dash of courage and stubborn tenacity, because in spite of everything she does want to make a future for herself, she carefully studies what the switch to organic farming could be like for Schokland and what kind of dairy farming would best suit her.

She's in the headquarters, watching a short film about a farmer who's switched to organic and has decided to leave the calves with their mothers for a few more months.

Trijn watches the film over Femke's shoulder. The farmer is cheerfully talking about the pleasure he gets from his farm, how much quicker the calves are growing, how much healthier both the mother and child are. 'And above all,' he says, 'it's done wonders for my image. I'm seen as the most animal-friendly dairy farmer in this area.'

Trijn gives a scornful laugh. 'As if that's what it's about. You don't hear him say anything about a drop in milk production, or unsupervised colostrum intake, or accidents with calving. It's not possible in our cow-stalls. You need a completely different kind of set-up.'

Femke pauses the film, turns round and says: 'So have you thought it over?'

'What?'

'Renting a place somewhere.'

'Of course not. As if there could be any question of that now.'

A light-blue, hump-backed figure comes into the shed. It's

Fokko. His hair is dripping wet from the rain. He pulls off his boots outside the headquarters, and then takes off the blue refuse sack he's pulled over his head and rucksack as a kind of waterproof. Trijn holds the door open for him. He has the buzzard in his hands, soaked through and grey with debris.

'Jesus, man,' Trijn says in greeting, 'you look really bad.'

'Cold,' he says, teeth chattering.

'Where've you come from?' Zwier asks, checking him out from top to toe.

Fokko stays in the doorway, helpless and completely drenched. Trijn tells him to take a warm shower. She's got dry clothes for him and they'll just have to work out somewhere for him to stay. She asks him to come with her and while he's in the shower she sorts out some clothes for him.

When she comes back into the headquarters Zwier says firmly: 'I'm going to sleep in my own room again. I've got rid of that plaster-cast now, and I was planning to go back there anyway.'

'Nothing doing,' she says. 'Fokko can sleep there.'

Zwier frowns and says threateningly: 'Femke's just told me that my room has been declared unfit to live in. And you want to put Fokko there! You should be ashamed of yourself.'

She shakes her head.

'You women think you can call the tune for everything.'

'Well,' she says, 'so it's us women at fault again. I don't want you to sleep in your own room.'

He shakes his head. 'The whole place is a mess anyway. We'll put Fokko in the farmhand's room.'

Trijn shrugs her shoulders. Fokko comes down wearing dry clothes. Trijn makes him tea and a couple of sandwiches, and asks him what everyone has been asking each other recently: 'Where were you during the earthquake?'

He was outside, on the land, fortunately not in Siepke's Sleepstead, because then he'd have got a sheet of corrugated roofing on his head. He got the buzzard out from under the debris and now he's sorry he hadn't left it with Trijn to look after.

'It wouldn't have been safe then either,' she says and tells him about the special investigatory officer.

'And they took all of them away?'

She shakes her head. No. He registered them and put together a report, and now he's consulting with the public prosecutor to see whether there'll be a fine, or whether the birds will be confiscated.

'No court case, then?'

'He says there won't be.'

'And will that guy come back?'

Trijn shrugs. Perhaps. Or perhaps there'll be a letter. 'But to be on the safe side,' she says, 'I'd hide that buzzard in the farm-hand's room.'

He coughs.

'That doesn't sound good,' she says. 'Have you got something for it?'

'Just this.' He digs out his pouch of tobacco.

Zwier chuckles.

'Look,' he says, 'Fokko is a man after my own heart.' He gets his own tobacco pouch.

'Shall I make some grog for you?'

'Grog?' Fokko asks. 'And what sort of stuff is that?' Trijn is already standing there, kettle in hand.

'Hot water, lemon juice, honey and a little jenever. It's good for your throat.'

He grins.

'The jenever seems like a good idea. But don't bother about the rest.'

Zwier and Femke laugh. Trijn goes to the cupboard, gets out the bottle of jenever, and puts it on the table with two glasses, then gets two mugs and makes tea for herself and Femke.

Zwier fills the glasses and asks: 'Fokko, what's going to happen now?'

'To me? Or to you?' Fokko points into the shippon. 'There's a lot more damage now, right?'

Zwier tells him about the leaking slurry store and says that the farm was built on a proper foundation, put in place to resist tempests. How could their forefathers have foreseen that the ground beneath it would be sucked dry, causing the farm buildings to subside along the fault-lines, by fits and starts?

'And that scum keep shouting that they're not going to look at what's happening below ground level,' he says bitterly.

Fokko knocks back his glass of jenever, pours himself another and says: 'I've got a plan.'

'Again?' Trijn smiles.

'I've got two plans,' he corrects himself.

'To get yourself a house?' Zwier asks.

'My van's still here.'

When he was with them before they'd put it behind the shippon, on the grass. His old Mercedes.

'If you'll let me keep it here a little longer, then I'll convert it. Put a bed in it, a little table, a kitchen area, a woodburning stove. And a worktop. House and workplace all in one. Then, if I need to, I can make a bolt for it.'

'Where to?'

'That's to do with plan two.'

'And what's that then?'

'Nobody fucks with Fokko.'

Femke giggles. Zwier mutters and Trijn asks: 'And are you going to tell us anything more about it?'

Fokko shakes his head.

'No info from the management as yet.'

'Right then,' Trijn says. 'You'll stay here for the time being. Till your van is ready.'

'Yes, please,' he says, 'and then we'll settle the account.'

'Us?' she asks, surprised.

'No. Me and them.'

*

Femke is visiting the architect she heard in April, speaking at the meeting in the village hall about how quake-damaged farms can be restored. She's driven there without making an appointment. She's in luck. He's in his office and he's prepared to listen to her. She tells him about the leaking slurry store, the kitchen they're not allowed to enter, the cracks in the cow-stalls and farmhouse.

'Leaking slurry stores are a sign of subsidence and indicate that the walls are out of true. Really hazardous – just like those horizontal cracks in the brickwork. You said the roof has been properly supported,' he continues. 'Right?'

She nods. 'But no one knows if it's safe enough.'

He sketches out various possibilities, speaks about steel frameworks, piled raft foundations, hipped roofs, trusses and purlins, and about repairs and reinforcement and possible new build, and how they could hire him as an expert and draft a plan together. While he is speaking it's as if a light has been switched on again. Here is someone who gives hope, and who has enough experience, and knowledge, and good will to try to help them put an end to this miserable state of affairs. If the riggers settle with them, that is to say. Because reasonable compensation is crucial, of course.

The man promises to come and look at the place at some point, but because it's incredibly busy they'll have to be patient.

'How long?' she asks.

'I hope,' he says, 'I'll be able to find some time at the start of next year.'

'And if we can't manage till then?'

'It sounds as if you really should leave the place,' he says. 'You should ask for temporary accommodation.'

'We've got a farm with one hundred cows. We can't just give that up. They don't have any kind of solution for that.'

'I'll do my level best to come and look as quickly as possible, so at least I can advise you.'

As she's driving back she longs to go and see Danielle to tell her about the architect, who she's managed to find because of the meeting in the village hall. She's already driving toward the sea dyke, but then stops by the verge, thinking back to the night after the earthquake. How she didn't get any answer to her texts, and how she'd driven to the sea dyke, feeling extremely worried. Danielle partying. A rotten little text was all she'd got from her.

She turns the car round and drives towards Schokland in the falling dusk. She sees an immense cloud of starlings above the fields. She gets out and walks onto the land. Countless wings are vibrating in the evening sky. The air is full of a mysterious rustling. She watches the thousands of small creatures pirouetting in a black, wheeling, fluttering sky-ballet that constantly changes form: an ellipse, a cylinder, high in the air, along the ground, in a long straight line, with smaller groups of starlings constantly flying towards the bigger mass, flapping and beating their wings at an amazing speed, deftly joining in. A wondrous performance in which every shining speck of starling becomes a part of that enormous quivering ball without any apparent effort at all.

Only when the pulsating, stippled cloud has vanished beyond the horizon, as if swallowed up by the purple-orange flaming sunlight, and shadow falls over the land and a chilly damp instantly rises up from the ground, does she get into the car and drive to Schokland. She turns the radio to top volume and sings along with Haim: *I'll give you all the love I never gave before I left you.*

When she's back in the farmyard and takes the key out of the ignition and the music stops, she's shocked by the sound of blaring sirens and she sees a trio of fire engines tearing up the concrete track towards their lonning. The moment she opens the car she realises that something is horribly wrong. She races through the yard to the shippon and it feels as if she's somehow floating above herself, watching herself run, but there's a delay in the running, as if her body can't keep up with her brains, or perhaps it's the other way round, at any rate something isn't in sync, and so it takes a while before she understands what she's seeing, when she comes to a stop by the shippon's wide-open doors.

The grating has toppled down into the slurry store, taking the cows with it, and in the deep, dark brown, fuming, stinking abyss the cows dazedly hold their heads above the sludge, their necks outstretched, their bodies buried under gleaming slurry. The animals are stock-still, trapped by the sharp stench of excrement that is emanating a deadly gas. They're not making any sound at all. Only the shining whites of their wide-open eyes betray their panic. Trijn and Zwier are standing on the other side of the shippon, on the solid concrete floor in the cubicle section, separated from her by a chasm of slurry, full of dazed cows. Zwier is gripping onto a feed rail. Trijn is busy phoning. Fokko comes out of the old byre with an enormous amount of rope. Their faces are deathly pale.

What follows is an endless nightmare that continues far into the drab-grey morning. A night in which they mechanically do all they can to save what can be saved. Femke, wearing waders and an oxygen mask, plods back and forth with the firemen, up to her waist in slurry. It takes a while for the crew to realise that Femke is the one who best knows how to fix the straps around the animals without causing panic; after which they're hauled, cow by cow, out of the muck, washed clean with the garden hose and then led by Fokko and Trijn behind the railing to the cubicle section of the shippon. Then the poor beasts, suffering from hypothermia, are put in the cubicles, with extra straw around them to warm them up. And Femke wades through the muck and plays God, while the tears run down her cheeks behind the oxygen mask. She points out the cows with the greatest chance of survival, who are therefore the ones that have to be hauled up first, until she's chilled to the bone and has to come out for a while to warm up, just like the firemen, who every now and then change over. Help has been drummed up via the Nest Protest App. Siewert comes immediately, with a couple of farmers from the village. The farming woman who isn't allowed to enter her own house anymore brings an enormous pan of stamppot. Someone has warned the milking robot supplier and called a carpenter to make a new route through to the robot. And amid all this hectic activity Femke stands in the ice-cold slurry with the men from the fire service, and the work becomes more gruesome as the hours pass. The cattle are hauled up with their legs or hips broken, overcome by poisonous gases, and then they lift out the dead cows, already lying with their heads under the slurry. The corpses are piled up in a corner and the vet puts an end to the suffering of those animals that won't make it.

And Zwier is shivering and whimpering, in the middle of all this commotion, on a chair that someone has brought him from the headquarters, his hand on Allie, one of the six cows safe inside the cubicles when the place collapsed. The morning is nearly over by the time all the cows have been hauled up, and Femke and the fire crew, shivering with exhaustion, come out of the pit, let themselves be hosed down outside, peel off their waders, and have coffee and bread in the headquarters.

Femke and Trijn take the cows that are strong enough into the pastureland, even though the nights are cold and the earth is soaked through. A few of the weaker animals are put in the straw pen. The rest stay in the cubicles in the shippon. And all that time Zwier sits in the headquarters weeping. He's being doing that all night already, all night and all morning, as if he himself has become a leaky milk-tank, and no pat on the hand, no arm around his shoulder, no friendly word can stop that leaking.

Finally, Femke lets Trijn send her to bed. With a weary tread she hauls herself up the stairs, pulls off her clothes, and lets the warm water of the shower clatter down over her. When she creeps under her downie a little later she too can only weep, until she has no more energy left for that, and at last release comes in the form of pitch-black sleep.

November 2017

AFTER THE SLURRY STORE DRAMA huge numbers of people are milling around the farm again. Journalists, film crews, insurance experts, disaster tourists, building contractors and experts come and go. The Koridons are bombarded with contradictory advice. All the visitors have an opinion. Some accuse them of negligence because they didn't evacuate the cows after discovering the leaking slurry store. Journalists keep asking them what they think about it. But they have no answer.

The experts advise them to clear their farm, to take the forty-eight remaining cows elsewhere, and tell them they should go and live in temporary accommodation, in one of the little prefab houses set up at the edge of the village for quake victims, but they're refusing to leave their home and so they're seen as being awkward so-and-sos.

They can't leave, because they're absolutely convinced that leaving will mean the inevitable destruction of Schokland. Fokko's presence reminds them how important it is not to give in. Leaving means betraying their stewardship. They're not like Captain Schettino and Schokland is not their Costa Concordia.

Thanks to their stubbornness they don't have to be cooped inside a prefab, for the time being, and they're allowed to live in a small section of Schokland until further notice. Perhaps they're given this concession because there is no current provision to help businesses that go under because of quake damage, and there's nothing at all to indicate that anyone sees any urgent need to create such a scheme.

Access to the top floor is strictly forbidden. Femke is now sleeping in the front part of the farmhouse, in the parlour, alias kitchen, alias drift mine. Zwier is back in the farmhand's room and Fokko is living in his converted van. They've set up a shower cabin and generator in the farmyard and have moved a bed for Trijn into the Dead Bird Museum. When they shifted it into a corner there, Trijn said to Femke: 'Well, am I in rooms now? Or not?'

They've improvised a deep litter house, in the section of the shippon that hasn't collapsed. New layers of straw are continually having to be put over the cow muck. That means there'll be much more work soon, in the spring, and their daily routine has already gone to pieces, but there's no choice. They're all pale and worn-out. But Femke is more determined than ever.

The day after the disaster Femke and Zwier, both in tears, had watched fifty-two dead bodies being loaded by crane into trucks. They didn't go back to the headquarters until the last one had been taken away. Since then Zwier has been sitting on his chair at the head of the table, without anything to do. He rolls one fag after another and doesn't put any more work into his nail pictures. His breath rasps and wheezes, his back is more and more bent, his head is disappearing between his shoulders. He's subsiding, like old clay.

Trijn is in the headquarters with him. Femke is showing the architect round Schokland. After the slurry store incident he did, in fact, come sooner. Trijn thinks he's a good sort of chap. He drives a normal medium-sized car and he's wearing a pullover and corduroy jacket with elbow patches.

When Femke and the man come in after the inspection, he says, addressing Zwier, that they have a beautiful and very distinctive farm here. Trijn notices he's speaking in the present tense and that moves her.

Zwier nods.

'You're living', the man continues, 'in a farmhouse that is an important element of the cultural heritage of this area.'

'Aye. Right enough.'

Femke nods enthusiastically. Trijn serves the coffee.

'Just suppose,' the architect says thoughtfully, 'that some billionaire comes to the Rijksmuseum and slashes Vermeer's Milkmaid to pieces. What punishment would a judge impose on him?'

No one answers. Femke gives him a questioning look.

'Three hundred and thirty-three billion has been earned by the state and the multinationals from pumping the ground dry. It shouldn't pose any problem at all to repair, restore, and strengthen your farm. It would cost more than demolition, certainly. But damn it! This region is full of really beautiful and distinctive buildings. Farms like yours, magnificent old churches, villages that escaped the flood-wave of modernisation in the sixties. So much beauty. And they're letting it all go to hell.'

They nod quietly.

'I can't look inside your wallets,' the man continues, 'but if you can manage it, I'd say, don't take this lying down.'

'You mean take them to court?'

He nods at Femke.

'It's a long and expensive battle with an uncertain outcome. They have the most expensive lawyers. They'll drag everything out as much as they can. You've got to have plenty of staying power and lots of money.'

'Yes,' says Trijn, 'I'm afraid we can't do that anymore.'

And then, with some shame, because it sounds like betrayal: 'We're finished.'

The man nods. 'That's the biggest outrage of all, that they've killed off your stamina, your ability to resist.'

Now all three of them are looking down in embarrassment, because it's so uncomfortable to be seen as victims, even when someone's on their side. To be seen as people who couldn't cope.

There's no sound of disapproval or disappointment in his voice as he continues to speak, and they're grateful for that.

'They haven't sorted out the new protocols yet. When that's happened, you can probably demand an arbitrator for your case. If he's made of the right kind of stuff, then you'll certainly get a judgement in your favour. But even then, you won't be finished. After that the haggling about payments will start. It's extremely important to do your own homework on this. Don't depend on their contractors. Those people have already come to an arrangement with the riggers and they estimate the structural costs as being much lower than they really are. Employ your own contractor and architect and pay them in advance. And when you know exactly what you need, that's when you should get around the table with the riggers and your own negotiator. Be clear in your minds that you'll never get everything you want, that you have the right to. But set your lower limit and stick to it. Very strictly. That can be scary, but it's absolutely necessary. And it won't be sorted out in a day either. You'll need plenty of staying power.'

'We're so tired,' Trijn slips out.

'Mam,' Femke says, annoyed, and Trijn says: 'Sorry.'

The architect nods. 'I'd really like to be able to do more for you.'

A silence falls. The only sound in the headquarters is Zwier's rasping breathing. Then Fokko pops his head round the door of the shippon and calls out that there's someone for Trijn in the yard. She says goodbye to the architect and goes outside. She sees the impeccable figure of Hessel Sjoerdsma standing there: special investigative officer of the Food and Consumer Products Safety Authority. She sighs. Now this too.

She greets him listlessly and leads him towards the Dead Bird Museum, but then remembers that her bed is there, so she stops in the barn and explains that they can't go into the Dead Bird Museum anymore.

He nods understandingly.

'I've heard about your problems, Ms Koridon,' he says, 'and that's why I wanted to come and tell you about the decision the public prosecutor has made. I thought it was better than sending a letter, which I've also brought, of course, because it's a legal duty to give the decision in writing.'

He waves an envelope.

She leans against the grass mower. 'I really can't take much more.'

He nods again. 'I read about it in the paper. Such a tragedy. Wouldn't it be more sensible, perhaps, to accept temporary accommodation, instead of having to sleep in the barn?'

She wearily shakes her head. 'We don't need any well-meant advice. You really have no idea how many people think they know better than us what we should do.'

He apologises.

'Yes,' she repeats, 'I really can't take any more.'

'I understand that,' he says, 'and that's why I've dropped by. Perhaps I can bring you a little relief. The public prosecutor has decided not to prosecute you and also not to fine you. You've managed to make perfectly clear that you were acting in good faith, that you didn't deliberately break the law, and that you had no commercial intentions.'

'That's a relief,' she says, without any sign of joy. 'Thank you. You must have put together a very nice report.'

He nods. 'That wasn't difficult.'

'And what will happen now?' she asks. 'Will the birds be taken away from here? After the death of fifty-two cows, that's quite likely too.'

'No, no,' he hastens to tell her, 'that's the other good news. Although the birds are state property from now on, you will be allowed to keep them.'

She smiles. 'Thank you very much. That really is very kind. At any other time I'd be very happy about it, I know that for sure.'

She can feel tears welling up. Because there's someone, even though it's just a dull dog like this, who has done his level best for her. She sniffs and wipes the back of her hand over her eyes.

He digs a handkerchief out of his pocket, ironed in knife-sharp folds. She thanks him and wipes her eyes with it, blows her nose, and then hesitates.

'Keep it,' he says, smiling. 'I have plenty of them.'

'Please thank your wife then too,' she says. 'I've never seen such a beautifully ironed handkerchief before.'

'That was done by the laundry,' he confides in her. 'I don't have a wife.'

She offers him her apologies. Then there's an uncomfortable silence.

'I –' she starts saying, hesitantly, and then points to the yard, '– they're waiting for me.'

'Of course,' he says. 'Apologies. You're busy. I do understand. That's why I came to tell you this, then there's at least one thing you don't have to worry about.'

He laughs awkwardly but doesn't make any attempt to leave.

'What I wanted to ask,' he says hesitantly. 'I don't want to embarrass you, but I thought, perhaps –'

He goes quiet again. She looks questioningly at him and then hastens to help him: 'Would you perhaps like to choose a bird for yourself, as a thank you present? That's perfectly fine by me.'

'No, no,' he says, with a shocked gesture. 'Those birds are the property of the state. You're really not allowed to give them away. No, I was wondering, so you can briefly escape from these problems, and do something a little different, if perhaps, well you know, I'd really like to take you out to dinner some time, that's what I thought.'

He screws up his eyes in a painful expression, and frowns.

She gives him a look of incomprehension. 'Excuse me?'

'I thought, a bite to eat? Somewhere? Just once?' He sounds more and more hesitant. 'Or do you think that's inappropriate?'

'Inappropriate?' she asks, thoughtfully, and then continues: 'No, not that. But it's incredibly busy at the moment, and difficult to see what will happen. I really don't know.'

'Of course,' he says. 'I completely understand.'

His face falls and it's silent again for a moment.

And then suddenly, to her own surprise, she says: 'What an incredibly sweet idea. Go out for a meal… yes, I'd really like to do that.'

He looks at her in amazement for a moment, and then his smooth face breaks into a broad grin. They arrange a specific evening. He insists he'll come and pick her up at the farmhouse, and she watches him walk out of the barn. When he's outside and thinks he's out of view, she sees him give a little hop.

*

When were the leaves blown from the trees, when were the berries on the bushes devoured by the redwings? When did the colour vanish from the reedbeds and the harriers fly south?

Drab autumn begins each day with a stubborn mist, a grey veil swamping the land in a white vapour that drips and drops and mizzles and only slowly starts to lift halfway through the morning, when Femke's already been working for hours, and then finally a little bit of light and landscape appears. It's a chilly dampness. She goes into the headquarters and pours coffee for herself and Zwier. He nods a silent thanks. She sits down beside him, shivers a little, and then asks if he misses Klaske too.

He nods. 'And Trudy,' he says.

'And Patch-face,' she adds, 'and Tuesday.'

He nods. And then he says, thoughtfully: 'I do understand it, why people believe in heaven.'

'Are you starting to think that there is one?'

He shakes his head vehemently. 'I wouldn't dream of it. Believing in that sort of thing is just an antibiotic against fear.'

'What are you scared of?'

He shrugs his shoulders and she takes his hand and gently strokes it. She notices how pale he is, how hollow his stubbly cheeks are, and how dark the bags are under his eyes.

'We'll come through this, Grampa,' she promises him.

He nods, but without conviction. She also doesn't know if it's true. The anxiety gnaws at her, especially at night, and then it feels as if insects are scratching around in her bloodstream, because she's so scared that everything is doomed to failure and that they'll still end up on a housing estate somewhere.

She hears a ping.

Hey Blondie, she reads, *I heard about your problems.* Three little kissy faces. And then: *PS The dragon has gone for good.* A raised thumb. A little volcano followed by a question mark.

She looks at it for a long time and then finally texts a thumbs-up back.

No more than that. Then she turns off the sound and stuffs her phone away.

Fokko flings the door open. 'I wanted to ask, have you got any paint brushes?'

'Are you going to paint the van?'

'No. I've got more important things to do.'

She tells him where all the paint stuff is stored in the barn.

'Have you got red paint? Oil paint?'

'Why do you need that?'

He sniggers. 'Just a bit of badgering.'

'Badgering who?'

'Nobody fucks with Fokko.'

'What're you going to do?'

A broad grin. Femke looks at him anxiously.

'Just driving around a bit. Like to come?'

'If you tell me what you're going to do, yes, maybe.'

'You won't regret it,' he says. 'I could do with some help. We need brushes too. And a charged phone, so we've got light.'

Femke thinks about the map and the well-thumbed recipe book. The whole of her body is prickling.

'Is it dangerous?'

'No,' he answers. 'Absolutely not.'

'Okay,' she says. 'I'll come along. When do we leave?'

'After dinner?'

She nods.

'Keep your lips zipped. No one needs to know anything about it.'

'Then you're in luck. Trijn won't be eating here tonight.'

'Where's she going?' Zwier asks.

'I think', Femke answers conspiratorially, 'she's got a date.'

'A date?'

'Some bureaucrat or other has asked her out to dinner.'

'A rigger?' He sounds indignant.

'No,' she says, 'the guy who came about the birds.'

'What the heck would someone see in a bureaucrat?' he grumbles.

'Oh Grampa,' she says, trying to smooth things over. 'It's just a date. That's nice for her, isn't it?'

'That remains to be seen,' he growls, 'especially with a bureaucrat.' And then he focuses on rolling another fag.

*

It's already late when they drive back into the farmyard. Femke turns off the engine and she and Fokko look at each other.

'Well,' Fokko confirms, 'that was fun, wasn't it?'

She chuckles.

'This is just the start,' he says, grinning. 'There'll be laughter tomorrow.'

They go inside the shippon. The light is still on in the head-quarters. Zwier is sitting in his usual spot, at the head of the table.

'So,' he says, 'back from the secret mission.'

It's an observation. He doesn't even sound curious.

Femke nods and walks to the sink, gets a bottle of turpentine and a scrubbing sponge from the cupboard, and scrubs the red paint off her fingers. Meanwhile Fokko has poured three glasses of jenever. They drink in silence until Femke suggests they should tell Zwier what they've been up to, in the hope it will cheer him up. Fokko asks Zwier if he can keep a secret. Zwier stares into the distance.

Fokko gets the map out. He points out all the skull and crossbones he has drawn on it. 'Those are all the rigging locations, here in the north,' he explains. 'Nineteen in all. And we left a message at all of them.'

'What was it?'

Fokko grabs a pen and some paper and scrawls in large letters: FINAL WARNING: LEAVE MY GROUND ALONE. NO MORE RIGGING. And then a kind of signature: THE WORM.

'The Worm?'

'The Worm,' Fokko confirms. 'In the end we all become what we once were.'

'And you've scrawled these words in nineteen different places?' Zwier looks from one to the other with a frown. They nod.

'In red oil paint,' Fokko says with satisfaction. 'They won't easily get that off. They'll have to hire a cleaning company to do that.'

'And now?'

'And now we wait and see.'

'What are you waiting for then?'

Zwier doesn't sound very enthusiastic. 'Do you really think they'll stop, because some worm or other', he says the word with scorn, 'has made a few threats?'

'No, I don't think that.'

'Threats only make sense if you carry them out.'

'That's right,' Fokko says.

Zwier gives him a questioning look.

'If they don't stop, The Worm will take action.'

'And what will The Worm do then? Is he going to play around with paint again?'

'No,' Fokko says, and his eyes are flaming, 'those who won't hear will have to heed.'

'So?' Zwier asks with increasing agitation.

'No info', Fokko jokes, 'from the management as yet –'

Zwier shoots up like lightning and hammers his fist on the table. The glasses wobble. He yells with greater fury than Femke has ever seen from him before: 'We're trying to bloody well keep our farming business afloat. I don't want any illegal activities going on here. Understood?!'

Fokko looks at him in shock. Femke stands up and puts her arm around Zwier, and hushes him. 'Calm down Grampa. We've just daubed a bit of paint around. He won't do anything else, right Fokko?'

Fokko doesn't answer.

Femke repeats: 'Fokko, it won't go any further than this, right? You're not going to do anything dangerous, are you?'

He shakes his head, without saying anything at all. Zwier sits down again, limply.

But there's a new energy burning in Femke, and she remembers how wonderful it felt to be doing something, however simple and innocent it might be, after all those moments when she was consumed by powerlessness, as if she was just one of the fallen apples under the trees in the garden that the fieldfares devour.

*

The three of them are sitting in the headquarters. Zwier, with his head bowed, is looking thoughtfully at his broad hands. His coal shovels, as he used to call them, are deeply grooved and grimy, as if the earth and his hands have become one.

Trijn asks him whether he wouldn't perhaps like to work on one of his nail plaques, because although the hammering irritates her, her alarm at his apathy is stronger. He listlessly shakes his head. She is busy composing a letter to the insurance people, in which she is protesting about the fact that they've been told to contact the riggers about the damage to the cow-stalls and the livestock. What have they spent years paying out a fortune in insurance premiums for?

Femke pours out the coffee and asks how her date went. Trijn smiles.

'The restaurant had ochre walls and ornate plaster-work and chandeliers. There were damask tablecloths on the tables, and napkins, and different kinds of wineglass, and tall candles in silver candlesticks.'

'Was it nice?' Femke asks.

'It was the most delicious meal I've ever had,' Trijn continues. 'It was a set menu. You just got what you were given. I found that a bit strange. But it wasn't a problem. We had a little Parmesan cheese quiche, followed by ravioli with pumpkin and pork sausage, nicely arranged on the plate like a work of art, and I thought the meal was over, but then the main course came, and then cheesecake and limoncello. And coffee and chocolates.'

'But was it nice?'

'The craziest thing was that he didn't just order a bottle of wine, but a complete selection. They serve you a different wine for every single course. Really unusual.'

'But was it nice, I mean with him, with that man?'

Trijn is silent for a moment.

'Yes,' she then says. 'You wouldn't expect it. He looks so impeccable, so boring really. But he's much more fun than you'd think.'

It almost sounds as if she is apologising and perhaps she is. Hessel Sjoerdsma has nothing at all in common with her Harlequin Romance dream heroes, her knights in shining armour.

His courtesy had surprised her. He held the door open for her, helped her take off her coat, and pulled up her chair for her. No one had ever been so attentive with her before.

Once they were seated he asked her, without any beating around the bush, about her daughter's father, and that was also something no one had ever done before. On the rare occasions she'd had to answer such a question, she always said that she and Femke's father had split up when Femke was still very young, but she couldn't get away with that now. He wanted to know if there was still any contact between them and whether Femke perhaps might need that.

'Of course not,' she answered firmly, and then he gave her a questioning look.

She corrected herself, feeling a bit uncomfortable. 'I don't really know. Femke and I never talk about it.' And then she confessed that she hadn't simply left the father, but that she'd fled from him.

'I'm so sorry,' he said, and he carefully put his hand on hers and cautiously stroked it, and she remembered when Femke had been about eight and Zwier and Femke and she were working in the byre. She'd heard Femke asking why she didn't have a father.

'People sometimes swap things,' Zwier had answered. 'Marbles, Wuppies, or one heifer for two bull calves. And your mammy has swapped your daddy for Ootje and me.'

Hessel listened attentively while she recounted this memory. She was surprised it had suddenly surfaced. He stopped stroking, but kept his hand on hers. It was a clean, warm hand. Stronger than you'd expect for a brainworker like that.

'But why?' Femke had asked. 'Why did she swap my daddy?'

Trijn had stopped forking the hay and watched her delicate little daughter who was looking up at her Grampa with a frown.

'Because', was his answer, 'your father couldn't look after you.'

'But isn't that sad for him?' Femke persisted. 'Doesn't he miss me?'

Trijn wouldn't have had any idea how to answer that, but Zwier said calmly that it wasn't sad at all. He pointed to the cows in the shed: 'All the baby calves are taken away from their mammies after they're born. And are those mothers sad?'

'Perhaps,' she said doubtfully.

'Yes,' he concluded, 'for a short time, but it doesn't last long. And that's how it is for your daddy.'

Hessel kept looking straight at her, his hand still on hers. Not uncomfortably, but it was unusual.

'But,' he asked, 'haven't you spoken to her about her father yourself?'

'Once,' she says, 'when Femke was studying at the agricultural college, she asked me to tell her something about him. And I said: "You have no father. I made a mistake when I was still a girl and I spent some time living with a feller I really should have kept my distance from. He impregnated me and you were conceived. But you've got nothing else to do with him. And you should be pleased about that."

"But I do have his genes," Femke pointed out.

And then I told her there was nothing in her that was at all like him, thank God.

"Your bloodline is one hundred percent Koridon," I told her. And then we never spoke about him again.'

Hessel nodded thoughtfully. 'That makes her an extremely unusual person,' he said, and raised his glass to toast the Koridon bloodline. Then he tucked into his main course with gusto, a dish of pork belly and pancetta.

She asked if he'd ever been in a relationship with anyone.

'Not a soul,' he answered. 'I was tied to my mother's apron for far too long,' he explained, a little embarrassed. 'I looked after her for years. She died two years ago. Love', and he spoke this word with some exaggeration, 'didn't get a look-in, with that kind of life.'

They toasted each other again, with a new glass of wine from the wine-pairing.

At the end of the evening he brought her back home and after he stopped the car in the farmyard he asked if they could see each other again some time.

'That's fine,' she answered, and for a moment it looked as if they were going to kiss. Their heads slowly drew together, but almost as a kind of reflex she drew back and gave him her hand, which he kissed passionately, and then she got out of the car, her heart thudding, and waved goodbye while he drove off up the lonning.

But she didn't say anything about all of this. She doesn't reveal anything more to Femke than: 'He's much more fun than you'd think.'

'And are the two of you going to see each other again?'

'Who knows,' she says blandly and then they fall silent, because on the radio they're saying that threats have been graffitied in nineteen rigging locations.

Femke pricks up her ears and Zwier also raises his head. Trijn looks from one to the other. The newsreader says that all the threats have been signed by The Worm and that phrase makes Trijn peek back in time: she sees a group of young people round the fire basket in the Wide World's farmyard, listening to the amazing adventures of Fokko in Siberia – the worm who bores down into the sludge, looking for black gold. The era of exploding tennis balls and stories about unquenchable thermite fire. Trijn looks questioningly at Femke, who leaps up and calls for Fokko.

He comes into the headquarters while the police spokesman is speaking and several glances flash between Femke and Fokko and Zwier. Trijn asks what's going on.

'Nothing,' Fokko says and looks aside a little bashfully, and then: 'Just a bit of badgering. Nothing more.'

'Are you sure?'

He nods.

'Because that's one extra thing we can't have, any illegal nonsense.'

And she asks Femke: 'What have you got to do with this?'

Femke looks her straight in the eye. 'I'm an adult, Mam.' And then: 'I think I'd rather be a worm than a victim.'

She can't hold it in anymore and bursts out laughing. Fokko chuckles and then Trijn can't help joining in too. Only Zwier is sitting in his own spot, all hunched up and sighing.

'The Worm,' Trijn laughs. 'How did you come up with that? But I'd completely forgotten, Fokko, that you were a rigger too, pumping oil up from the ground.'

'I hadn't.'

'What now?'

'Now we wait and see.'

Zwier slowly shakes his head, staring at his open hands.

'What's wrong, Dad?'

There are tears in his eyes.

'Do you still remember it?' he asks. 'The Accident?'

'Yes,' Trijn says curtly, 'I remember.'

'If I hadn't –'

'Dad,' she says sternly, 'it was an accident. Don't talk about it.'

He shakes his head.

'It shouldn't have happened. If I –'

'Dad,' Trijn says, and it annoys her that her voice breaks, 'don't.'

He looks at her. 'You were just a child still. You couldn't see the full picture. But I should have known better.'

Trijn suddenly starts crying, and she's furious about it. She gulps and sniffs and then hisses: 'Stop it, Dad, stop talking about it.'

Fokko and Femke look silently from one to the other.

Zwier gazes at his big hands again, as dark as the earth itself. And then he straightens himself and looks directly at Trijn. And he says in a frail voice: 'Do you think that Jort would have managed it?'

'That Jort would have managed what?'

'Saving Schokland?'

Trijn's cheeks go bright red. Her eyes spit fire.

'Dad,' she says, sputtering with annoyance, 'we're doing everything we can. You, Femke, all of us.'

'I think Jort might have managed it,' he continues, 'but we'll never know.'

'Jort is dead, Dad,' she says, 'and he's been dead now for twenty-seven years. Because of an accident, not because it was anyone's fault.'

He nods and softly repeats: 'Yes, Jort is dead.'

In the meantime, the weather report is being read out on the radio. More fog, rain and night frost are coming.

*

Good with animals and awkward with people, clumsy with words, a born farmer, too soft for normal life, these are the typical things that are said of Femke, the way she is described by her mother and those few others who think they know her.

And then she became a victim too, although she has always resisted that term. She associates that word with the musk-rat. Such a wretched creature, although it's one that digs the dykes to pieces, a wee beastie that patters into a deadly trap via a friendly-looking little house floating on the maar, and then drowns in a cage full of water before it can even take a bite of the apple, in a slow, horrifying death-struggle.

But not every rat lets itself be trapped, and some manage to somehow fight their way out while they're thrashing around in the cage.

She's like that too. She's helped by her increasing fury. Fury at the failure to recognise the problem. Fury because the Centre from Here to Nowhere, set up only two years ago to help the victims, has earned millions by not helping them. Fury about the indifference overshadowing the land like a gloomy sky. The more fury she feels, the greater her determination never to be a drowning muskrat.

What her evening with Fokko has most given her is the discovery of how much energy you get from doing something, rather than slowly drowning.

Femke has mucked out the shippon and given the cows their feed. She has seen to Allie, who'll be calving at any point now, and she's on her way back to the headquarters. Zwier has started a new nail picture.

He doesn't look up when she comes in. She fills the kettle with water and hears a ping.

Hey Blondie. I miss you. Three hearts.

Too late, she thinks.

She puts a tea bag in the teapot, pours boiling water onto it, cuts a couple of slices of gingerbread, spreads them with butter, and puts them onto the table.

Her phone pings again: *I really miss you. I'm not joking.* A couple of kissy lips.

She allows herself to send back a thumbs-up, but she won't give her any more than that.

Zwier seems to be making a kind of a snake, shaped in a big S-shaped curve. That's what she thinks at least.

Another ping. Zwier looks up and shakes his head.

'Don't let her drive you round the bend,' he says. It's not a warning, but an order.

'No, don't worry,' she replies. 'I don't let her do that anymore.'

She shuts the text message app, puts her phone on silent, and asks him if they ever had their own bulls, before land consolidation, when they were still a mixed farm.

'Of course,' he says, frowning, because he's trying to remember. 'Back then,' he says, 'we used to breed them. But we only had bulls from cows that survived in really difficult conditions. Only from the very strongest.'

'So what did you do to the others then?'

He makes a gesture with the flat of his hand, like a knife cutting a throat.

'What would you think,' she continues, 'if I started a soil-based sort of farm, when we finally get out of this mess I mean, with a family herd and cows that calve in the spring, what would you say to that?'

He looks at her for the first time in ages. She sees his dark blue eyes under his grey bushy eyebrows, old eyes, with red rims and little black pupils, which could flash fierce sparks in the past, and which are now dull and weary. His face is furrowed. His skin is like crumpled paper.

'Would you really like that, a family herd?' he asks, and she asks him if that's something he'd mind.

'As long as you've got this awful state of affairs here, then it's madness to think of it.'

She notices that he's no longer talking about "we". As if he's said farewell to Schokland. As if they've already lost it.

And after a short silence he continues in a flat tone of voice: 'You need to realise it'll take a long time before you've got a herd that's fit for that. Your income will plummet. You've got to select strong calves to breed from. Everything with diarrhoea has to be chucked. Every cow in heat at the wrong time has to go. You've got to want that. You've got to be able to do it.'

He makes that gesture again, slicing his hand across his throat. A callous sign.

'Yes,' she says eagerly. 'The best breeders are the biggest killers.'

'You never liked that,' he says. 'You always wanted to save all the animals.'

'That's right,' she says, 'but for a new and healthy farming business difficult choices have to be made. I understand that now.'

'Aye. Right enough,' he says. She doesn't know this is the last time she'll hear him say that.

She wishes, she thinks later, that she'd asked him how he was feeling, that afternoon. Perhaps then he'd have let something slip that might have alerted her. There must have been signs, after all. Or perhaps not? Can a heart really give up from one moment to the next. Without him having noticed anything at all?

In the evening they all retreat to their own spots, as they often do: Trijn to the Dead Bird Museum, Zwier to the headquarters, Fokko to his little van, which he's taken away from the farmyard and has parked some distance away, by the side of the lonning. As if he's already begun to leave them. He's fiercely tinkering away there. Trijn warns him time and again that she doesn't want any illegal business going on and then he shakes his head and swiftly disappears into his van. And Femke recalls the old book with its recipes for explosives, but she doesn't know how to reveal her suspicion that he's up to something fishy, without giving away that she was nosing around in his stuff.

In the mine passage Femke is working on a plan for the farm, for the umpteenth night in a row, so that when the riggers are finally finished with their protocoleering, when the arbitrator comes and it's acknowledged that it's quake damage and that it must be compensated, she can shove her business plan under their noses and the reinforcing, repairing and restoration work can begin. After which she can start her soil-based, organic dairy farming. At least, that's what she hopes. That's what she promises herself.

Before going to bed she pops into the headquarters to say good night to Zwier, as she does every night. As she comes in he puts a newspaper over the nail plaque. She asks him if he's making a surprise for them. He shrugs his shoulders and mutters that he wouldn't call it that. She would really have liked to ask him more about it – he's never hidden one of his nail pictures before – but she knows how awful it feels when Trijn tries to worm her secrets out of her, and so she asks him no further questions and kisses him on the cheek. He takes her head in his hands, those hands that smell of earth and shag tobacco and smoke, and he kisses her forehead and says: 'Sleep well, darling,' as he does every night.

*

Later she asks herself how come there are so many computer apps that can tell you what the cell count of the milk is, if there's a threat of mastitis, or when a cow is on heat, but that there's no contraption to warn you if the person who is perhaps dearest of all to you is in danger, because his heart is too weary and too goaded. An app that makes an alarm bell sound, so you know: someone has to be saved.

It's the middle of the night. Femke has set her alarm so she can check on Allie, and before she goes into the shippon she pops into the headquarters, where the light is still on, to get her work gloves.

Zwier is there, his hands folded under his head, leaning against the nail plaque. As if he's asleep. She gently calls him, lays her hand on his shoulder, then on his cheek, and only when she feels his skin, far too cold, does she feel alarmed. She takes his wrist and searches for a soft pulse and can't find it, and she rings the emergency service number and Trijn, and screams into her phone; and then she puts him on the ground and does what she once learned how to do, she blows her warm breath into his cold body, she pushes down on his chest to press life into him until Trijn and Fokko and the paramedics are there and a machine takes over from her and only after quite some time has passed do they give up. Zwier Koridon, the true father of Schokland, is dead.

And it's not a snake that's been nailed onto his last plaque. For once he has tried to put into words the guilt he has dragged along with him for half his life – he has hammered out his message in little nails, all of the same size, nicely smoothed and shiny, but his heart stopped before he was finished. And so his last nail picture is the unfinished penance of a man who did everything he could to please the people he cared about. Who could forgive everyone's errors, except his own. On his last nail picture, written in nail-letters, it says: SORRY JOR–

December 2017

THEY'VE HAD TWO HUNDRED EXTRA mourning cards printed, cream-coloured, with deckled edges. The card and the death notice have created quite a stir, because not only did they announce an unexpected death, but they were unmistakeably a protest. Femke was against it, but Trijn got her way.

It was made impossible for a good steward to fulfil his duties. Zwier Koridon died from sheer indifference. He was sixty-eight. We miss him greatly.

Trijn looked up the names and addresses of all the board members and commissioners and a number of politicians in their uncracked dwellings, wrote the labels, stuck on the special dark-grey stamps, and brought the box full of mourning cards to the sub post office counter in the village supermarket.

She's been wondering if her comments about Jort had perhaps hurt her father more than she'd realised. But she doesn't want to think about it too much. One of the things she's finding painful is that it was Femke, of all people, who found him. He was far more than a grandfather for her.

And when Trijn had the chance to look at the unfinished nail plaque, on which, for once, Zwier had tried to put into words the unutterable thought that must so often have plagued him, she wondered if he'd realised that his 'Sorry' was the same word she'd used twenty-two years ago, in her scribbled goodbye note, left in his tobacco pouch on the selfsame table.

*

On the dull grey morning after that calamitous night they laid Zwier on his bed in the farmhand's room with the undertaker's help, and Femke and Trijn dressed him in his corduroy trousers and best guernsey. They combed his untidy grey hair a little, but not too neatly, and wondered what they should put on his feet. His smart shoes, which he hardly ever wore, his clogs, or his wellington boots? Femke chose the wellingtons. Once the undertaker left, Femke sat by the bed and started to cry.

Trijn would like to feel sorrow, but only fury rages inside her. She can't free herself from the thought that the only reason she has lost both her parents is the hopeless situation that Schokland is in.

Every day the post box is full of letters of condolence praising her father to high heaven. Even Spotty-tie has sent a card, expressing his sorrow and saying he wishes he had been able to do more for them. Nice words don't cost a thing, Trijn thinks, adding a 'right enough' to the thought.

She has also received a small parcel. It contained a dark-green cardboard box, with a golden border, and there were three men's cotton handkerchiefs inside it, red, brown and green, with a watered pattern, and a little note: WITH SYMPATHY, HESSEL. As she held the chic little box in her hands and read his message, for a brief moment sorrow did overcome her anger. She fluttered the red handkerchief open and dabbed her eyes with the soft, fine cotton.

*

After the well-attended funeral service, they gather together in the headquarters. Fokko, Femke and Trijn. They've swapped their smart clothes for their usual thick sweaters and overalls. Even when they're mourning there's still milking to do, feed to give out, calves being born, and things to clean.

They're sitting round the cleared table. No piles of nails and no more hammers. All the nail pictures have now been placed in the old byre. Femke put Zwier's tobacco pouch in the coffin with him.

Every now and then they secretly peek at the empty place at the head of the table. Trijn and Femke have a mug of tea in front of them. Fokko has poured himself a large glass of jenever.

Trijn and Fokko are talking about all the people who came to the funeral: the farmers and farming women from the area, the people who took part in the Nest Protest, the people living in the village, the former contract workers and suppliers, people who'd been on work placement, all the people who come by during a lifetime, even if you live in a sea of clay, two kilometres down a concrete track.

When Brian came into the auditorium he flew into Femke's arms, weeping. He kissed her on both cheeks and called out: 'Sun always comes after showers.' The tears trickled down his cheeks. His mother pulled him along to a bench at the back of the hall.

Fokko compliments Trijn on her speech. It was more a furious indictment than a eulogy. She spoke about a war of despoliation, continual plundering, increasing affluence and cold indifference.

'Zwier Koridon, our beloved father and grandfather, died because of years of official neglect. Because of the indifference of the gas companies and the government to our fate. Not a single speck of hope remained in him. After that kind of despair there's nothing left but death.'

That's how she finished her speech. Some of the people there had nodded in agreement and a muttered 'right enough' could be heard from different parts of the hall, a mark of respect that sounded like the 'amen' of a prayer. Others looked down, embarrassed.

Trijn also compliments Fokko who played the guitar and sang the well-known song by Ede Staal, a world-famous troubadour, in these parts at least. He had altered only one word of the text. By adding the word 'cursed' to what was originally an ode to their region, the song had become much grimmer: *Until the night of this cursed land lays a black cloth over us*. And when the last note had died away Fokko said into the microphone: 'They'll have to pay the penalty one day, I promise him that.' He nodded at the coffin.

The words echoed threateningly in the silence that followed. The undertaker's footsteps tapped on the tiled floor as she stepped decisively forward to announce the final piece of music and the end of the gathering. But suddenly Femke stood up, in her unusually smart clothes, her dark trousers with their sharp creases, the shirt and the little black jacket, her blonde hair in a tight, severe ponytail, her mouth a thin line. Her cheeks were pale. She walked to the lectern with her head held high. The undertaker made a sign to the man at the control board and Femke took a piece of paper from her jacket pocket, unfolded it, and looked into the hall. Her gaze crossed Trijn's. Then she turned to face the coffin, on which their bouquet had been placed, a meagre version of a wildflower bouquet, impossible to make in this chilly winter month. And then she read out a poem in a soft but steady voice.

'Who wrote that poem?' Trijn asks.

'She did,' Fokko says. 'That was obvious, wasn't it?'

Femke nods, without looking at her mother. Trijn asks if she'd like to read it to them again. Femke shakes her head. Trijn insists, and then Femke takes a piece of paper from her pocket and gives it to her mother. Trijn quietly mutters out the words.

If I could make the reedbeds blossom
and turn the cloudy skies to bright,
if I could change the rain to sunshine
and make the sun's fire burn at night,
if I could make the stiff clay crumble
and make volcanoes laugh in joy,
if I could set the swallows dancing
I'd hold you tight, you wouldn't die.

You taught me how to see in darkness
and helped me hear how silence sounds.

You showed me how to read the skyscapes
and when the wind sings rainy songs.
Because of you I love the fire
that crackles in the stove at home.
Because of all the tales you told me
I love the creatures on our land.
Because of you I grew to realise
that love and care go hand in hand.
I would have liked to walk beside you
for far more years than I can count,
if everything could only be
safe and certain once again.
I promise you that we'll look after
the farm you've left us to defend.
I promise you that your life's ending
will never be Schokland's end.

Trijn swallows. 'That's a beautiful promise.'

She sighs. And then it's silent.

Fokko taps his foot on the floor, an angry rhythm.

'It's a beautiful aspiration,' he then says, his voice sounding tense, 'but to achieve it something really does have to happen. Your mother was right with her words about war. It's high time to –'

'Fokko,' Femke begs. 'Please. Not now.'

Then they hear a car draw up in the yard outside and race off, its tyres squealing.

Fokko leaps up and runs out, and Trijn and Femke watch him through the window and see him walk back into the shippon with a big cardboard box in his hands. He puts it on the table.

FOR FEMKE it says, in curly felt-tipped letters.

She stares at it a moment, suspiciously. Pushes it back and forth. Something is moving inside it and there's a soft whining sound.

'Open it,' Trijn insists.

Femke is doubtful, hesitates a moment, opens the cardboard lid, and then the velvety-black snout of a puppy appears. She lifts the little dog out. It has long floppy ears and dark eyes, and is dappled like a Holstein cow. She takes it onto her lap. The small, furry creature whines and wags its tail. Femke strokes it and examines the soft little head and bites her lip, and Trijn points at the red collar which has a little copper-coloured canister hanging from it. Femke worms out a tiny note and reads it in silence. Trijn can't control her curiosity and asks her what it says.

'It's a present from Danielle,' Femke says without looking up. 'To comfort me. She's called Bayo.'

And then she begins to weep and the little creature sniffs at her face and that makes her laugh, and then she laughs and cries in turns and Trijn wipes a few tears from her own cheeks. For once, Trijn thinks, that flibbertigibbet has done something right. And she wishes she'd thought of giving Femke the only gift that can cheer her up a little now.

*

Femke leaves the headquarters with the puppy in her hands. She puts on her bodywarmer over Zwier's old guernsey, which she's worn since that awful Thursday. There are holes in the elbows and the cuffs are tattered. They weren't ever repaired after Ootje's death, but that didn't bother him any more than it does her now. There's still a trace of his earthy odour in the stitches. It's strange, really, she thinks, that his smell is still here when he isn't. When someone's dead everything eventually disappears. What someone sounded like, how he felt, and what effect he had on her. An heir has the duty to keep the memories alive, like a stiff cervical collar holds a broken neck in place.

She puts on her woolly hat and fingerless gloves. It's icy cold.

A hard frost has set in since the day she lost Zwier.

In the barn she looks for something to use as a leash. The puppy is wagging its tail. She knots a piece of rope round its collar and walks onto the land, across the rock-hard clay and white rime. The puppy is making funny little gambols with its short little legs. Its tail wags unceasingly. It keeps looking up at her, joyfully and full of expectation.

She steps out along the maar which has a film of ice on it. The wind scours her cheeks, roughened by the salt of the past days. It's really too cold to sit outside, but she has to be alone a while and she sits down on the remains of Siepke's Sleepstead. Nothing is left of it other than a pile of icy bricks and fragments of corrugated iron. Another beacon in the landscape shaken into ruins. It had long been neglected, but it was once a handsome sheep barn. Why is it, she thinks, that in this world the only things that get protected are things you can make money from?

She again reads the mini letters in which Danielle has printed her message: A LITTLE DOG FOR FEMKE, TO CHEER HER UP. HER NAME IS BAYO. KISSES, YOUR DANNI. And below that: PS, I'M TURNING ROUND, LIKE A FEARLESS DUCK.

The tears start flowing again and the puppy sniffs and licks herself silly.

Don't let her drive you round the bend.

She takes her phone from the inner pocket of her bodywarmer and texts: *Thanks for Bayo*. She takes a photo of the puppy and sends it with the message, tickles Bayo behind her ears, and Bayo tries to bite her hand. Then there's the sound of a little ping.

Do you know what her name means? Three question marks.

Then a second ping: *Joy is Found, in the Yoruba language*. Three thumbs-up.

She shivers.

Don't let her drive you round the bend. She really mustn't forget that.

It's thirty-five days now since Danielle walked away. '*I'm not afraid of anything.*'

It's a hundred and nine days since they last lay in each other's arms.

Another ping.

I'm sorry. A row of hearts and kisses.

Don't let her drive you round the bend.

Bayo is wagging her tail. While she scratches her behind the ears, she looks at the broad landscape and sees a grubby plain, terrifyingly empty, grey-white with rime and hardened by frost, with gigantic dark clouds above it, so immense that everything here on the clay soil below, trees, ditches and farmhouse roofs, seems small and insignificant. She remembers her fear that one day the clouds would fall down. Perhaps, she thinks, the clouds are already falling, perhaps all that time I've been afraid about something that's already happening. Immediately after this thought hailstones clatter down, hurled onto the land with a furious force. Bayo whimpers, creeps close to her, sheltering from the vicious balls of ice. She stands up, tucks the little creature under her bodywarmer, bows her head, and walks back along the maar into the wind and hail. The soft warmth of the puppy's nose against her chin makes her feel tender and confused.

The best breeders are the biggest killers. Would she have noticed more if she hadn't been so angry? Did she miss signals from her Grampa? Could she and should she have known there was something wrong with his heart, in spite of his battery of tablets? Should she have warned a doctor? Could she have prevented his death? Drenched through she steps into the shippon and shivers. She's cold to the marrow.

*

No, he isn't disturbing her. It's nice of him to call. And of course Trijn isn't annoyed that he wasn't at the funeral. She really values it, that kind handkerchief gesture of his, and in one sense he was present, in the form of those cotton hankies, which she certainly made good use of. Yes, she'd like to eat out with him again, but this time they'll go to the Chinese in the village. They have the best spring rolls. The wine is terrible but there's nothing wrong with the beer. And she'll pay.

He laughs and says that the only thing he can do is yield to her demands. They agree to go out the next evening.

He's already sitting there. They give each other three kisses on the cheek in greeting. He's wearing corduroy trousers and a light blue shirt with a dark blue sweater over it, unmistakeably the casual clothing of a civil servant. She's dressed in a simple black dress. She's put a little make-up on her eyes and is wearing some lipstick. Femke gave a wolf-whistle when she came into the headquarters to say goodbye.

He puts both his arms round her as they greet each other, looks at her with a beaming face, corrects himself, composes his features, offers her his condolences, before pulling out a chair for her, and they sit down in the otherwise empty restaurant, among the red lanterns with their yellowy-golden fringes and behind the aquarium where neon-coloured fish swim round and round without any goal. The aquarium forms the barrier between themselves and the Chinese family killing time at a table at the back of the restaurant. They order spring rolls and an Indonesian *rijsttafel*. Beer is brought to the table. They toast each other and he says he finds her father's death really sad.

'Yes,' she says, 'it's a big shock. It's so unexpected.' And no, she doesn't mind talking about it. After all, it goes round and round in her head all the time, especially the fury.

'Fury?' He sounds surprised. 'At him?'

'No,' she says, 'at the riggers, of course. They really do have his death on their consciences. Just like that of my mother, nearly three years ago.'

At that point the spring rolls are served. They're still piping hot, and so there's a lot of blowing at them and careful testing, and then he agrees with her that these are the best spring rolls he's ever tasted.

'What do you mean,' he asks hesitantly, 'that the riggers – it was a heart attack, wasn't it?'

While the hotplates are put on the table and a train of children, guided by their mother, brings the various dishes, Trijn bursts out in a tirade against riggers, bureaucrats, the government, and general indifference. Until she sees that the waitress is waiting for her to pause, so she can explain the different dishes to them. She listens politely and, when the waitress has gone to the back of the room with their order for more beer, they serve the food to each other and start eating.

'I've been working for the state for thirty years now and I know, better than many, that we do make terrible mistakes. That the interests of the individual are often set aside in the interest of the country.'

'It's not in the interest of the country,' Trijn snaps back. 'That's exactly the problem. It's to do with the interests of a couple of multinationals. They're the ones ruling the roost here.'

He nods calmly. 'Yes,' he says, 'but put yourself in the position of the government. You people say: stop pumping the ground dry, and then you go to your thermostats and set them at a higher temperature. That stuff has to come from somewhere.'

'I didn't mention 'stopping'. I'm talking about giving compensation for what has been destroyed. An honest compensation, which does justice to the damage they've caused. Instead of having to sit in the waiting room for years. And what do you think the accusation of poor maintenance did to my father and mother?'

He nods again and gives a light smile.

'That unjustified feeling of guilt was the death-blow, the stab in the back for both of them. I call that murder.'

And to her fury she can't hold back her tears. She weeps. She can't stop herself anymore. She stammers out, between her sobs: 'My father gave up the ghost because he couldn't bear the weight any longer. Like with a rafter.'

The family sitting at the table at the back peeks at them through the aquarium water, trying to catch something of the drama playing out in their normally quiet restaurant.

He takes her hand. She pulls it away, irritated by his kind understanding.

'What do you know about it? What have you had to suffer?'

He lowers his eyes, a moment, then looks straight at her and says: 'I was ten years old when I found my father's body.' And then his eyes drift down to his plate again. Her cheeks go red.

'Sorry,' she says softly. 'I didn't know that.'

'No,' he answers. 'You couldn't have known it either. I don't find it easy to talk about.'

Now she's the one who hesitantly puts her hand on his and carefully strokes it while the tears gently drip from her cheeks onto the plate.

'Was it his heart too?'

He shakes his head. 'He hanged himself in the attic room. Next to our Meccano train set. He'd just bought me a new loco-motive and tender.'

She keeps quiet but presses her hand more firmly on his. He carries on talking, without looking at her, tonelessly: 'It took me a long time to realise it wasn't my fault. That my father thought he wasn't good enough. Not that that really was the case.'

'But why did he think that?' she asks.

'Oh,' he says, 'it's so long ago. He'd reported an irregularity at the company where he was working. And it wasn't appreciated.

Not by his employer, not by the state, and not by my mother.'

'Is that the reason you carried on living at home so long, then?'

He nods. 'She could be quite intimidating.'

He rubs his eyes.

'The meal will be a bit saltier than usual,' he jokes. And then: 'And I was planning to suggest something to cheer you up.'

'That will have to be a bloody good suggestion, then,' she replies.

'It is.' He smiles and carries on eating, as if he hasn't just made her feel incredibly curious, and he doesn't seem to notice her restlessness, but thoughtfully chews his *babi pangang* and says nothing.

'So,' she can't control herself any longer. 'What is it?'

He raises his head and gives a broad smile that shows his even teeth. Then he slowly stands up and walks with a spring in his step to the coat stand. The waitress stands up and asks if she should bring the bill. He shakes his head. Another beer perhaps? He looks briefly round at Trijn and she nods.

Then he places an envelope in front of her. 'You can open it.'

She opens the envelope with a knife she's cleaned on a napkin and takes out two train tickets. To Paris. A voucher for a hotel on the Place des Vosges. And a coloured postcard of the shop whose yellowing photograph has been pinned to the wall in her Dead Bird Museum for nearly thirty years.

She looks doubtfully up at him.

'Don't worry,' he says. 'I've booked two rooms.'

And then she starts beaming. She takes his head in both her hands and kisses him full on the lips.

The Chinese family tries to follow as much of this unusual scene as they can, through the sauntering fishes. Closing time is long gone.

*

It's growing light. Femke is standing in the yard with a mug of coffee, dressed in thick clothing, looking out over the land. Greyish blue clouds tower up into the sky from the horizon. The earth is white with hoar frost. The strips of land stretch out in taut strands, like an exercise in geometric forms in which you're only allowed to make a sparing use of colour: a vague tint of light green, an indefinite brown and beige. The reed plumes are lumpy with white ice-crystals.

The deep clay furrows look like a miniature mountain range, the tops covered in snow, the brown sides impassable steep slopes. The soil recently dredged from the maar, dumped onto the land by the contractor, lies beside the bank like a black trail of lava. Two crows are irritably stalking back and forth, sometimes pecking at the frozen clods.

Bayo is sniffing around the farmyard, occasionally leaping up at her. She sends Danielle a photo every day. Bayo with a slipper. Bayo next to a cow. Bayo growling at Fokko. Bayo in her basket in the headquarters, which is still the only place that can be properly kept warm.

Every day Danielle sends her a photo back: the shippon and the loader; the place on the dyke where they first lay together in the summer; an empty bed; the utility room with a bottle of beer lying smashed on the ground; and under every photo there's a caption: *do you remember?* And after that there's always a picture of her open front door, with the doormat that says *Welcome*.

How can she know if Danielle really has changed? That it isn't just that she only wants her for as long as she's unreachable?

Sometimes, when she's almost at the point of getting into the car to drive to the sea dyke, she thinks back to what it felt like to be sent away. Because clearly the intimacy they'd just shared had to be immediately wiped out.

Don't let her drive you round the bend.

The sun appears. The thick grey layer of clouds turns light

blue. Above it there are pale pink tatters of cloud, like veils in the sky. The earth is buried under a white layer of coldness and glazed frost. The ever-brightening rosy sky doesn't alter that at all.

She thinks about the visitors they had yesterday and while something crunches inside her, like the sole of a shoe stepping on shards of glass, she wonders if Zwier might still perhaps be sitting at his place at the head of the table if the arbitrator had come a month earlier. Or did the man come precisely because Zwier's heart had given up? Perhaps the mourning cards her mother sent out did indeed signal to the people in that office-bunker that, for once, someone had to do something? Did Zwier manage to achieve with his death what all those years in the waiting room and fifty-two dead cows couldn't?

The fact is that yesterday they had a visit from the arbitrator and two aides. One of the aides had the job of taking photos, the other made notes on everything that was discussed. The arbitrator was independent, by his own account, and at any rate the three men took plenty of time to listen to them, without any obvious bias. The men worked their way through the drift mine with them, the forbidden kitchen and the rooms upstairs, through the farm buildings and across the farmyard. The arbitrator displayed understanding for the fact that during the past five years it had been very complicated to decide what maintenance work should or shouldn't be done on your crumbling farm. That it's not a sign of bad management.

The arbitrator and his aides were visibly shocked by what remained of the once proud shippon and by all the improvisation they've been forced to carry out since then. Forty-eight cows in less than half of the shippon, with no access to slurry stores: a deep litter house in a space intended as a free-stall barn.

When they were warming themselves up in the headquarters, Femke imagined Zwier sitting in his usual spot and him seeing that they'd finally come, and that they empathised with them, and that these chaps could perhaps sort out things for them, so that an end would finally come to their life in suspended mode.

Sunlight falls across the land. The day is getting ready for a little warmth. The cold is retreating into the hollows of the earth, under the film of ice on the ditches, inside the inmost parts of the frozen tree boughs, in the white plumes of the old reeds, in the darkness of the pool, and in the air, where ice crystals are gathering and growing into the next snow shower and a new attack of frost.

Before the arbitrator and his men left, Femke told them she had consulted an architect and that he'd said their farm was important, that it was specific to this area. She'd cited his analogy of Vermeer's Milkmaid, and the arbitrator had smiled and said that it wasn't perhaps the most well-chosen analogy since there was, after all, just one Milkmaid, while the number of Head-Neck-Rump farms that still survived would astonish you.

Trijn spoke fiercely about the Wide World, less than a kilometre away from here, a beautiful farmhouse, of which not one single brick was now left over. One of the very many with this fate. All these iconic farms are falling by the dozen.

The arbitrator nodded.

'I'll do my best,' he said, 'and I'll make sure you'll have some kind of certainty as soon as possible. As far as lies in my power. At any rate you can expect a result from me by the beginning of next year.'

'Well, well,' Trijn said, 'so fast. And that's something you'll manage even though we seem to be a complex case.'

'Things have to move quickly, particularly for complex cases,' the arbitrator said. 'Nine out of ten times, a complex case means too little has been done to sort things out and too slowly. But of course, I didn't say that.'

A delivery van is coming up the drive. Another package for

Fokko, who barely comes out of his van anymore. He's busy doing something, and rather obsessively too, and Femke has a worrying suspicion about what that might be. But how can she say anything about it, without giving away that she's secretly been poking around in his stuff?

With the parcel in her hands she walks back into the headquarters, where Trijn is sitting with a cup of coffee and a newspaper.

Trijn looks up. 'Again,' she says, when she sees the box. 'What the hell is that man up to?'

'I've no idea.'

'He's brewing something. Something that's not right,' Trijn says with certainty. 'Have you noticed how shifty he's been recently? I'm even wondering whether I can leave you alone with him.'

'Mam, you're going to Paris for three days. You'll be home before you know it.'

She pours coffee for both of them and sits down.

'Do you think,' Femke asks hesitantly, 'that if an arbitrator had come earlier, it wouldn't have happened? Grampa, I mean.'

Trijn shakes her head. 'I think that a sliver of hope like this wouldn't have made any difference anymore. He was finished.' She smiles and says gently: 'But the two of us can find some hope in this, and that's what we should do, right?'

Femke nods. 'If the arbitrator supports our case, if they do compensate us, then next year, perhaps, we can start building things up again.'

Bayo is whining. Femke lets her jump onto her lap. Bayo gives her a lick, full in the face.

'Have you actually ever been away from home for three days before?'

'No. Just once for three years, and then for no longer than a day. Are you pleased about it? Three days without that nosey mother of yours?'

Femke thinks it over. 'I'd have been pleased before Zwier, I think... now I feel as if I can't take pleasure in anything anymore.'

'And yet we do have to start doing that again, taking pleasure in things.' Trijn sounds very sure of herself.

Before Hessel Sjoerdsma came into Trijn's life, Femke never thought of her mother as a woman who could have anything going on with a man at all. But now she's going to Paris with that fellow.

'Are you in love with him?'

Trijn shrugs her shoulders. 'I don't really understand that sort of thing – love. And what about you?' she continues. 'Did you like being with... with her?'

She nods her head at the puppy.

'She's called Danielle, Mam. Why can't you ever say her name?'

It stays silent.

'Is it because she's a woman?'

'No. I don't think so.'

'But you don't like her, do you?'

'She seems hard as nails to me'.

Femke laughs. 'Yes, and you chose so much better.'

They giggle, a little awkwardly.

'Anyway, we're better at breeding cows than at this sort of stuff,' Trijn says.

'Ha!' Femke sounds triumphant. 'A compliment for my breeding programme. Off you go to Paris, then, and I'll find out more about the family herd system.'

Trijn shakes her head.

'Working with a family herd is just asking for trouble.'

'That's the case for every family,' Femke concludes. 'Yet you can't do without them.'

*

Her travel clothes are hanging over a chair in the farmhand's room. Her comfortable walking shoes are underneath it. Her suitcase has been packed with the cobalt blue dress, among others, and the high-heeled shoes, and with the newly purchased glimmering sleeveless thingamajig, sexier than the old flannel shirts she normally sleeps in, mainly intended for warding off the cold.

Trijn is drinking a cup of tea in the headquarters. Femke went out with Bayo after the meal. She was going to drop in on she-who-must-not-be-named, Femke joked, to let her see how the puppy had grown.

Trijn had suggested saying goodbye there and then, but Femke said she'd be back tonight, that she wasn't going to take it too fast, that she was just going to dip a toe in the water, nothing more.

There's still one thing Trijn has to do before she leaves early tomorrow morning. She puts her thick woollen cardie on, because there's a hard frost, and shuffles across the yard with its frozen puddles. The moon is almost full. Stars are glittering in the clear night. She walks down the lonning and knocks on the door of Fokko's van. The curtains are carefully shut tight.

'No,' he calls out impatiently. 'I'm busy.'

She pulls the door open, without hesitation, and immediately encounters three big flowerpots, packed one inside the other. She looks with some perplexity at the junk inside. It looks like a laboratory. There are storage jars everywhere, tins of powder, tins filled with rust flakes and with iron or aluminium filings. She can see a pestle and mortar, a roll of shiny cord, small metal plates, a soldering iron, safety goggles, all kinds of tools, empty bottles, and packets of shag.

While she's looking at everything, Fokko rushes forwards, half tripping over the mess and his own legs, the blow torch in his hands held in front of him like a revolver. She retreats. He grabs the door handle and pulls at it, roaring at her to fuck off.

'I need to talk to you, now,' she says, gripping the door tightly.

He yells that he's busy, but she insists and eventually he turns off the blow torch, follows her out into the freezing cold, carefully shutting the door, and shivers.

'Well,' he snaps, 'what do you want?'

'I want to talk to you properly a moment. Come inside with me.'

He goes with her, swearing, and when they're in the headquarters he plonks himself down on the bench and starts rolling a fag. She puts a mug of tea in front of him and says: 'So, now I want to know what's going on. What are you up to?'

'That's nobody's business,' he says, focusing his brooding gaze on his twisting fingers.

She remains standing, with her mug in her hands.

'I thought as much. You're parked in our yard. You're using our electricity. You've been our guest for months now. And it's nothing to do with us?'

'Trijn, you don't want to know about this.'

He's jerking his head back and forth, like a barn owl on the lookout for danger. A bag of nerves. Why hasn't she kept more of an eye on him?

'What are you up to?' she repeats sternly.

She tries to catch his gaze, but his eyes are flicking from left to right.

'The Worm is back,' he says grinning and lights his cigarette.

'I thought so. And in my opinion he's busy doing something that'll go a lot further than daubing graffiti onto a pavement.'

He nods, grimaces. 'It's war,' he says. 'You said so yourself.'

'Yes,' she says, 'but I didn't mean we should arm ourselves. What are you doing? Is it what I think?'

'You have to arm yourself in wartime, otherwise you're slaughtered.'

'Fokko, of course I didn't mean that stuff about a war literally. I said it to show that something terrible is happening here to us.'

'Yes,' he says, 'and you're right about that.'

'I don't want this,' she says sternly, 'and definitely not in our farmyard.'

'I'm not in your farmyard anymore. Just in your lonning.'

'I don't want that either.'

'It won't take much longer now. It's almost ready. I've just got to do a trial run, a little test, and then *pouf!*' He says it jokingly.

'No,' she says. 'You've got to stop this.'

He shakes his head. 'They've got to be taught a lesson.'

She suddenly knows with absolute certainty that Femke mustn't be left alone with him. 'Then I want you to leave.'

The headquarters is crackling with his suppressed anger.

'Oh, man,' he says annoyed. 'It's a bit of fireworks. Nothing more.'

'No,' she says. 'It's not right.'

'In contrast to that scum,' he rages, 'I really won't be putting people's lives in danger. Nothing more than a bit of material damage. Paying them back in the same coin. They ruin our houses. Their stuff will get ruined too.' He goes silent a moment, then his face breaks open in a nasty grin and he says, coaxingly: 'An office block, at night, no one there. Bit of thermite. Boom. A few of those rigs, sent to high heaven. Whoosh… That kind of stuff. Nothing more. No lives lost.'

Now she really does start to feel panicky.

'I want you to leave,' she says tightly. 'Early tomorrow morning, at the very latest. When I leave, you've got to be gone as well.'

He starts to get up, and says grumpily: 'Trijn, calm down. Nothing's going on.'

'No!' she screams. 'I don't want this. I. Don't. Want. This. Clear? No explosives on our farm. No illegal nonsense. We've just fucking well got a bit of hope again. You leave tomorrow morning. Understood?'

'Okay,' he says. 'I was on the point of leaving anyway. Just you wait, Trijn. Just you wait till The Worm speaks. I'm not just doing it for me, but for him too.'

He points to the empty chair at the head of the table. Then he stands up and walks agitatedly out of the building.

She wonders if he really will leave. If he won't actually abuse the fact that she'll be gone tomorrow. She remembers again how he used to make tennis balls explode.

Feeling worried she phones Femke, who has clearly turned off her phone. She immediately gets her voicemail. She irritably tells her to call back, but she knows from experience that Femke never listens to her voicemail. So she sends her a text: *Phone me now!*

All the excitement about her forthcoming trip has vanished. How can she trust that this unguided missile really will leave? She drinks her tea and keeps looking at her watch. Time seems almost to be standing still. Every now and then she stands up and peers into the shippon to see if Femke is already coming. Until she realises that it's impossible for her to go on her trip tomorrow. She can't leave Femke alone with him.

Hessel cheerfully answers the phone and asks her how many suitcases she's packed. She tells him, her voice breaking, that the trip can't go ahead, because Fokko's brewing something, and she doesn't trust it one little bit.

'Trijntje,' he says, trying to calm her down, 'what's the matter?'

'Fokko,' she stammers, 'the man who lives in the van on our farm. He's up to something.' She tells him about the tins of powder, the iron plates, the shiny cord, and her suspicion, which has just been confirmed, that he's making explosives. That he'd already daubed threats at the rigging locations. That he's The Worm who the newspapers wrote about at the time. And she daren't leave Femke alone with him.

'Hey, hang on,' he interrupts, 'if what you're saying is true, then there's only one thing to do.'

'And what's that?'

'Phone the police. They'll come immediately and if they find a van with explosives inside it, then the problem is swiftly solved.'

She doesn't answer.

'Trijntje?' he asks.

'Yes?'

'You've got to phone them.'

He says it very forcefully.

She still doesn't answer.

'A van full of explosives on your property. What's stopping you?'

She hesitates and then says softly: 'He's one of us.'

'Nonsense,' Hessel says. 'If he's making bombs, then he's nothing more than a terrorist. And if you know that, it's your duty to report him. Otherwise you're aiding and abetting him.'

She remains silent. A feeling of dismay rises up in her, about what she has just done.

'Trijn,' he says forcefully, 'if you won't do it, then I will.'

'What?'

'Phoning the police. Now.'

'But...' she begins to say and then doesn't know how to continue.

'I mean it,' he continues, with undisguised sternness in his voice. This is what a law enforcer sounds like, a man of statutes and rules. And he goes on: 'That madman will put all of you in danger. And God alone knows who else.'

She keeps quiet and without saying anything more she breaks off the call. The only thing she wanted was to tell Hessel that the trip couldn't go ahead. And now she has betrayed Fokko, their Fokko. Because even though he's an unguided missile, even though he's a maladjusted non-conformist and a loner, even though he's never managed to live a life that most people would call normal, he's still one of them. When it comes down to it, she realises, the world is made up of two kinds of people. And she has just delivered Fokko to the other camp. And by doing so she has betrayed their cause.

Her head spins.

Her phone rings. It's Hessel and she rejects the call. She paces up and down in the headquarters. Back and forth. That feeling of guilt again, which always surfaces, always at exactly the point when life is finally going to smile at you for once. She has created yet another victim with her eternal lack of foresight.

And then a clear thought: she has to warn him – perhaps it's not yet too late. Perhaps he can flee into this clear frosty night. Get rid of the explosives. Cross the border, it's not far from here. Lie low a while, until other urgent issues arise again. She looks for the key to the safe: in the desk drawer, in the small change glass, and then she finds it in the old cigar box on top of the desk. She crouches down, takes a few hundred euros out of the safe – escape money, a pack-your-bags-and-leave bonus – stuffs them into an envelope, throws her woollen cardigan around her shoulders, pulls on her boots, races through the shippon, where there's the familiar snuffling sound of cows, the rattling of the feed-fence, and their sleepy mooing.

Trijn opens the door of the shippon. The freezing cold hits her and she runs quickly across the frozen yard, into the lonning. She can see Fokko's lanky form not far from the van and she hears his heavy footsteps crunching across the icy lane. A flame flares from the blowtorch he's holding in a hand protected by a heavy work-glove. In the flickering light he looks like an astronaut. The blowtorch's spooky flame is reflected in the safety goggles he's wearing, but his face is more or less concealed by his grey hoodie. He's walking backwards, away from the big flowerpot standing on the ground of the lonning. The roaring blowtorch is in one hand, in the other he's holding a shiny cord leading into the flowerpot, which he's winding out as he walks.

She screams out his name. He looks up and bellows: 'Go away, Trijn, get back. It's The Worm Test.'

'No,' she calls out. 'Fokko. You've got to go.'

He doesn't listen to her and bends down, and sets the cord on fire with the blowtorch.

'The police are coming,' she calls. She sees him start.

'Fucking bitch,' he shouts and at that moment they hear the sound of sirens blaring through the clear freezing air.

Fokko takes a quick look behind him. At the end of the concrete track, two kilometres away, they can see the flashing blue lights of three police cars, tearing at breakneck speed along the track.

He runs forward, cursing, and with his distinctive half-lurching tread he tries to stamp out the fire, but the ribbon of fire has already reached the flowerpot, which is standing on one of the frozen puddles. And to her horror Trijn sees Fokko trip over his heavy boots as he's kicking at the flame and fall forward with a terrifying cry at the very moment that the tongue of fire reaches the pot, and a cloud of smoke rises up and a gigantic flash of flame shoots up with tremendous force, bright yellow and fierce orange, edged with red, as if it's trying to reach a universe. The sparks spatter onto the ice and make it explode, bang after bang – fire on ice. Fokko is ablaze. He tries to scramble up again but is flung back onto the ground by the next explosion. He hasn't got a chance. Trijn flees onto the farmland, away from the shower of sparks. It's as if a Vesuvius has suddenly sprung up in this flat clay country, spewing out a singeing fire, flames that no wood or iron or steel plate or van can withstand, let alone the skin of a man who has never found his place in the world, a world where, in his opinion, too much importance is placed on money and not enough on care, where the individual is defeated by the system, compassion by self-interest, imagination by inflexibility, quietness by tumult, love by fear, humanity by cruelty. The man with a good heart, which month after month has been increasingly poisoned by bitterness and sucked dry of all hope, that man is being consumed skin and bone by a fire he himself lit, but whose sparks were first stirred during all those years of powerlessness and of being disregarded. The man who once thought he'd finally come home, on his own farm, the Wide World, which he'd restored with care and attentiveness to its former glory, that man is now being consumed by thermite fire. Because thermite can only be quenched when it has burnt itself out.

And hours later, when the fire has subsided, when the clear night sky has made way for a grey blanket of clouds from which thick snow will later fall, in the lonning where the Mercedes van once stood there is now only charred earth.

An icy stillness falls over the farm of Schokland.

January 2018

A FEW WEEKS AFTER the catastrophe, and after the police investigations and the disaster tourists and the TV crews, all of whom eventually disappear from the farm, the clapped-out Old Year changes to the New. The only reminder of what has happened is the charred black hole in the middle of the lonning, that looks like a bomb crater, as if a war has raged here.

Trijn and Femke mechanically do what has to be done, because even when you're in mourning there's still milking to do, feed to give out, calves being born, and things to clean.

Every day Trijn is plagued by the question as to why she can never save anyone, why she always somehow sends people to their death. The trip to Paris didn't happen, of course. Hessel reassured her and told her on the phone that they could do it later. But Trijn isn't at all sure that anything will come of it.

And Femke wonders whether things would have turned out differently if she'd raised the alarm about the map and the cookbook. Or perhaps she could have saved things if she hadn't gone to the farm by the sea dyke, or if she hadn't stayed there longer than she'd intended.

Sometimes there are no more words.

And in those silent days an image increasingly looms up inside Femke: her forefather – the lad driven away from his island, still a child, and completely alone. If he'd stayed where he was, then twenty years later the state would have forced him to leave, because they didn't want to invest any money in an island that was in such a bad state. He didn't stand by and wait for help that would never come. He left his native ground and, with a dash of courage and stubborn tenacity, he built his life in a sea of clay on this ice-cold soil, once no more than sea and salt marsh and muddy sea-margins, in this vast landscape where there's nearly always a cold wind blowing that makes people shiver. A lad with Koridon blood in his veins and perhaps that's the reason he succeeded in leaving Schokland for his descendants, that characteristic Head-Neck-Rump farmhouse with its ancient cloister bricks, the elegant keystones, the beloved owl board, the proud swans, the weary beams, the big wooden barn, the battered byres, the dark-green shutters, the high attics, the large windows that are under far too much strain.

Sometimes Femke goes with Bayo into the reedbeds, and listens to the pinging of the bearded tits, the trilling of the reed buntings, and the honking of the geese, and then she thinks about that lad, so much younger than her, and so much more alone than she is now, because she isn't completely solitary. And the thought of that resilient lad fills her with hope. She must persevere. Even though it will still mean a long struggle, even though she'll have to stand firm and strong, stronger and firmer than ever before, because big businesses and a heedless government work against people rather than with them, even though there'll be countless concessions she'll have to make in the future, through gritted teeth; and, even though she doesn't yet know if having a family herd is realistic, if that's only asking for trouble, giving up is not an option. Schokland 2018, or 2019, or 2020 must be built again: a family farm in a sea of clay. And she will do it. Femke Koridon.

Epilogue

An article in the New York Times of 23 March, 1914 states that the tragic death of Giuseppe Mercalli was perhaps not a dramatic accident, but a brutal murder.

A substantial sum of money was missing, which Mercalli had kept in a steel box, and the police had found clues suggesting that the volcanologist and seismologist had been strangled and doused in petroleum, after which he and his notes and his bed were swallowed up in a conflagration, deliberately started to camouflage a banal robbery with murder.

It was a gruesome ending for a dedicated scientist, who with great courage had rushed to earthquake regions to study the state of the ground there, and the buildings, the animals and the people. He was a man who didn't hesitate to risk his life by venturing to the very edge of volcanoes on the point of eruption, driven by his intense will to understand what was happening under the ground. Someone who perceived his far from risk-free research as a duty, as his life's task, by which he could minimise the danger for people living in seismically active regions; yet he discovered, to his great disappointment, that the state continuously turns its back on the interests of those citizens.

He was a man who understood how important it is to consider things carefully. A man who preached that what is essential for creating good policies is a knowledge of history. A man who only wanted to use his tireless labour to serve and protect the population. A man who didn't want endangered citizens to lose their faith in government. But governments didn't listen to Giuseppe Mercalli.

That people refuse to learn from history may be humanity's greatest tragedy.

Translator's Note

Shocked Earth is a translation of Saskia Goldschmidt's novel *Schokland*, first published in Dutch in 2018. As Goldschmidt makes clear in her acknowledgements, the book is absolutely rooted in the landscape she so lyrically describes. The research she carried out in preparation for the writing of the novel was based not only on textual, audio-visual and internet sources, but also on intense lived experience. During the period in which she was writing the book, she rented a small cottage in the heart of the area hit by the induced earthquakes and became deeply involved in the life of the community, participating in farming activities and attending action-group meetings about the effects of the earthquakes. She immersed herself in the surrounding nature, and through close daily observation and walking in the clay and reedbed landscape taught herself to see and write about what was there.

The novel is set in a very specific place – not the stereotypical Dutch landscape or cityscape that most people call to mind when they think of the Netherlands (no tulip fields, no closely-woven webbing of city canals, no rows of seventeenth-century patrician canal houses). This is not Holland – the western part of the country where the majority of the Dutch live and where the government is based – but the province of Groningen, in the north-east of the Netherlands. Groningen is already perceived as being far distant from the major Dutch cities, but the specific region in which the novel is set is almost as remote from big city life as it is possible to be in this small country. This is Het Hogeland, a fertile farming region, with a very distinctive landscape and a specific culture and way of life with its roots in antiquity.

The word Hogeland means 'high land', indicating that it lies above sea-level, yet height is a relative concept here: the land is actually flat and low-lying, and while some areas within the region are a few metres above sea-level, a substantial part of it lies below.

The area has always been subject to sea-flooding, something that before the building of effective sea dykes was relatively common and sometimes catastrophic. The land itself has been formed by both sea and rivers, with siltation gradually building the land up along the sea margins and by the riverbanks. Over the course of millennia, regular tidal deposits of mud and sand formed the Old Marine Clay on which the farm of Schokland is built.

Although the modern landscape of Het Hogeland has been shaped by farming, the watercourses which were once the gullies and creeks of the tidal flats, but are now inland, are also an important feature. These are the 'maars', winding channels of water that add an element of wildness and nature to the cultivated land. Over the course of time, some of these maars have had a helping hand from humans and have been deepened to form drainage channels or land boundaries; some are so straight that it is clear that they have been artificially created, acting more like canals and waterways, although still retaining their drainage function. Where these maars once led to the sea to the north, after the sea dykes were created in the Middle Ages many were diverted, via a system of interlinked channels, to the east, where the estuary of the Ems river forms the border with Germany. In the novel, Femke's maar, with its side-channels and reedbeds, where she so enjoys walking and birdwatching, forms an effective nature reserve within the farmland.

A distinctive aspect of the landscape is that many of the older farms and villages are built on artificial mounds – known as *wierden* (sing. *wierde*) – which protected buildings, animals and stands of trees from rising waters. These enabled farming to develop even in prehistoric times, well before the building of dykes in the Middle Ages. The medieval dykes were broken through by the sea at several points by storm floods, being severely damaged by the Christmas flood of 1717, in which more than 14,000 people, across the northern Netherlands, Denmark and northern

Germany lost their lives. As a result a new dyke was built, further out to sea, on what had been sea-marsh, which meant that land was gained and the old, damaged dyke became a second line of defence, an inner or 'sleeper' dyke. This reclaimed land is the area in which Danielle's farm is located, close to the sea and somewhat less susceptible to the tremors caused by the gas extraction.

In the late 1950s a gas field was discovered in Slochteren, in a region to the south of Het Hogeland. This was eventually found to encompass most of the area to the north and east of the city of Groningen, one-third of the entire province, and including Het Hogeland. At its discovery, it was one of the largest gas fields in the world, and is still the largest single gas field in Europe. Production started in 1963 and soon the Netherlands became a major gas producer, not only supplying domestic use but selling gas to neighbouring countries. The economic benefits to the country as a whole have been enormous, but the people of Groningen argue that the majority of state revenue won from this gas field has profited projects in the west of the country, rather than in the north.

This area of the Netherlands is not subject to natural seismic activity. The first earthquake registered as a result of gas extraction occurred in the neighbouring province of Drenthe in 1986 and the first to occur in the Groningen gas field took place in 1991, yet although an official study published in 1993 demonstrated the link between the earthquakes and gas extraction, it was claimed that the material damage caused by such earthquakes would be limited and light. The official perception of risk was low and exploitation of the field continued; it was believed that the main environmental impact would be from subsidence rather than seismicity, and that this could be managed. Yet in the past quarter of a century the number and severity of induced earthquakes has substantially increased. These in turn have led to an increasing amount of damage to buildings, often of a historic character, and have created a situation of stress and insecurity for the inhabitants. Even more stress has been caused by a lack of fair compensation, a situation that is so dramatically described in the novel.

As Goldschmidt makes clear, the effect of these earthquakes is much more severe than might be expected from their measurement on the Richter scale. The strongest earthquake so far recorded in the Groningen gas field area took place in 2012 and had a magnitude of 3.6. In fact, there have been several earthquakes since then of a similar size. However, while the Richter scale is suitable for measuring the size of a natural earthquake, with its source deep below ground level, it is not very good at measuring the impact of shallower, manmade earthquakes. Shallow quakes and tremors release more energy to the surface, creating a greater impact on buildings and structures than might be expected. The clay soil that lies above the Groningen gas field also spreads and intensifies the effect, increasing the amplitude of the shaking. As the frequency of earthquakes has increased further stress has been added to structures already damaged by previous tremors. The effects of a manmade earthquake may appear to be less catastrophic than that of a natural one, but they produce situations of insidious damage, ongoing stress and real suffering. This is the reason why it has been argued that a scale, such as the Mercalli scale, that measures the intensity of an earthquake, rather than its magnitude, would better represent its impact, which is ongoing in spite of recent changes in government policy.

As the translator of this novel, it was clearly important to me to understand the background I have outlined above, but it was even more important to find a way of conveying the distinctive character of the setting and, especially, the people as naturally and easily as possible, both in their 'northernness' and in their humanity and individuality. Words which refer to features of the landscape, such as the maar, were therefore not translated but borrowed into English, with a small explanation added on first use ('a winding watercourse'). Similar decisions were made with regard to other important cultural elements, such as food and drink.

The name of the farm, 'Schokland', has been retained throughout the text, while the title of the novel has changed from Schokland to Shocked Earth. It was essential to retain the name of the farm, of course, because of its symbolic force. As most Dutch readers know, Schokland is a former island in what was the Zuiderzee, a bay of the North Sea that has now been dammed, forming the freshwater Ijsselmeer and a complete new province, Flevoland. Before this major feat of engineering was completed in 1932, Schokland was still an island, although one increasingly subject to encroachment by the sea. It had suffered continual flooding and attenuation throughout the nineteenth century, until in 1859 the government decided that its inhabitants would no longer be allowed to live there. The island now forms part of the reclaimed polderland and has become a UNESCO World Heritage site, yet in the nineteenth century it seemed that it had no future.

The farm and its surrounding environment are central to the atmosphere created in the novel, to the sense of place and rootedness, and even to shaping of individual character. I found that in order to convey that rootedness in English it was important to understand the ground plan of the farm, how the various rooms and buildings related to each other, where and what its boundaries were. This was partly because I had made a decision to render the names of the buildings or elements of the farmhouse using terms which would be used in the north of England; old terms, which are still current in spite of changes in farming practice. There are parallels in the Dutch for this, for example in the term 'stee', which is related to the English 'stead' or 'steading', or 'grupstal', literally a 'gutter stall', but equivalent to what is usually called a 'tie-stall'. In most places I have translated that as 'byre' or 'old byre', particularly when it was clear that the housing for the animals interconnected with the farmhouse itself. This kind of housing has in many places been superseded by cubicle housing or free-stall barns. In the novel, the Koridon family has invested in this new form of cattle housing, a modern cowshed that, while not part of the original 19th century farm complex, has been built beside and is linked into the older form of cattle housing via the farm office, the Koridon's headquarters. This is the building that the family in the English version refer to as the 'shippon', a term still used for similar housing throughout much of the north of England, and certainly where I live, in Cumbria. Saskia Goldschmidt was kind enough to help me in this decision process by providing a detailed plan of the fictional farm she had created.

The use of dialect words and farming terms in the original text is sparing, but distinctive. I have not necessarily aimed to recreate this usage at every point, but to reflect it in specific turns of phrase and in the speech rhythms, without, I hope, modifying the sense that the story takes place in a specific region. The north of the translated text is, linguistically speaking, a generic (and hybrid) north and I have aimed to layer the familiar with the unfamiliar, the here with the elsewhere. After all, here and elsewhere are deeply interconnected: the fate of one particular family in a remote corner of the Netherlands is absolutely linked into the fate of humanity as a whole.

Antoinette Fawcett
November 2020

Acknowledgements

This novel couldn't have been written without the stories, expertise and feedback of very many people. I am very grateful to all of them.

I was extremely lucky to be able to rent Marijke and Uli Künzli's little house in the grounds of their former farm, two kilometres down a concrete track, after you reach the Plus supermarket. I lived there for two years. While I was sitting by my dormer window writing, looking out across miles of arable land and across the maar and a small nature reserve, or when I was out walking, I could see marsh harriers hunting, a drenched griffon vulture, and timid roe deer. The house became a home.

I was adopted by Anita Jongman and her daughter Agnes de Boer, both dairy farmers. Anita was an inexhaustible information source, and much more: she let me shave the cows, mix the slurry, and repair the pump. She warned me if things were in the pipeline and took me along to organic farming meetings. I was also made very welcome at other dairy farms: by Klaas and Truus Pastoor; Adrien and Annely Langereis van Koe; Max and Annelies Tilburg van Waddenmax; Martina Sprienstra; and Truus Pettinga.

In Friesland I visited Graasland, a farm belonging to Sierd and Joke Ensing and their daughter Welmoed. Once they were one of the top ten Friesian dairy farms. They've now switched to organic dairy farming and are a font of information for other farmers, and for writers too.

Ton Brandsen, Aafke Sterenberg, Toke van Oorsouw, Pie Oosterbeek-Harmsen and Jack Schurer, who all live in the Hogeland area of Groningen province, told me what it's like to live there, both now and in the past.

The psychologist Eike Meiborg filled me in on the impact the earthquakes have had on her clients.

I was a guest at several meetings about the earthquake problems. Many of the speakers impressed me: Hiltje Zwarberg; Annemarie de Haan; Sijbrand Nijhoff; Hilda Groeneveld. Willem Meiborg, a civil engineer, told the story of his grandfather who as early as 1960 had warned about the consequences of gas extraction, making the case for a provisory fund. Peter van der Graag, a geologist, explained very clearly why the earthquakes have had such a tremendous impact in Groningen province. Something the authorities have long ignored.

Annemarie Heite became the standard bearer for the people of Groningen. Her farm and family were filmed for Piet Hein van der Hoek's impressive documentary *De Stille Beving / The Silent Quake*. She is still working tirelessly for a just and generous settlement for all the victims of industry-induced earthquakes.

Kor Dwarshuis has created really clear animations that make the consequences of the gas extraction visible.

Klaas Nanninga welcomed me to his natural history museum in his own house in the city of Groningen. On two swelteringly hot June days he taught me how to prepare a bird. He let me make a botched job of a woodcock and put up with my bad language. I'm very grateful to him for both.

The lectures and excursions organised by Ben Koks, the father of the Montagu's Harrier Study Group, with the help of the peerless Madeleine Postma, were inspirational and instructive.

Bert Jalving checked every single word of the different versions of the manuscript, first alone and then with me. I cherish the memory of our daylong meetings.

Kim Goldschmidt and Liesbeth Iest read the text very closely and gave extremely useful feedback.

Jaques Muller and Frank Verbeek are my 'new neighbours'. I went for long treks in the countryside every week with Frank,

ACKNOWLEDGEMENTS

and was always treated to a perfect cup of coffee and a piece of Groningen spicy gingerbread at the end of the walk.

Piet Hein van der Hoek made a wonderful trailer for the book, with the help of a keen film crew and enthusiastic actors. The passion of everyone who collaborated on this project was unparalleled, as was the generosity of the fifty individuals who made donations for the film.

Krijn van Noordwijk was the photographer of a new set of author portraits.

Christoph Buchwald, publisher and word-surgeon, was as critical and enthusiastic as ever – a wonderful combination. The comments and suggestions he made about the structure and content of the book were really important.

I am also grateful to the rest of the team at Cossee Publishers: Eva Cossée, Eva Bouman, Nienke Timmers, Melle van Loenen, Hanna Breukers and Pim Waakop Reijers for their faith in the Dutch original of this novel and for all the work they did to bring it into the world.

And then Gerard Rijper. It isn't difficult to live by yourself in the clay country if you know that there's someone two hundred kilometres away who'll always make you welcome and who's always there for you if you need him, and even when you don't need him. We've been together thirty-seven years now, and we're still not tired of each other. That's a real blessing.

Many books, films and websites were valuable for the writing of this novel, including *De gaskolonie* (The Gas Colony) by Margriet Brandsma, Heleen Ekker and Reinalda Start. All the titles and web addresses can be found on my website: www.saskiagoldschmidt.nl.

Saskia Goldschmidt
February 2021

ANTOINETTE FAWCETT is a literary translator from Dutch to English. She was educated at the Universities of St. Andrews, Durham, Lancaster and East Anglia, where she was awarded a PhD in Literary Translation. Her interest in Dutch language and literature is lifelong; she is the daughter of a Dutch mother and spent some years living and working in the Netherlands.

Antoinette has translated for a number of literary publishers, as well as for the British Film Institute, the Dutch Foundation for Literature and the Holland Festival. Her translation of *Bird Cottage* (Pushkin Press, 2018), by Eva Meijer, was shortlisted for the 2019 Vondel Prize. Her most recent publications are her translations of Eva Meijer's *The Limits of My Language* (Pushkin Press, 2021) and *Bigger than the Facts* (Arc Publications, 2020), by the Dutch poet Jan Baeke.

Antoinette has gained numerous awards for her original and translated work. She is a member of the Society of Authors and of the Translators' Association.

Saskia Goldschmidt (Amsterdam, 1954) debuted as a writer with *Verplicht gelukkig: portret van een familie* (*Obliged to Be Happy: a Family Portrait*, Cossee 2011), which concerned survivors' guilt in the postwar generation. Her first novel, *De hormoonfabriek* (Cossee 2012), was on the longlist for the Libris Literature Prize 2013 and was also nominated for the Euregio Prize. It has been translated into several languages, including German, French, Afrikaans and Turkish. Its English translation, *The Hormone Factory*, translated by Hester Velmans, was published in the US by Other Press (2014) and in the UK by Saraband (2016). It was broadcast in 2014 as a twelve-hour-long radio serial on the Netherlands' Radio 1 channel and released as a podcast in 2018. Goldschmidt's second novel, *De voddenkoningin* (*The Vintage Queen*, Cossee 2015) has also been translated into several languages and is a bestseller. Her most recent novel, *Schokland* (2018), translated into English as *Shocked Earth* (Saraband 2021), is the first major novel about the effects of gas extraction on people living in the Dutch province of Groningen.